Praise for *Best-Laid Plans*:

'With her usual mixture of huge heart and humour,
[Kathy Lette] rips the stigma out of autism.'
Ruby Wax

'Deliciously rude and darkly funny, but with compassion
and humanity at its heart. Read with relish.'
Nicole Kidman

'Kathy Lette can turn from raunchy farce to the most tender
emotion in a trice: this unputdownable book wrenches the
heart and the laugh muscles with stunning panache.'
Stephen Fry

'An important and poignant subject – a mother's search for
the perfect girlfriend for her grown-up son with autism – that
is also a hilarious and entertaining page-turner, written
with Lette's inimitable irreverence, brio and wit.'
Jill Dawson, author of *Fred and Edie*

'As her fans will expect and newcomers discover, this
tale is perspicacious, pithy and witty. A tale of
mother love which will twang your heart strings
before making you laugh out loud.'
Sandi Toksvig

'For the good of your immortal soul, and all your other
vital organs, read this deeply touching tale.'
Billy Connolly

Best-Laid Plans

Kathy Lette

BANTAM PRESS

LONDON · NEW YORK · TORONTO · SYDNEY · AUCKLAND

TRANSWORLD PUBLISHERS
61–63 Uxbridge Road, London W5 5SA
www.penguin.co.uk

Transworld is part of the Penguin Random House group of companies
whose addresses can be found at global.penguinrandomhouse.com

Penguin
Random House
UK

First published in Great Britain in 2017 by Bantam Press
an imprint of Transworld Publishers

A CIP catalogue record for this book
is available from the British Library.

ISBNs 9780593071359 (hb)
9780593071366 (tpb)

Typeset in 11.75/15.5 pt Palatino LT Std by Jouve (UK), Milton Keynes
Printed and bound in Great Britain by Clays Ltd, Bungay, Suffolk

Penguin Random House is committed to a sustainable
future for our business, our readers and our planet. This book
is made from Forest Stewardship Council® certified paper.

1 3 5 7 9 10 8 6 4 2

To my darling kids, Jules and Georgie

Contents

PART ONE

1

Kerb Your Enthusiasm

It was never my intention to take my son kerb-crawling to pick up a prostitute. Nope. Kerb-crawling was definitely not on my 'To Do' list after 'Buy hummus, sort sock drawer, do Pilates'.

A mother does many things for her son – running trays up to his bedroom for nothing more serious than a stubbed toe, detecting lost bits of sports kit, secretly completing overdue homework ... But soliciting a prostitute shouldn't be one of them. 'So, how much to initiate my son sexually?' are just not the words a bookish, cake-baking, cryptic-crossword-ninja, law-abiding mum of one ever expects to say to a working girl in thigh-high boots and leather hot-pants in the dead of night in a seedy backstreet.

So how did this sick scenario come about? Well, earlier that night, over dinner, I'd casually mentioned the plans I was making for my son's twenty-first birthday party. As soon as I mentioned the word 'party', Merlin's face shattered like breaking glass.

'No. No party! There's nobody to invite because I'm worthless. I'm nothing . . . The boys at school said I was a freak. And it's true . . . That time I came home with a sign sticky-taped to my back saying "Kick me, I'm a retard" . . . Well, they were right. I *am* a retard. No wonder no girl will ever go out with me. Those girls who laughed at me at school were correct – I'm shit on a shoe.'

I can't quite explain the fierce onrush of tenderness I felt then for my strange, beautiful boy. It overwhelmed me. I tried to hold his hand, but he recoiled as though being doused in boiling water.

'I can only apologize to you for not being the son you deserve. Why did you ever have me? I bet you wish you'd never had a child.' My son's tone was metallic with self-loathing. 'Why can't I be normal?' Each word he uttered was like a bullet to my heart. 'I'm so sorry I ruined your life, Mum. Without a girl to love, well, I just don't want to live any more.'

His annihilated voice filled me with desolation. A kind of sludge formed around my heart. Then this sob just wrenched out of him. And, well, it broke something open inside me. I was gripped by a protective, lioness-like love for my gentle, tortured boy for all the years of rejection, bullying and humiliation, for all the misery, isolation and lost dreams. I felt my claws come out . . . And the next thing I knew those claws were clutching my car keys and I was driving him towards the city to fulfil his inalienable right to the pursuit of life, liberty and human sexual contact.

I'd read in the papers that, since the gentrification of King's Cross, which was now all gastro-pubs and Pilates studios, the area close to Liverpool Street had become the new red-light district. As we drove closer and my mood cooled, I did register the fact that this was rating rather high on the Oprah-ometer. I mean, what kind of mother gives her son party tips championed by Donald Trump and Berlusconi: 'Take off pants. Mingle.' I'm an English teacher at a secondary school . . . And before you start picturing a boring, pedantic, predictably dull English-teacher stereotype, let me assure you: you are one hundred per cent correct. Was soliciting a prostitute for one's son a seriously abnormal thing to do? Well, yes, but mothering a child with autism tends to recalibrate one's view of normal.

When the twin spires of Liverpool Street Station loomed into view, I veered off the main road into a labyrinth of dark streets with low, dilapidated houses huddled together conspiratorially. I nosed my car into a lane-way that resembled a beach after the tide's gone out – plastic bags, broken bottles, rusting cans and crisp packets, and drunks lying by the wall like drowned sailors.

What the hell was I doing here? I was more likely to be found at a Quilting Bee than on a kerb-crawl. I felt I was going for an interview for a job I didn't want. This was such a foreign world to me, I might as well have been on Jupiter. It suddenly became an effort to keep hold of the steering wheel. The bitumen seemed to billow under my tyres like a mattress. I could think of a million things I'd rather be doing on this drizzly, grey May evening – a book club, a hot bath – Jesus, reordering my condiment cupboard while doing my tax return looked irresistibly attractive right now.

'Maybe this wasn't such a good idea . . .' I admitted to my son, who was slumped despondently in the passenger seat beside me. 'I'm sure someone lovely will come into your life soon, darling.' My second-favourite mothering experience is lying to my son about his chances of ever having a girlfriend – my favourite being beating my head on his locked bedroom door until drawing blood.

'It's so much easier for animals, Mum, isn't it? Animals are always in pairs. I can't even go to the zoo any more, because it just reminds me how lonely I am.'

Since puberty kicked in, Merlin has attempted *every*thing to attract girls . . . Well, everything bar smothering himself in cupcake icing and sauntering through town holding a placard saying, 'Free Designer Shoes!' . . . And still nothing. To girls his own age, he's just too exotic . . . The poor boy might as well be a sherbet-winged flamingo flying down the high street.

'I can't fathom why no girl wants to date me' has become his sad mantra. 'Do you know why, Mum?'

Of course I knew why. Because saying you're autistic and socially isolated is like saying that you're on a diet *and* hungry.

With Merlin's birthday only a month or so away, his hormones had gone into overheated, obsessive overdrive. When he wasn't asking me if dogs do it 'people-style' or why his penis kept making him touch it, dark moods began to dominate his quick-silvered wit.

'I'm failing to add up as a person, Mum,' he'd said a few days before. 'The constant rejection, it's breaking me down. I compliment women all the time. I talk to every female I meet . . . "Are you a woman of experience?" "Do you moisturize?" "How's the modelling going?" And they just laugh at me. A woman's sweet smile says nothing about her heart. I struggle, Mum.' He'd looked at me, his pale-blue eyes wide with confusion. 'The signals I broadcast make me hum like an amplifier but I'm just not on the same wavelength as women. What can I do, Mum? What can I do?'

What *could* he do? I'd racked my brains. Mail-order bride? Thai wife? Auction him online? I'd seriously considered this, and was discouraged only by the fact that it's illegal to sell live things on eBay.

Basically, if I didn't want his only hobby to be earning Boy Scout badges in Trouser Tenting and his passport to read, under 'Occupation', 'Crazed Loner', then I had to help him . . . Which is why I was now kerb-crawling behind Liverpool Street Station.

'The male kingfisher courts the female by bringing her small fish. They mate even before she's had time to swallow her wedding present,' Merlin elaborated.

'Uh-huh,' I said, wondering where I could park. The irony of worrying about getting a ticket for parking on a double-yellow line while illegally picking up a prostitute was momentarily lost on me.

'The male wolf spider presents the females with morsels of food gift-wrapped in silk. Although copulation for spiders must be difficult. How does a male spider let a female arachnid know that he wishes to be her mate and not her meal?'

'Uh-huh,' I said again, preoccupied about how I would negotiate the transaction and where the escort would take him. I glanced up at the sooty Victorian buildings crumbling away behind their grey façades. Would she have a room in some seedy B&B, the static electricity from the cheap acrylic carpet providing an impromptu perm? Or – oh God – maybe they'd do it in the car and I'd have to go for a walk somewhere and do a crossword? But surely if I walked around here I'd be brutally mugged and my battered corpse tossed into a filthy canal.

Women were skulking out of the shadows now. My heart drilled against my bra. All I could think about were the night-hunting snakes Merlin had shown me on YouTube, and how their infrared sensors allow them to strike at anything warm in the dark.

This was a bad, bad idea. I waved my hand back and forth like a windshield wiper to shoo the women away. White-knuckled, I'd just decided to turn the wheel for home when a statuesque blonde in the clichéd uniform of thigh-high boots and leather hot-pants emerged from a murky whirlpool of pimps and prostitutes.

'Botticelli's Venus rises,' Merlin sighed wistfully, as the woman homed in on us with the nocturnal accuracy of a bat.

I braked abruptly so as not to hit her. By the time I'd established that I hadn't wet my pants with nervousness, Venus had put one high-heeled foot on my bumper bar like a conquistador. Her beautiful, ice-blue eyes were clear and cold and as hard as mint candies. They were framed by eyebrows plucked into two sceptical arches. Her luscious pink lips were enhanced with the most emphatic lip-liner but I couldn't quite decipher the exact tone of her smile. It seemed to be held stiffly in place as if for an invisible photographer.

As she leant into the window, I opened my wallet,

preparing to launch into the brute vocabulary of the sordid transaction. 'So, yes . . . um . . . so what are your rates?' I asked, feigning insouciance.

Venus levelled a searing glare at me that only just fell short of igniting my hair.

'Fifty for a headie. A hundred for the full service. Five hundred for the night . . . For a thousand, you can have dwarves and a donkey, as far as I'm concerned.'

'Um . . . The full service, I guess.'

I extended a fan of twenty-pound notes in her direction. Her hand shot out like a tentacle and wrapped around my wrist. With the contemptuous suavity of a diplomat, she then stated: 'You're nicked.'

I dropped the money, the notes scattering over the car floor, and drew back from her as if she were a live socket. *'Nooooo!'* My volume rivalled the voice of Moses parting the Red Sea. Panic punched my chest. If I were a nuclear reactor, I'd have been going into meltdown. What to do? Pleading seemed the best option. Either that or abandoning the car and sprinting off down an alleyway . . . an option Merlin now took, leaving the passenger-side door swinging wildly on its hinges.

'Merlin!' I called out after him. As he disappeared from view at the far end of the dingy street, I made a noise like a tyre going flat. Couldn't the undercover officer see that I was more deranged than St Deranged, the Patron Saint of Single Mothers of Special Needs Boys?

'Please, I must find my son!' I pushed out of the door to run after him, but Venus blocked my way. The pimps and prostitutes had instantly evaporated back into the shadows, leaving an eerily empty silence.

'Your son? Jeez, Louise! Tell it to the custody sergeant. He's gonna love this one.' The click of the handcuff snapping on my wrist had a dull and final sound to it, like a lead door shutting.

I shouted Merlin's name again. I tugged the officer in his direction. I flailed about to no avail. 'Let me go, you idiot!'

'Do you want me to add resisting arrest to the charges?'

'You don't understand! My son is out there alone!'

Venus flashed me her identification badge and began reciting my rights, as a back-up police van pulled up.

As she spoke, I stared at her in shocked silence for what I estimated to be about a million years, then interrupted, 'But . . . you can't arrest me. I have thirty-two English essays on Moral Education Through Literature to mark before morning.'

I'd hoped this would make me appear a sensible, sane, supremely competent career woman and decent member of society rather than a kerb-crawling crazy. But there was no more talk. Despite my squirming protestations and writhing anger, I was told to 'secure my car' and was then bundled into the caged back of the police van and dragged off to the local cop shop for questioning.

'But my son!' I cried out, beating on the sides of the van. 'We're going the wrong way! We should be looking for Merlin!'

When I thought of Merlin alone in the city, a burning sensation skittered through my stomach and my toes curled. How could this have happened? God had clearly taken a sabbatical and left some hopelessly unqualified intern in charge. I felt the wild terror of losing my moorings. Even worse, I'd lost my child. I was a bad, bad, hopeless mother. Kerb-crawling – I mean, what had I been thinking? Clearly, from now on, when it came to parenting I would have to wear a paper hat reading 'Trainee'.

2

Best-Laid Plans

As I bounced about in the back of the police van, my nerves were shrieking like unoiled hinges. As we swerved through a quarrel of traffic, I pondered the best way to explain the build-up to tonight to the police. How could I adequately express the frustrations my boy had endured in his effort to make female friends for so long.

By his sixteenth birthday, despair had already started creeping in. 'Mum,' Merlin had said to me, 'I think I have an enthralling and charismatic demeanour, don't you? I'm also at the pulchritudinous pinnacle of my career ... It would make me feel amazing inside if a girl loved me. It would just be so majestic ... Do you think any woman will ever throw me a lifeline of love?'

I said, 'Yes, of course,' but I was thinking, *Yeah, the day kangaroos start playing croquet.*

After another year of rejections, his voice became even

more plaintive. 'Mum, will I ever feel the lick of love's tiger-ish tongue?'

Then, on his eighteenth birthday, he'd beseeched me, 'Mum, will all women forever find me geekish and freakish?'

I told my son to think of all the wonderful, inspirational people who have been misunderstood – Galileo, Luther, Jesus, Pythagoras, Socrates, Copernicus, Newton, Van Gogh . . .

He'd interrupted my rattling roll call with the words, '*I'm* not a genius, Mum . . . If I were a genius, I'd know how to pretend to be normal.'

I said something platitudinous about how there was no such thing as normal and abnormal, just ordinary and extraordinary . . . And how exciting, tangential, intriguing, creative and unique I found his mind to be . . . But it was to no avail, because on and on they came – the normal everyday knockbacks, the endless everyday put-downs.

On his nineteenth birthday, Merlin had asked, 'Why don't any love goddesses want to chat to me?' He was gangling in the door, all legs and elbows. 'Why do girls always say no to a date? Why do they reject me as a retard and a spaz?'

Merlin's luminous eyes had fleetingly held mine. The green bowler hat he'd chosen to wear that night (he often dressed eccentrically, for 'good luck') was tilted at an awk-ward but absurdly touching angle that tore at my heart.

On his twentieth birthday – just Merlin and me and a chocolate cake – he'd confided, his voice heavy with weary exasperation, 'My personality is a dazzlement of surprise. I feel I'm at the zenith of my charismatic beguilement. It really hurts when you compliment a girl and tell her how exquisite and delectable she is and she just shoots you down. Or laughs at you. It happens a lot and, most importantly, I don't know why. Without love, existence is futile. If I don't lose my virginity before I turn twenty-one, I won't be able to go on.' He wrung his hands. 'Rejection is like a repugnant odour you feel instead of smell. I torture myself, remembering hurtful things women have said to me . . . If the body is designed to vomit up what is contaminated, why not the brain? Why can't my brain throw up, Mum? Why?'

How I'd ached with love for my eccentric son. I had to help him. And so began the mission to *Get Merlin Laid*.

At first I'd tried dating websites. But Merlin's profile – 'Adore space–time continuums and tennis scores, plus have encyclopaedic knowledge of Amazonian moths, mathematical equations and black holes' – tended to put girls off. As did his accompanying declaration suggesting that women 'Come and join me in my magic world where relationships are at their very zany best.'

His profile picture didn't help either. The shy, delicate glance he gave to the camera was just right. His tender blue eyes, the flawless lapis of an Italian summer sky, peeking out through his mane of golden hair, coupled with his other-worldly, ethereal aura, gave him the look of a mischievous cherub. If it weren't for his suit-of-armour-plated six-pack, the result of his obsessional sit-ups (six hundred a day), the kid would have looked under-dressed without angel wings . . . Except that he was wearing a Sherlock Holmes deerstalker hat and a monocle. 'My most lucky look,' he'd explained.

After running the usual online gauntlet of paedophiles, predators and money launderers who prowl the Web, the only woman who responded was an eighty-eight-year-old great-grandmother whose byline read 'Time wasters need not apply.'

My sister then proposed that I just 'Think French.' It was wine o'clock and we were sitting at her kitchen table mulling over Merlin's options. My younger, prettier sister, who's as glossy and flighty as a racehorse – I'm like a plodding Clydesdale beside her – assured me that, if we lived in France, my husband would simply take Merlin to a brothel. Phoebe is very worldly. Literally. She's a flight attendant. Although right now, I was the one who had done something stratospheric – stratospherically stupid. I was the Sensible Sister. It was so out of character for me to be caught with my synapses down.

Anyway, I'd reminded Phoebe that not only was I neither French nor married, but as a feminist, the exploitation of women wasn't high on my agenda. But Phoebe had already clicked open her iPad and found a list of twenty-five women within a five-mile radius offering everything from fetish work to adult mothering – whatever the hell that is. She then proceeded to read out the reviews, like TripAdvisor – only this was a walk on the wild side with the sexually dysfunctional, or, rather, the 'differently pleasured'.

' "The worker enjoyed the sex," ' my sister read out to me.

'Yeah, right. Academy Award-winning orgasms all round . . .'

' " . . . and offered FWE – the Full Wife Experience." '

'What's that, I wonder? Leaving hubby sulking on the couch eating crisps while *she* goes off to bonk the pool boy?'

We both snorted out a laugh then, the big, hearty kookaburra cackle we'd inherited from our bohemian Antipodean mother, who was away on another of her SKI – Spend Kids' Inheritance – trips, somewhere in the big, wide world.

'But seriously, Phoebe, I can't take my son to a brothel. What am I going to do? Sit outside the bedroom, knitting? Like some pervy Madame Defarge?'

'Well, clearly, *you* can't take him,' my sister had said, disappearing in a haze of cigarette smoke – the cigarettes she'd supposedly given up years earlier. 'Put the hard word on one of your male friends.'

And so, desperate and demoralized, the next day I asked some of my male colleagues if they'd take my son to a brothel.

Invisible tumbleweed blew around the staff room for a while before Philip, the Head of Maths, replied facetiously, 'Great idea. I'll just run it by my wife, shall I? *Sweetie, do you mind if I just pop off tonight for a few hours? I'm helping out Lucy's son, Merlin. No, not with algebra, football practice or driving lessons. I'm taking him to a whorehouse to get laid.* Seriously, Lucy, does the word "manslaughter" not mean anything to you?'

Undeterred, I next propositioned my lesbian journo pal from Yogalates, peering at her across our perineums while we did the upside-down lotus position.

'Jesus, Lucy! We're members of the Women's Equality Party!' Her Lycra-clad legs were suddenly as taut as an archer's bow. 'How can you condone prostitution?'

'I wasn't really seeing her as a prostitute but as a "sex care provider" who is presenting herself as a commodity allotment within a business doctrine,' I rationalized.

But the only result was that another friend bit the buddy dust.

Next stop, the gay boys, starting with Arron, my urbane and unshockable hairdresser. Well, he reacted as though I'd suggested he support Lance Armstrong's return to professional cycling. He positively convulsed at the notion. 'What? And start an ugly rumour that I'm straight?'

Finally, an actor friend *did* agree to take Merlin to a local brothel for me. He maintained that it would be good research. Off they drove, with high hopes (and low morals), to some suburban house in Kilburn ... but he was on the car phone to me half an hour later saying he'd chickened out because someone had recognized him.

'You're an actor, for God's sake,' I chided him. 'Why don't you just pretend to be someone else, you old ham?'

My son's voice had then piped up over the car speaker. 'Mum, is ham sick? Is that why it's got to be cured? Can loneliness be cured the same way? We just passed a dead fox on the road ... How do you know if animals are road-kill or suicides? Maybe they were just depressed?'

Most parents' biggest worry is that their child might get a nose piercing or a tattoo or dye their hair purple. Mine is keeping my son from hurling himself under a moving vehicle. This is the kind of worry that keeps me awake at night.

When Merlin's twenty-first was only a month or so away, my sister had another idea. 'With Merlin's lean, lithe physique and angelic looks, you should get him work as a male escort ... Apparently, professional women seeking sexual encounters have fuelled a three-fold increase in the male-escort business ... You could make money out of this libido of his. Merlin would make an excellent escort. He's so amusing.'

'Are you crazy? I am *not* pimping my son! Besides, he

might just want to sit around and talk about tennis, or comets, or meteors, or something totally boring. Then *she'll* charge *him.'*

As the police van shuddered to a halt, an idea came to me – a bit late, admittedly. As all my fifty-something, divorced women friends are chewing holes in the furniture with sexual frustration and all the young autistic boys I know are priapic, perhaps I could matchmake them on an app called – maybe – 'Square Pegs for Round Holes'? Or 'Tinder-ism'? Or 'Au-Tinder'? . . . But before I had time to write my app pitch to Mark Zuckerberg, the police had me clambering out of the van. As my sleeve caught on the wire mesh and tore, I looked up at the grey, grimy walls of the cop shop with foreboding. The whole place had the ambience of a Dickensian debtors' prison. Clearly this is why I became a mother – I couldn't resist the glamour of it all.

As I was frog-marched inside, I concluded that a seedy, inner-city police station is definitely not my natural habitat. My natural habitat is the classics section of the local library. Or the cheese counter at a French deli. How had it come to this? Even worse, my son, my vulnerable boy, was now out there, lost, in the big, bad world. It was then that I threw up. Right there on the linoleum floor. When I stopped retching, the 'prostitute'-turned-arresting-officer tore off her blonde wig and said brusquely, 'Are you okay? How do you feel?'

I felt like a fish left gasping at the bottom of a bucket.

3

If You've Got That Sinking Feeling, Then You're Probably Drowning

Kerb-crawling with your twenty-year-old son proved a pretty hard concept to explain to the jaded custody sergeant who took my statement half an hour later. Under normal circumstances, the man's mix of searing blue eyes, musculature and world-weary, rugged, leathery good looks would have meant I'd be tilting my head backwards so that my eyeballs didn't fall out, but all I could think about was my missing boy.

'Couldn't you just turn a blind eye and let me go, Officer?' It was a pretty gutsy thing to say, considering I was halfway through a major heart attack. 'My son is lost out there somewhere and I need to find him.'

'Sure,' the big bloke drawled sarcastically. 'And why don't I make a donation to the Oscar Pistorius defence fund while I'm at it.' The officer had clearly trained at the Smart Ass Academy.

'You don't understand. My son has autism, chronic anxiety and an obsessive compulsive disorder . . .'

'OCD? It must have been a very organized crime then,' he quipped sardonically.

I took a deep breath to stop me hyperventilating. I closed my eyes, trying not to be distracted by the rolling boil of noise around me. Phones were shrilling and people were yelling. The cacophony of voices and complaints, the clattering metal gates scraping along the floor, the doors slamming with a cymbal-like crash made me think of an orchestra tuning up. Police personnel manoeuvred laser-eyed pimps, furtive-looking in their hoodies and handcuffs, away from the grim-faced, skinny-legged sex workers who careered about like drunks in their too-high heels. The air reeked of despondency. Under the harsh fluorescents, other people's hopelessness wafted like BO from an armpit in a summer Tube at rush hour.

'Look, this is obviously a mistake. I didn't intend to break the law. I mean, do I look like a criminal?' I gestured at my flat sandals and ink-stained fingers. 'I'm an English teacher, for God's sake. I'm more likely to order a soupçon of ennui with a nuance on the side and a faux pas to go than a lady of the night . . .'

I'd been attempting to demonstrate my literary credentials, but clocking the custody sergeant's nonplussed expression, I diagnosed a serious irony deficiency and rephrased. 'The point I'm trying to make is that I don't even go on holiday to countries that have a bad human-rights record . . .' I peeked over at the officer, looking for some reaction. Nothing. 'Put it this way' – I tried a more relatable analogy to illustrate the true level of my dullness – 'I'm the type of woman who goes to a male strip show and looks at the audience.'

Still nada. I sighed loudly and started again.

'The point is, it's my son's twenty-first birthday soon and he's obsessed with losing his virginity. He told me that if he didn't experience any horizontal refreshment, he just wanted to "wake up dead tomorrow". But sadly, girls are acutely allergic to him . . . Not that he's not charming and handsome. He is. But, unfortunately, females his age just can't see beyond his chronic foot-in-mouth disease and inability to read social situations.'

Judging by the sceptical curl on the lip of the big, beefy sergeant sprawled in a man-spread before me, I wasn't doing a very good job of reading social situations either.

'Girls tend to act as though my son's just been beamed down from Planet Weird and has lost his guide book to understanding earthlings . . . which is why he often says the wrong thing . . .'

Like me right now, I thought, blundering on. 'He has no filter, you see, and tends to say whatever he's thinking . . . in the case of a girl, about her breasts or her legs or . . .'

Where was *my* filter? Why was I blabbing on like this to a man clearly sired by an armoured tank and a grizzly bear? Obviously, autism was genetic and Merlin must get it from *my* wilting branch of the family tree and not, as previously thought, from my arctic-hearted, upper-class ex-husband.

'Although, don't get me wrong,' I corrected, 'my son often says the right thing, too. When he was four he wanted to know what to call a male ladybug . . . When he was six he asked me why "phonetic" isn't spelled the way it sounds – you know, with an "F" . . . When he was eight he asked if I'd ever imagined a world without hypothetical situations . . .

When he was ten we discussed at length just how important a person has to be before they're considered to be
assassinated instead of merely murdered? . . . The kid's
intellect is so towering it constantly makes a thwacking
sound as it bumps into ceiling fans, which is why girls
think he's representing the universe in the Intergalactic
Whacky Alien category . . . Does that make sense?'

Sense? I had a feeling that the custody sergeant was going
to arrest that last sentence and have it sent down for life. He
ostentatiously checked his watch with end-of-shift weari-
ness. Nerves and exhaustion were causing me to blurt out
my words, so I steadied my breathing and tried to refocus.

'What I'm trying to say is that my son's been on a mission
to get laid. Sex is all he thinks about. And I just thought that
an encounter with a prostitute might calm him down, alle-
viate his depression and, I suppose, slake his curiosity. You
know?'

My interrogator clearly *didn't* know, judging by the
increasingly deep frown lines on his forehead. It's at times
like this that I wish I lived in an earthquake zone. With any
luck, there'd be a fortuitous meteor strike or a zombie apoca-
lypse to get me the hell out of here.

'I've read you your rights. You're aware you're entitled to
legal advice. So, why not just wait in the cell for a duty solicitor?' The officer yawned.

'In a *cell*!' My life seemed to have suddenly turned into a
scene from a Solzhenitsyn novel. 'Good God, no! I need
to go and find my boy. This is all a mistake. Um, look,
Officer. I think we got off on the wrong foot. Let's start
again, shall we? You see, the mother of a kid with special
needs has to be his advocate, standing up for his rights.

She has to be his scientist, challenging and questioning medical solutions. And his full-time executive, making all his decisions—'

'And part-time pimp,' the custody sergeant rebuked me gruffly.

I why-me'd my eyes heavenwards. It was after midnight and people were now foaming into the police station like suds from a sitcom washing machine. The sergeant glanced up at the queue of miscreants awaiting his attention which had formed behind me.

'So are you planning on giving me your name and address any time in my actual lifespan? I gather these ramblings are representations as to whether or not I should charge you?' he said in a blasé tone.

I suddenly felt the longing to confide like a raging thirst. All the years of pent-up anxiety and desperation just erupted out of me.

'My son's mental well-being was at stake. You've got to understand that Merlin's despondency is so great I should be able to claim that hooker as a medical expense, instead of being arrested by your lot. The red-light district – believe me, it's not an area I would ever frequent if it weren't an emergency. When I stopped the car in that street, I felt as though I was in one of those nature docs where the shark circles the shoal of fish, except we were a shoal of only two in a car and the sharks were pimps and . . . undercover police, it turns out.'

'Rrrright.' The policeman swirled a grey teabag around in his mug and watched the curls of black spread through the water like ink. 'So if this is all some innocent misunderstanding, why did your son run away?'

'In Merlin's mind, he wasn't running away, he was being *chased*. When the prostitute produced handcuffs and arrested me, he just went into spooked-deer mode and bolted off into the shadows.' I pictured him, running so fast it was as though his feet had taken steroids. 'And he's out there now, scared, discombobulated, in danger . . . Which is why you've got to let me go, so I can start looking for him!'

The custody sergeant opened one jaundiced eye and scrutinized me. He rocked back in his chair, arms folded, scratched his prime pectoral real estate and said, 'All very interesting, but it doesn't detract from the fact that you were illegally procuring a prostitute.'

'Look, Officer, my son was desperate. He had a meltdown. I panicked. How else would a middle-aged English teacher end up driving through back alleys looking for a woman to initiate her autistic son into the joys of carnal pleasure? Where's *that* chapter in the child-rearing manual, I ask you? Huh?'

The arresting officer stopped by the desk and tapped her watch. I had the distinct feeling that if I didn't cut to the conversational chase I'd be test-driving dildos in a peniten-tiary, pronto.

The custody sergeant picked up his pen. 'So, is that it, then?'

'No. No, that is not *it*! Look, I called my son Merlin because I wanted him to stand out and be different, but I had no idea just how different he was. When I realized he wasn't normal, at first I blamed myself. I worried that maybe motherhood just wasn't coming as naturally to me as to others. But nobody could have loved that baby more. I lost my marriage over how much I loved him. His father wanted to put him in a home, but I would rather die! Over the years, 'experts' diagnosed lead poisoning, sensitivity to food colourings, to additives, to refined sugar . . . I was accused of smoking during my pregnancy and drinking excessively. Only one thing's for sure: my darling boy doesn't fit into the world. He's so hyperactive he sleeps with one eye open in case he misses anything. It's exhausting, trying to protect him. The anxiety, the panic attacks, the self-loathing . . .' The tangy taste of sweat crept into my mouth. 'I just hope he dies before I do, because who is going to look after him when I'm gone? That's the thought which haunts me in the small hours. So, yes, yes, yes! I *do* want him to find someone who loves him as much as I do. Yes, yes, I *do*. But *how* and *who*?'

I peeked up again at the custody sergeant, who seemed on the point of giving me a commiserating pat. He was just licking his full lips in readiness to speak when he was interrupted by a long, lean streak of acned aggro in uniform who approached the desk, chewing gum ferociously. He fidgeted and jiggled as if he'd been pepper-sprayed. His eyes raked over the custody record. 'Autistic, eh?'

Now, there are three things you should never say to a mother of a special-needs child: 1) it's clearly genetic; 2) it could be worse – he could be in a wheelchair; and 3) autism is nothing more than Cold Mother Syndrome.

'It's genetic, ain't it?' The younger policeman squinted at me. 'Mind you, it could be worse. It's not as though he's in a wheelchair . . . It's cold mothers, right? That's what causes it . . . So where's the kid then?'

'Scarpered,' the custody sergeant clarified.

'Are you sure there was a kid? Maybe she was just lookin' for a bit of lezzer action . . . That undercover cop, she's hot.

Or maybe some kinky threesome with her old man? Or were you kerb-crawling for a gig-ilo?' He jigged about a bit, groping his own crotch lasciviously. 'I've seen all them telly shows about all youse desperate housewives.' He let rip with a machine-gun laugh, spraying spittle.

'I'm a teacher!' I exclaimed illogically, squeezing as much hauteur and disdain into my voice as possible, as though my profession immunized me against committing any possible misdemeanour.

'Yeah, well, I've read about youse cougars. Out on the prowl in the urban jungle for hot, young male flesh.' The cocky cop struck a suggestive pose before firing off another humourless haw-haw.

Of course, if I'd handled this whole booking-in procedure at the police station with more diplomacy, that might have been the end of it. But, that fateful night, I was about as disarming as a Russian hit squad in the Ukraine. I felt my anger boiling over, like milk.

'And what would it matter if I were? My husband couldn't cope with his only son not being normal. He said he felt lost and needed to "find himself" – which meant he soon found himself in the knickers of a woman twenty years younger than me. Jesus, I wasn't sure if he was going to *date* her or *adopt* her! But imagine if *I'd* done that? Abandoned my autistic child for a toy boy? I'd have been crucified by public opinion. I'd be tabloid toast. *He*, on the other hand, was promoted by his bank and back-slapped by his mates.'

'Okay, calm down,' the custody sergeant warned, but I'd mounted my high horse and was galloping towards both policemen, flat out.

'I hate the assumption that older women are never

allowed to have younger men. Why are mothers made to feel we've been put out to sexual pasture? Especially when fat, hairy blokes are allowed to strut about in trousers so tight you can detect their religion. I can't believe Rod Stewart and Mick Jagger's testicles haven't put in for a transfer. Keith Richards, Iggy Pop, Steve Tyler, Hugh Hefner . . . Christ! I've seen better-dressed salads! But nobody ever makes cracks about mutton dressed as *ram*, now do they? If one more ugly, beer-bellied or boring bloke like you two calls me a cougar, I'm going to hit him repeatedly over the head with a copy of *The Female Eunuch* until he bleeds to death, repenting! Got it?'

To say that my rant went down well with the two officers is like saying that Austria was a little upset about the assassination of Archduke Ferdinand.

'Finished?' the custody sergeant finally drawled.

My words hung irretrievably in the air. I nodded.

'Funnily enough, I *was* gonna let you off with a caution. But not now. Now, this' – he used his fingers to imitate inverted commas – ' "ugly, beer-bellied, boring bloke" is gonna bail you and send the file to the Crown Prosecution Service, recommending that you be charged, as you're clearly unfit to be interviewed. So I'll see you in court . . . Mother of the Friggin' Year.'

4

Wine o'Clock

Being arrested for pimping prostitutes for your progeny was off the scale on the Parental Anxiety Gauge. A fast-track scheme to clear up cases of kerb-crawling meant that, after a perfunctory hearing, the magistrates' court date was set for four weeks' time. I felt so relaxed I was only changing my underwear, oh, every half an hour or so.

'Don't beat yourself up,' my sister Phoebe soothed a few days later. 'I mean, it's not as though you've clubbed a seal, or been outed as a cross-dressing Scientologist or something. And hey, at least you'll get a strip-search. That'll be the most action *you've* had in years! ... Too soon?' she asked, screwing up her nose at my stony expression.

The thick skin I'd grown from raising a child with special needs meant that I was no longer intimidated by much – well, apart from the tax department, the menopause and

Muslim extremists. But a full-cavity search before incarceration in prison? Who wasn't afraid of that?

'I don't want to be strip-searched – not without a date including dinner first.' I made a half-hearted attempt at humour. 'Besides, the only contraband I'd want to smuggle into prison are the complete works of Shakespeare, which are notoriously uninsertable. And how will I survive without them? I have a pretty strong suspicion that prison libraries are chronically short of the Bard and Jane Austen and are quite parsimonious with their Proust.'

'Oh, Lu-Lu, nobody's going to send you to prison. You have no more business being in a prison jumpsuit than, I dunno . . . a dolphin in stilettos.' My sister turned to the bemused teenage waiter who was hovering nearby. 'I'll have a magnum of Mum Juice, please. Chardonnay,' she decoded. 'And sharpish, there's a lamb.'

As soon as Phoebe had landed back at Heathrow from LA I'd insisted she meet me in my local wine bar, named, appropriately, Sloshed – The Grape Escape, so that Merlin (who'd thankfully survived the kerb-crawling escapade unscathed after catching a taxi home) couldn't overhear our conversation. My son's anxiety disorder is triggered by the smallest things – what colour shirt to wear, which trousers, or DVDs, or walking routes will bring him the most good luck – so I felt pretty sure that his mother's imminent imprisonment was not the most helpful information for someone of his fragile state of mind.

Sloshed was where we always met when disaster loomed. It's where we came to dissect Phoebe's MBD (Marriage Bed Death), when her husband of twenty years, Danny, stopped making love to her. It was where we came when Phoebe found out the reason *why* she was flying right under Danny's romantic radar, namely, because he'd joined the Mile-High Club with her best friend from work, a gay air steward named Trevor. (Apparently, on a flight to New York, they'd liaised in the loo the moment the captain had turned off the 'YOU MAY NOW UNFASTEN YOUR PANTS' sign.)

It was where we came when Danny filed for divorce, and when, a year later, he announced his engagement to Trevor the Trolley Dolly. And where we retreated when Phoebe's teenage children – Dylan and Julia – decamped (no pun intended) to their father's house after Phoebe banned them from attending his engagement party. 'Your father is not gay,' she'd told them. 'No one who's gay could ever possibly dance that badly . . . Plus, he doesn't even like musicals or Madonna!' she'd tut-tuttedly surmised.

Needless to say, the waiters always gave us a corner table, a box of tissues and a vineyard of vino. Tonight we would need a Loire Valley's worth, minimum.

'But seriously, Pheebs, what if I *am* sent to prison? A prison which recruits the kind of Neanderthal wardens who got sacked for employing tactics deemed too brutal at, say, Guantanamo Bay? I've watched *Orange is the New Black*. What if I get dipped in anchovy paste and thrown to the bull dykes? What if I have to share a cell with a psychopath who writes me love letters about Fallopian tubes and full moons in menstrual blood?'

I suddenly realized that other customers were looking in our boisterous direction. My sister and I have inherited our mother's motor-mouth tendencies, lobbing banter back and forth at Wimbledon ball speed. I lowered the decibel level and continued my moan.

'And how will I survive on the food – Split Pea and Sewage-rat Soup, Hot 'n' Hearty Microbe Mash, Birdseye Assorted Vagina Parts, Bitches-Who-Crossed-Me Casserole . . .' An even more terrifying thought then crossed my mind. 'And who will look after my darling son while I'm inside? How will he cope without me? I'm his carer, his companion, his rock. And, more importantly . . . *what will that rough prison soap do to my skin?*' I concluded on a note of sarcasm, in lieu of some stiff-upper-lip gloss.

'You are *not* going to prison.' My sister's warm hand was on mine.

'But I could. I've read *The Trial*. I know how these things go. Situations like this tend to snowball into Kafkaesque confusion. I mean, seriously, Phoebe, how will I survive? I'm a teacher. The only wound I've ever received is a paper cut.'

'Hello? Waiter! Can you hurry up with our wine, please?'

'Speaking of which,' I quavered, 'you do realize I have to plead not guilty. Teachers can't have criminal records.'

'You can always just attend Parent–Teacher nights under an assumed name,' she joked.

'Phoebe, you're not getting how serious this is. A guilty verdict means I'll be sacked and will never be able to get another teaching job.'

My sister's blonde hair hung in a neat little curtain around her pointed, slightly elfin face. She brushed it from her eyes to see me more clearly. 'Oh shit. Okay. Yikes. But, well, you have been cheesed off at work for yonks now. All that increased bureaucracy and paperwork. I took a look at those essays you're marking on T. S. Eliot. The exercise books were lying open on your kitchen table. I just thought

31

I'd poke about for the odd errant comma or whatever . . .
Well, every bloody essay was full of "anaphoras", "poly-
syndetons" and "enjambments". What the hell are they?
Mild urinary infections?'

'A mild urinary infection would be less painful, I'm telling you.'

'What a brilliant way of taking the pleasure out of reading.
Job well done, Education Department! Maybe retrenchment
could be a blessing in disguise?'

'Oh, yes. Once I'm kicked out of teaching I can just
revert to my true calling as a round-the-world solo yachts-
woman,' I snapped sardonically. 'Or maybe I'll take up
my rightful place on the British Olympic Synchronized
Swim Team.' I put my head in my hands. 'Teaching is the
only thing I'm good at – besides angst and apprehension,
that is.'

Phoebe lit up and took one prolonged inhalation of her
cigarette, rocked back in her chair and bloomed smoke.

'What are you doing? You know you can't smoke in here.'

'Why not? We always do everything together, so we
might as well both get arrested.'

The bottle arrived, along with an admonishment from
the manager. My sister stubbed out her fag, then slurped a
generous amount of wine into my glass before wrapping
my fingers around the stem. 'I'm sure that if you tell the
judge about your disastrous – I mean, your, ah, *interesting* – life, he's bound to just let you off with a caution,' she
joshed.

'Oh, you mean tell him how my husband flunked the
practical exam for his marriage licence, in that he shagged
someone younger, then abandoned me with a handicapped

child and no maintenance money?' I swigged deeply at my Chardonnay. *'You may think I sound bitter, Your Honour, but that's because I **bloody well am**. Oh, and surely killing an absentee, manipulative, lying, philandering ex-husband must only be a class-B misdemeanor, m'lud?'*

Phoebe laughed. 'Maybe you can get your jail sentence commuted to a few psychiatric sessions? I mean, you clearly bloody well need your head shrunk for ever marrying that ponce in the first friggin' place. I've never understood why you fell for Jeremy.'

I shrugged. 'He was a hotshot financial lawyer, incredibly posh, with a vintage wine cellar . . . Three traits I'm always drawn to in a narcissistic psychopath.'

'Still . . .' My sister has a tendency to pull at her hair when she's thinking and has been known to suck on a strand when plotting, both of which she was doing now.

'Oh God. You're planning something, aren't you?'

'You know what' – she topped up my glass – 'maybe we should call him?'

'Call Jeremy?' I was so shocked by my sister's suggestion that wine spurted out of my nose – which was such a great look on a middle-aged woman in a bar called Sloshed. 'Are you insane?'

'Think about it, Lu-Lu. Going to court is so expensive that clients should really get a truffle-and-lobster sandwich with each legal conference, maybe washed down with a glass of vintage Krug. Jeremy's a trained lawyer. He could represent you. Or at least give a character reference about what a good mother you are. After all, Merlin is his child, too.'

I thumped down my wine glass with such intensity it almost shattered. 'Sis, let me phrase this in a way you can comprehend: *I'd rather be pinned down by mortar fire in the middle of a genocide atrocity in the Congo than call that prick.'*

'Okay, then, do you have a better idea? Do you think that if maybe you just stand there in court and look well-dressed in pastel, clutching a copy of *Les Misérables*, the judge won't jail you?'

'I am *not* calling Jeremy.'

'Well, then, there's much planning to be done, isn't there? Perhaps your first priority should be to start thinking about what kind of gang you're going to join in prison. If you have any hopes of blending in, you'd better get a tattoo, and a piercing of some kind. And lesbian tendencies wouldn't go astray. Although I am kinda worried about how the orange colour of the prison uniform will clash with your skin tone. And you'd better write a will. I read that an inmate was recently whacked in the face at dinnertime with a piece of meatloaf. Some of it got into her mouth and she died.'

A sob erupted out of me with such unexpected ferocity that other drinkers turned to stare.

My sister, who majors in empathy, sympathy and hugs, had her arms around me in a second. 'I'm sorry, Lu-Lu. I'm just joking. Darling, don't cry. Forget I even mentioned Jeremy. Shhhhh, hush.'

'B–b–but you're right. How will I afford to pay court costs?'

'Don't worry about that. I'm going to get extra money by flying weekends with that Russian budget airline – *Flight-o-flop*, or whatever it's called.'

'You are not!' I wiped my eyes with my sleeve. 'Even *terrorists* are afraid to fly with them! They have a frequent-flier Near-Miss Programme.'

'Good. Then I'll get flying-by-the-seat-of-my-pants air miles, too.'

'No! I am not letting you fly with them. And anyway, let's look on the bright side. If I *do* lose the case, at least I'll get sent to an all-women prison, so the toilet seat will never be up.'

And we were laughing again, because that's the way we are. Laughing in the face of adversity. It's something our mother taught us. Laugh and the world laughs with you. Cry and you get salt in your Martini.

5

Social Siberia and
Paraskevidekatriaphobia

For the next few weeks I was wound up tighter than a Californian facelift.

Merlin, meanwhile, seemed oblivious to our impending doom, preoccupied as he was by his relentless search for a girlfriend.

'I'm at the most handsome point of my career,' he announced over breakfast one Monday morning. He cocked his head, gave a pouting half-smile and narrowed his sparkly eyes, selecting the smouldering Blue Steel look from his catalogue of rehearsed expressions. We were both running late – me for school assembly and him for his horticulture class at the local tech.

'Have you eaten any cereal yet?'

'I think I have a mesmerizing personality, don't you? I am actually a very nice person, you know. Mum, what does my future hold for me?' Merlin gave me a puzzled smile as

I whisked away his teacup. 'In this era, sex is crucial. But I seem to be the Artful Dodger of romantic warfare. Maybe if I wore my cap backwards I'd get a result? The cap backwards is the best look for male tennis stars. They get loads of females. Why don't young women approach me and ask me how old I am? I *will* meet a woman with experience at some point in the future, won't I?'

He pulled his pyjama top over his head, his slim, muscular arms crossing his chiselled body. 'Why can't I get a girlfriend? Am I not a smoking-hot sensation?'

Merlin smiled at me, that blinding, heartbreaking smile he used when trying hard to fit in. His smile filled the room. It filled me, too. As he shrugged on his T-shirt, I also wondered why no other female on the planet seemed able to glimpse the funny, quirky kindness that I could see in him.

'Of course you'll get a girlfriend.' I winked. 'No worries, kiddo.' It was a Lauren Bacall and Humphrey Bogart-esque line, and sounded as inauthentic as tinned asparagus.

Distraction. That's what he needed. But what? Hobbies? Sports? Birdwatching? Anything to take his mind off romance ... and the mission became even more urgent when I got home from school later that day and walked in on a conversation Merlin was having with my sister in the kitchen.

'So, exactly how big is your clitoris, Aunt Phoebe?'

This time, it was tea, not wine, that was shooting out of a nose – my sister's. 'Well, I've never had any formal complaints,' Phoebe said finally, once she'd stopped spluttering.

'But are clitorises different sizes, like penises?'

'That question is way, way above my pay grade,' Phoebe

whispered to me as I placed the shopping bags on the kitchen counter.

'Is it wrong to tell a girl that you think about her while you're masturbating?'

'Yes!' my sister and I chorused.

'Wouldn't she take it as a compliment?' he added, perplexed.

'Merlin, darling, why don't you have a long, hot bath . . . or, possibly, a cold shower, before dinner?' I suggested.

After he'd bolted up the stairs, Phoebe turned to me. 'Okay, you have *got* to get him a girlfriend. Speaking of which, *you* should hook yourself up with someone, too. It's been so long since you've had sex, if you get killed in a car accident nobody will be able to identify your body.'

'Oh, cheers, sis.'

'I'm serious. If you're ever called upon to give a sex talk at school, you'll be lecturing from *notes*. Your G-spot has taken to sending the odd sexual SOS, along the lines of "Remember me?" The Dalai Lama could ring you up for tips on celibacy.'

'There are worse things than celibacy, you know.'

'Yeah, like Ebola and death. Since my born-again-gay hubby set sail up the windward passage with my best male buddy and became a middle-order batsman for the other side, I've been sowing whole *plantations* of wild oats.'

'Well, *my* only erogenous zone is the second shelf of the pantry' – I opened the door with a flourish – 'where I keep the gin. Want one?'

'You're smart, you're slim and trim. Plus, you can rewire a house, jack up a car tyre and mow your own lawn. What's not to love? Shall I slice the lemon?'

'Will lime do?' I scooped one up from the fruit basket and arced it overarm in her general direction. She caught it with expert ease.

'Although your hair does need a cut, Lucy. You're starting to look like a kale-eating, vegan ceramicist, or something equally dull. Which is a shame, as you're such a handsome woman.'

'Handsome?' The tonic seemed to fizz with laughter as I unscrewed the top. 'That's just a euphemism for "plain but with a brain". *You're* the looker in the family, Pheebs. Besides, dating was bad enough in my twenties. I don't even want to think about it in my forties. Honestly, I sat out more dances at the school disco than Stephen bloody Hawking. Don't you remember that?'

'You just never seem to go out anywhere. Or meet anyone any more. It's not good for Merlin. I mean, he's the kind of kid who might well grow up to invent some astonishing math formula or—'

'Or get a maximum life sentence for hacking into the Pentagon computer. It's kinda too early to tell, I know.'

'Well, yes.' Phoebe dropped a slice of lime into my glass. 'But the way things are going, the two of you, hermetically sealed in this house, with no friends or partners – well, he could also just end up living alone on benefits forever more in your basement.'

It was true. I often worried I'd be bound to my son like an indentured servant for the rest of my life. Other mothers, post-menopause, are free to roam the world having adventures, like our mum. But I would always be anchored, earthbound. My son would always be in my basement, or in my attic, like an autistic Anne Frank. Plus, there was also the nagging nightmare that all this social isolation could turn him into a loony loner, the type of guy whose answer machine says, 'Hi, I can't come to the phone right now as I'm plotting the downfall of Western civilization as we know it.'

And so, heeding my sister's advice, I began accepting every invitation that came my way. Staff barbecues, birthday parties, gallery viewings, talks at the British Library – with my son as my permanent 'plus one'. And Merlin would try his best. He'd smile, and ask questions, and dazzle with his knowledge of pulsars and tsunamis.

You see, whereas most people's thoughts plod, Merlin's positively shimmer. My son didn't talk until he was four, but once he'd found his vocal chords he just babbled away as garrulously as a brook. Words streamed out of him, a geyser of words and stories and tangential, lateral, literal, lovely lunacy. Aged seven, he wrote me a card reading, '*I have such supiriour intelligence. I am a bit of a genious, you know*', a card that clearly would have prime fridge-magnet position for life.

I loved the way my 'genious' son's mind worked. But in the big, wide world, his precocious, unique, idiosyncratic intelligence fell on deaf, multiply-pierced ears. Girls his age eye-rolled and recoiled, invariably giving me the old '*She's created a monster and just doesn't know what to do with him*' look.

'Autism's not contagious, by the way,' I said to one haughty, judgemental woman as she drew her daughter away from us at a neighbour's garden party. 'He didn't get it from a toilet seat.'

Merlin flinched. 'Why are you torturing me by making me stay at this party, Mum?' he pleaded urgently.

'Look, if all the guests are as rude as that woman, we'll just say you're not feeling well and leave before dessert, okay?'

In desperation, I then suggested that Merlin try to mingle with an all-male group so that he could meet girls within the protection of a pack, but he was quickly made to feel as if he'd crash-landed into a culture to which he wasn't native. The main conversational topic for boys his age – namely, football banter – just parted Merlin's hair on the way over his head.

'I feel as though I'm looking at things underwater,' he whispered to me as I passed him on the way to the buffet. And that's exactly how he spent the rest of the day, forlornly floating about in the world like some sad, abandoned aquarium fish.

When the hostess told us what cakes she was serving for dessert, Merlin replied, 'Mum said we're going long before then, because your guests are so rude that I will be feeling sick soon.'

Exit stage left, but not before Merlin helpfully pointed out to the nearby party-goers that as many as one in ten of the sausages they'd just eaten would have been infected with hepatitis E virus, 'which can cause anything from flu symptoms and liver failure to death' . . . and our exile to Social Siberia was complete.

'Please don't ever again make me go to one of your boring friends' barbecues in the hope that one of their daughters might take pity on me,' Merlin declared the minute we were out the gate. 'I can't ascertain why you want to stand around in the freezing cold pretending the sausages aren't half raw and that you half like the boring people who are standing around pretending to like the half-raw sausages.'

The kid had a point. I joked that it made me want to start a charity called 'People with Autism Who Want to Help Dull, Dreary Neuro-typical People to Stop Pretending to like British Barbecues', but Merlin didn't react. He was closing in upon himself, the way quicksand swallows a pebble.

'Am I actually your son?' he asked me over dinner the next night. 'It's amazing, isn't it? I find it astonishing that I'm your son. So, who introduced us? Where did we meet?'

'Um . . .' I tried not to visualize it.

'We met back in the 1990s, didn't we, Mum? As you're one of my oldest friends, tell me truthfully . . . have I always been a freak and a geek?' Even though we were now sitting safely at our kitchen table, he looked as though he was being buffeted by the fiercest winds. 'If you'd known I'd be autistic, would you have aborted me?'

I felt the punch of his words in the pit of my stomach. 'No! No! Of course not, darling!'

'How many more nights will I lie alone, unembraced?' he asked tautly. 'I worry so much about not having a girlfriend that I'm starting to feel as though my brain is leaking out of my ears. It's the endless routine that numbs me. Breakfast, lunch, dinner, breakfast, lunch, dinner. Is this it? I'm working so hard to be part of this world, but maybe it's better if I retreat into my own universe, as there's no cruelty there.'

The night after that I came home from school to find him sitting in the gloom in his room, the light off. 'I am an abhorrent Gollum clone. No wonder no girl will go out with me. I'm a freak from Freakington. If I were a girl, not even *I* would date me,' he said sadly.

After much probing, I discovered that someone at college had stuck a sign to his back saying, 'Spit on the spaz'. This kind of abuse was, sadly, all too familiar. It started when he was eight. He'd come home from school crying, having been beaten up by the other kids for being a retard.

'What does it mean when people call you a "tard", Mum?' he'd asked, traumatized.

'Tardy. It means someone who is running a little late,' I'd lied at the time. But there was no softening the blow now.

Yes, I rang the head teacher at the horticultural tech and received apologetic assurances, but going to college now became Merlin's least favourite activity, besides maybe contracting the Zika virus or getting caught in crossfire in the Gaza Strip. He soon stopped going to class altogether. I came home from work later in the week to find him still in his pyjamas, slumped on the couch. Clouds were coagulating outside the window, and Merlin's mood was just as stormy. I could feel the ions of anxiety sparking off him. He sat hunched into himself, as if cold, even though it was a warm June evening. Then I noticed that all the framed family photos had been turned to face the wall.

'Why have you done that, darling?'

'I just don't feel I deserve to be in this family. I've quit that prison called "college" too. The point is, Mum, if I can't subtract from the world's sum of misery, do I have to add to it?' His voice seemed to have a puncture – it just got softer and softer. 'Jumping on to the tracks in front of a train can be a good way to get rid of someone you can't stand – yourself, for instance.'

My arms were around him in an instant. 'Darling, please don't talk like that! There's so much to live for!' I cried. But as there were articles in the papers every day about young people with depression killing themselves, I didn't treat it as an idle threat.

'The anxiety and loneliness defeat me, Mum. I don't necessarily feel like dying, but I don't feel a lot like wanting to be alive either.'

In an effort to short-circuit Merlin's angst, I'd been skirting the topic of love as assiduously as I would a mud puddle. Now, I avoided it like a giant sink hole.

From then on, two things obsessed me – my impending court case and Merlin's slide into self-doubt and misery. He'd even quit his obsessional Iron Man ritual of sit-ups and press-ups. Grasping at straws (which invariably turned out to be nettles), my next plan was to distract him from feelings of failure on the female front by finding him a job.

'Doing *what*?' Phoebe asked, over the phone. 'I adore my nephew, as you know, but his only skills seem to be press-ups, masturbation and faux pas.'

She wasn't wrong on the faux pas front. Apologizing for my son had become part of my daily routine. It was a default position. As soon as the phone rang or the doorbell buzzed, I immediately adopted the brace position. But job-hunting for him was about to take embarrassment to a whole new level.

It started in the Job Centre, where I soon discovered there are no prospects for people like my beloved boy.

'Don't get your hopes up, yeah? Only, like, fifteen per cent of autistic dudes are in employment, which is, like, much lower than other disabilities,' stated a dandruffy bloke with bad breath and terminal tedium. All I could think was, *If a* *waste of space like **you** can get a job, then surely my son can achieve **anything**.*

'Despite his high IQ?' I asked, amazed.

'Yep.'

'So, what you're telling me is that kids like Merlin have zero options and will be tossed on to the scrapheap of life, aged twenty?'

'Well, what options were you considerin', like, *realistically*?' the dandruffy, halitosised *dude* said with callous condescension.

'Options? Gee, I dunno. During his early years, I thought his true calling would be an astronaut, and if that didn't pan out, maybe a concert pianist,' I mocked. 'Although, *realistically*, I was just hoping for a job where he wasn't mugged, stabbed or sold large quantities of Class-A drugs on a daily basis.'

One thing I've learnt as a teacher is that arguments with brick walls are rarely effective, but this didn't stop me banging my head against one in frustration. Giving up on the Job Centre, I circled every employment vacancy ad in the local paper. And it started well, it really did. Merlin's spirits rallied at the prospect of having something to do every day and getting paid for it – even possibly making friends, some of whom might be female.

A conscientious, straight-A, goody-two-shoes student, I'd never truanted school – until I started teaching, that is. To accompany Merlin on his job interviews, I rang in sick one day and faked a funeral on another, promising to make it up to the disgruntled teacher who was forced to cover my classes.

At Merlin's first job interview, for the position of

supermarket shelf-stacker, he didn't just enter the office, he bounded into it with the enthusiasm of a golden retriever, imaginary tail wagging. Now, Merlin knows a lot of fantastic facts. He knows the right temperature for sperm whales to mate, and that seahorses are the only species whose males give birth. He knows that 'triskaidekaphobia' means extreme fear of the number thirteen. And that this superstition is related to 'paraskevidekatriaphobia', which means a fear of Friday the thirteenth. He knows that the shortest complete sentence in English is 'I am.' But the one thing he doesn't know is how to read social situations.

Here, for example, are some random comments Merlin made to his first potential employer on his initial foray into the workplace. 'Do you ever think about licking a gorilla's armpit?' 'Do you ever give your pelvis much thought?' 'Would you rather be buoyant or flamboyant?' 'Are you a woman of experience?'

When the thin, rangy boss of the local cinema asked him what his ambition was in life, he replied, 'To defrost Walt Disney.' At Pizza Express, the only question he asked the rubbery, baby-faced manager was why round pizza comes in a square box? And his only query of the Primark recruiting person was why 'bra' is singular and 'panties' plural? When asked how he would respond when asked a silly question by a member of the public, he replied that he'd simply pretend to be a painting in a gallery, because paintings must hear more stupid comments than anything else on the planet.

By the time each interview drew to an end, the interviewer was either glaring at us across the desk, arms folded, and with a bolted-on expression of polite disdain, or glancing around desperately for the nearest emergency exit – especially when Merlin pointed out their resemblance to startled emus, curmudgeonly armadillos or prissy poodles. (My son has the habit of giving people an animal totem which uncannily encapsulates their personalities.)

Other potential employers were simply cruel. When I put Merlin forward for a job as a cashier in McDonald's, a snide man with a sharp, satanic beard pointed out to him that his mental retardation meant he was suited only to scrubbing out the toilets. I felt the keen urge to force-feed the bloke his own burgers until they adversely affected his buoyancy in a quicksand scenario. Merlin wanted to buy lunch before we left, but only Prozac would have made that a 'happy meal'.

At a local hardware store, a short, bald, fat bloke who had about as much character as he had height, hair and musculature asked if Merlin had the mental capacity to empty the garbage, a task so simple it could be learnt by a 'toddler or an advanced hamster', he rudely pointed out. (If only his hardware store sold a missile with a guidance system that targeted condescension – 'which means "talking down to", I would tell him, just before blowing the bastard to smithereens.)

With each rejection I felt such desolation. Why did every potential boss seem to have Loveable Genius filters on their glasses?

When a recruiter for the council, an over-fleshy woman with a bad perm (which made her look as though she had pubic hair sutured to her cranium) coupled with the personality of a wilted pot plant, told my son that he didn't have the right 'people skills' to work as a street sweeper, I felt the heat of anger flush across my face. Merlin sat mute in the shadows, unregarded in his new shoes and best shirt.

The woman's heavy body was like a languid jelly. Bits of her wobbled as she swivelled back and forth in her smug little chair, waiting for us to vacate her office. Sensing rejection, Merlin tried to explain himself.

'I am working on my people skills. The trouble is, I get bored with conversations that don't contain information. Social chit-chat I find very tedious. But I have taught myself how to chit-chat about the weather. Did you know that hail forms when frozen water droplets get caught in updraughts of air and move through a cloud, collecting water on their surface then colliding with other ice particles to form ice balls?'

When the jelly just continued to just sit there, glassy-eyed and double-glazed, Merlin added desperately, 'Was I too direct? I can also be too direct, which Mum says can be inappropriate. But I aim to please and will try hard.'

I watched as he selected an engaged facial expression from his rehearsed repertoire of neuro-typical responses – which only roused Bad Perm Woman to new heights of apathy. When Merlin chose an overwrought ewe as her four-legged doppelgänger, simultaneously enquiring why sheep don't shrink when it rains, the jelly wobbled to the door at high speed. She then shooed us out into the hall like vermin, before smilingly ushering in her next applicant.

By the end of our job-hunting efforts, when Merlin encountered a gruff man, rendered egg-bald by alopecia, who was hiring hospital porters, a grump who glowered with one eye and glared with the other, it quickly became clear that my son had endured enough.

INTERVIEWER: What do you consider to be your greatest weakness?

MERLIN: Honesty.

INTERVIEWER: Honesty? I don't think that honesty is a
weakness.

MERLIN: I don't give a fuck what you think.

It was then that I started to consider the voluntary sector.

With my unemployable, undateable son obsessing about death, and my own incarceration imminent, was it any wonder Phoebe found me, the night before my scheduled court case, having a panic attack in my living room – a panic attack I was self-medicating with Mars bars.

'Relax. It'll all be fine,' my sister soothed. Phoebe has always been a one-woman task force for optimism.

'Then why do I have a sinking feeling that would make RMS *Titanic* look buoyant?'

'It's important to keep calm.' She placed her hands on my shoulders and gently bent my body forward. 'Put your head between your legs and breathe in, out, in, out. Breathe in—'

'I need a solicitor, not a bloody yoga lesson!' I shook myself free of her grasp.

'Yes, but solicitors cost money. How are you going to pay the court costs?' she asked me, triggering my own anxieties.

'I don't know.'

'I would lend you the money if I could, but since my hubby carelessly cast off his heterosexuality and leapt out of the closet in a feather boa and diamanté jock strap, I'm a bit skint. You could take out another mortgage on your house?'

'God, Phoebe! That's a bit extreme. We agreed not to do anything rash, remember? To take a considered, practical approach—'

'I rang Jeremy.'

I leapt bolt upright, as if electrocuted. 'And that would be your idea of *not doing anything rash*?' I asked, horrified.

'After a telephone plea featuring abject begging, Jeremy's agreed to come to court to give you a character reference. He's also offered to make a financial contribution. Says he feels responsible. After all you've sacrificed.'

This sentence made no sense to me, probably because I've never been bludgeoned over the head repeatedly with a blunt instrument. 'And you believed that two-faced, scum-brained, hypocritical toe-rag?'

'You could just say "my ex-husband".'

'I really can't fathom why you've dragged him into this.' I now gripped my sister by her shoulders. 'Specifically, when I asked you not to.'

'Look, we don't have to *like* the bastard. But let's just be grateful that he's agreed to help. Jeremy's your best option right now.'

'Best? That's like saying, *I've got cancer, but it's the best cancer to get as it kills more quickly and painlessly than a prolonged death.*'

'Well, do you have any other ideas, Einstein?'

'Perhaps I can simply ring the court and say that I'm having a breakdown and am being hospitalized?'

'Right.' Phoebe hitched a mocking brow. '*Patient has absentee husband and handicapped child . . . but no other discernible abnormalities,*' she added in a grown-up, stethoscope-wielding voice. She peeled my hands off her shoulders and squeezed them tightly. 'It will all be fine. Jeremy will explain to the judge the stresses and strains of raising an autistic child and you'll be let off with a caution. So, now, back away from the Mars bars and go and get some sleep. Ring in sick in the morning, and I'll pick you up at nine.' She kissed the top of my head. 'Okay?'

'Shit. What's the date tomorrow?'

'Ah . . . Thirteenth of June. Why?'

'Friday the thirteenth? *Great* . . . Do you happen to know where I can get a cure for peraskevidekatriaphobia?'

'What?'

'A Merlinism,' I sighed. 'It's just made sense to me for the first time after all these years.'

That night, I had a dream about reality. It was so bad I woke myself up.

6

A Day at the Zoo with My
Family . . . and Other Animals

'How are you holding up?' my sister asked as we walked into the north London magistrates' court.

'Great – but mainly because I have a nitroglycerin tablet ready to slip under my tongue.'

From the outside, the old stone courthouse was grimed with existence. But inside, it was all neoclassical froth, with gilded ceilings, lozenges of stained glass and wooden panels decorated with elaborately carved scrolls. We sat on benches in the foyer next to a black cast-iron staircase which curled upwards like a coil of smoke – along with my hopes.

'Maybe I'll just explain that I wasn't myself at the time of the arrest because I was light-headed from giving buckets of blood at the blood bank?'

'Yes, after catching the flu volunteering at a homeless shelter for war veterans, because that's the kind of self-sacrificing person you are,' Phoebe added, picking up my wily theme.

'Or maybe I could plead insanity? I'll simply respond to every question with: *I don't know. Let me consult the little alien who lives in my ear.*'

'How uncanny!' my sister joshed. 'That's pretty much how I always get off jury duty. I just keep pointing to different people in the courtroom, saying, "He did it!" then ask if I can execute the criminals myself.'

'Yes, or I might say . . .' But the banter died on my lips because, suddenly, there was Jeremy, all shiny-shoed and beach-tanned. He glided so effortlessly across the marble floor I thought he must be attached to invisible skis. He had always been like this, able to strut the world stage in gigantic strides. He wore trousers which hugged a posterior so pertly peachy it would cause a heart attack in a sloth. I instantly regretted my boring beige sack dress and sensible court shoes the colour of gravy. The wind had also made a comedy of my comb-up and left me with a listing tower of auburn tendrils.

I was ambushed by a memory of lying in my ex-husband's embrace, my head on his warm shoulder. How protected and safe I'd felt nestled in his arms – when, actually, it was the most dangerous place I could ever be.

'Lucinda.'

That silky voice. Strange in a familiar way, familiar in a strange way.

'Jeremy. Well, well, the years haven't exactly bypassed your face, have they? In fact, I'd say they've rather trampled it,' I lied. 'The way your cheeks hang all slack like that, they remind me of the breasts of Amazonian warrior women in a nature doc.'

The words left my mouth like poison darts. My sister jabbed me hard in the side with her elbow and surreptitiously pinched my arm.

'Thanks for turning up, Jeremy.' She smiled placatingly, rising to her feet to greet him with a peck on the cheek.

'Not at all. It really is the least I can do,' he said humbly.

They both looked down at me for a reaction. Clearly, I had to say something.

'You seem taller than I remember you,' I finally commented, making an effort to be civil, for Phoebe's sake. I stood up, too, but couldn't bring myself to shake his hand. 'Or maybe I've shrunk?'

'You're only five foot three,' Jeremy said tonelessly, 'so there's not a lot of height to lose.'

'I know. By the time I'm eighty they'll be able to use me as a decoration on my own birthday cake.'

Silence then fell like a snowdrift between us.

'We really are making "small talk", aren't we? Literally.' Phoebe attempted a quip. When neither of us reacted, she soldiered lamely on. 'Small talk, the height of pointlessness.' She sent me an urgent glance to spur me into saying something significant. When I remained tight-lipped and refused to take up the conversational baton, she confronted my ex-husband head on.

'We just need you to say to the magistrate what a good mother Lucy is. And how she always puts Merlin first. And how this was just a little error of judgement—'

'Of course.'

Jeremy's accent, which gives listeners the distinct impression that he has a moat around his home and possibly a maze and a helipad, made me seethe with sudden anger.

'And pay my court costs if I lose,' I chipped in. 'As I'm broke . . . on account of getting so little child maintenance from my ex-husband over the years.'

'I'm sure you won't lose.' Jeremy employed his calm, assured, *Trust me, I'm a doctor, four out of five experts agree* voice. 'Look, Lucy, I know I've not been the best father. But it's never too late to make it up to you and Merlin.'

Jeremy's life had been set out by his own parents on dynastic tramlines, the steam power of success driving him on. Merlin's diagnosis, aged three, had derailed all family expectations. Jeremy's imperious mother had wanted to sweep Merlin under the carpet (Persian, heirloom, seventeenth century) by locking him away with the sad ranks of special-needs children parcelled out to care homes. I'd clung ferociously to my son, but lost hold of my husband in the process.

On cue, the lift door *pschsss*ed open and Merlin appeared, clutching the hot chocolate he'd bought at the court cafeteria.

'Merlin, you remember your father,' Phoebe suggested appeasingly.

Merlin took stock of the man he only really knew from photographs. 'Are you actually my real father? I find that extraordinary. Don't you?'

'Sorry I haven't been around, old chap. Business abroad and all that . . . But I'm going to make it up to you.' Jeremy produced a brand-new iPhone from his pocket and presented it to Merlin with a theatrical flourish. 'Have you got the latest version? Thought you might like it.' Merlin's eyes glittered with excitement as he ran his fingers over the shiny new handset. 'So,' Jeremy ventured, 'do you still like your old Dad, then?'

Merlin considered this for a moment. 'Well, you're definitely the nicest husband Mum's ever had.'

I smiled inwardly at my son's wacky, off-the-wall diplomacy.

I now noticed a petite woman with a brown pudding-bowl haircut and flat shoes emerging from Jeremy's shadow. Her eyes, too big for her face, gave her an owlish look. She whispered something to him, but before he could introduce her – I presumed she was his PA – the robotic court usher boomed, 'Miss Lucinda Quirke'.

With the reluctance of a draftee crossing a minefield, I left Merlin in Phoebe's care and entered the courtroom. The usher led me into a court panelled in wood as dark as molasses. Various insignia gave off glinting gleams of brass and gold plate. The whole atmosphere was imperious and intimidating. Even the windows seemed cold and unfriendly. I stood in the dock at the back of the court.

To the words 'All rise,' the magistrate, who was in his early sixties and possibly always had been, entered the courtroom and lowered himself down behind the elevated bench. He peered out at the world beneath saggy, blue-veined eyelids. Coupled with his overbite, it gave him the look of an ancient tortoise. (Merlin's habit of describing people as animals was clearly contagious.)

'Would you state your name for the court?' the court clerk asked.

'I'm Lucinda Quirke,' I explained doubtfully. 'I'll be defending myself.' I tried to make it sound like a confident choice and not the desperate move of an underpaid teacher who knew that the queue for Legal Aid was now so long there were Cro-Magnon people at the front of it.

The clerk then escorted me to the front desk, next to the prosecution. I noted the smug smile my announcement had prompted in the prosecution lawyer, and my mouth went dry. The large old building slumbered on around me, blissfully unaware that my life was on the line.

The prosecuting lawyer, speaking with the lock-jawed diction of the aristocracy, set out the case against me. As the details of my night-time kerb crawl were itemized, I felt the condemnatory gaze of the hacks in the press box and the few spectators in the public gallery like a breath on the nape of my neck. Sitting there under the magistrate's judgemental ice-grey eyes, my face got so hot I thought I'd burst into flames.

When it was time to put my version of events to the magistrate, my whole body was trembling. Moving to the witness box, I was sworn in. Steeling myself, I launched into my own defence. I explained how I had always been Merlin's psychological fire blanket, constantly on hand to put out all flames in any social emergency. I described how my over-protectiveness meant that I never let Merlin out the door without a list of phone numbers longer than *War and Peace* and enough stuff in his backpack to set up a comfortable wilderness homestead. I revealed how I wished I'd never had the umbilical cord cut so I could keep track of my dear son more closely. I talked about Merlin's loneliness and sexual frustration and my increasing desperation. I tried to convey how out of my depth I'd felt cruising down an alley behind Liverpool Street Station looking for a prostitute. I talked about how the woman came to the car window and I got out the money to pay but was so nervous when she grabbed my wrist that I fumbled – 'which is why

I dropped the money on the floor of the car,' I insisted. The prosecutor's mouth curled in disbelieving disdain. 'And why no money changed hands,' I clarified quickly.

It was my only hope of getting off. But judging by the body language of the people in the courtroom, nobody seemed all that inclined to believe me. I knew things really weren't going in my favour when I heard the court clerk in the back row straighten her eyebrows. Phoebe was right. I needed a big gun. It was time to whip him out of my holster.

'I would like to call as my first witness Merlin's father, Jeremy Beaufort.'

After being sworn in, Jeremy agreed that I was a loving mother and a person of good character. For the first time that day, I felt my chest unknot.

'Thank you,' I said under my breath, and meant it. Maybe, after all these years, my ex-husband was undergoing a personality transplant and transmogrifying into a Nice Person. Weirder things had happened, right? I'd just been teaching my pupils about the aristocratic Leo Tolstoy, who rejected privilege, embraced pacifism and freed his serfs. Eton-educated George Orwell rebelled against the class system to live in poverty among the destitute. Communist leader Gorbachev embraced glasnost. Apartheid ruler F. W. de Klerk released Mandela . . . and a Kardashian had recently turned down a photo shoot! But when the prosecution lawyer began to cross-examine Jeremy, things took an unexpected psychological swerve.

'Actually,' Jeremy suddenly said, 'even though Lucy has always been a good mother, I suspect she's become so emotionally depleted by Merlin's condition that exhaustion is clouding her judgement. As much as I hate to say it, I'm worried that this does now pose a risk to our son. In all honesty, the welfare of our child is on my conscience.'

A voltage of fury pinioned me back against my chair. 'Scientists couldn't locate *your* conscience with the Hubble Space Telescope,' I said loudly.

The magistrate warned me not to interject and the prosecution lawyer urged Jeremy to continue.

Displaying a personality that had more natural oil than Saudi Arabia, Jeremy launched into a promotional campaign for himself as Father of the Year. Listening to his lies, the slow, thick drip of betrayal sank into the pit of my stomach. Playing up to the press box, he spoke with a fervour last encountered when Bill Clinton tried to convince us he wasn't having sexual relations with That Woman. Jeremy's voice coiled around the courtroom like toxic smoke, and he concluded with the lie that I'd cruelly kept Merlin from him all these years, and in so doing, denied the boy proper paternal guidance.

I jumped out of my chair with an alacrity my body hadn't experienced since I'd been forced to participate in a school aerobics class. 'That's not true! My ex-husband is to parenting – what? I dunno – what Spanx are to sex. A total impossibility.'

A titter ran through the public gallery, but the magistrate gruffly instructed me to sit down.

Jeremy steepled his fingers and continued, the full peacock range of his puffed-up importance on display. 'My ex-wife's monopoly over our child has been so complete that she wouldn't even allow him to accompany me to my mother's funeral.'

I shook my head so violently at this fallacy I was half worried it would fall right off and roll down towards the dock.

'Obviously, Merlin is too old for a custody case, Your Honour. But I'm suggesting that Merlin's residence be decided in a Court of Protection hearing. Clearly, the boy lacks the capacity to make up his own mind as to where he should be living. And, in my view – and in the view of the police, obviously – his mother currently poses a threat to his welfare.'

Hearing my ex-husband uttering these vile, nasty lies made me want to get my son's DNA steam-cleaned immediately.

'I believe that my ex-wife is putting our son in danger, as this court case proves. And I also believe that I can offer a safe harbour at this difficult time.'

I felt as though I'd been in some kind of nuclear explosion. My temples were pounding and my pupils were having difficulty finding their way back to the centre of my eyeballs.

Jeremy lifted his glasses and rubbed his eyes to indicate how long-suffering he was. 'If Lucy would just let me back into Merlin's life, there's nothing I wouldn't do for that boy of mine.'

'And that's exactly what he does. Nothing!' I called out.

At that moment, two things became clear to me: 1) I would never be eligible for a Neurologist's Best Brain Prize and 2) a law degree would always elude me.

'Any more outbursts and I'll hold you in contempt of court,' the magistrate boomed at me, before calling for a short adjournment.

'All rise!'

As soon as the magistrate had left the courtroom, Jeremy sauntered across from the witness box and loomed over me.

'You do realize, if you're convicted, you'll lose your job and your career will be over? Of course, I'd be willing to backtrack and sing your praises to the high heavens . . . if you agree to Merlin coming to live with me.'

'Why do you suddenly want Merlin after all this time, you prick?' I hissed. 'But hey, why don't you get back to me once you've talked it over with all of your personalities.'

'I've changed, Lucinda. Can't you see that? The point is, since my mother died, I've been so lonely. I know I've always put work first, and I bitterly regret that. Now, I just want to make up for my neglect of Merlin. I want to get to know my son. Also, you clearly need a break, whether you admit it or not. I'm just trying to help.'

I thought back to his supercilious battleaxe of a mother with her helmet of blue-steel hair and remembered how her haughty voice, reminiscent of the snobby character played by Margaret Dumont in that Marx Brothers movie, would constantly condemn and belittle me with lines like 'The only thing wrong with Merlin is his mother.' She told anyone who would listen that Jeremy had 'married beneath himself'. I would laughingly agree by pointing out my short stature. But inside I died – especially because my husband never defended me. I glared at him now with pure hatred.

'If you want to avoid jail and keep your job, Lucinda, all you have to do is ask the magistrate to allow Merlin to live with me.'

'The only thing I want to ask the judge is how to get the

stubborn bloodstains off my hands after I've killed you.' I lunged for him then, but he caught my fists in mid-air, cuffing my wrists firmly in his fingers.

'Being in prison is just like being at a hotel, I'm told' – he gave a mordant little smile – 'except that the other guests will want to cut you into tiny pieces and feed you down the sewage system bit by bit. Speaking as a seasoned lawyer, can I tell you my top prison-survival tip? Try not to give the finger to the female heads of any triads or drug gangs.'

'Phoebe said to give you a second chance. She said that you couldn't be all Dick Dastardly panto evil.'

'Very perceptive, your sister.'

'But I knew I couldn't trust you. You have the moral integrity of a flesh-eating microbe, do you know that?'

Jeremy leant backwards against my desk, arms confidently folded, legs casually akimbo, and continued with his intimidation tactics. 'Even a *minimum*-security prison is a notoriously ill-mannered place. I believe that nobody even says "please" before they rape you with a broom handle.'

'What I can't *believe* is how you manage to walk around with that huge ego,' I retaliated. 'I'm amazed it doesn't have to be manoeuvred by crane drivers using block-and-tackle rigs.'

Jeremy just smiled at me – the small, calculating grin of a man who's convinced he knows exactly what's going to happen next. The small, beige woman I'd presumed to be his secretary suddenly beetled across the courtroom towards us. She gave the definite impression that she collected snow-globe knick-knacks bought from cute little shops with names like Things 'n' Stuff; her only other hobby was probably feng shui-ing her aura daily.

'This is Sonia Wilbur. From Social Services,' Jeremy said, with lip-smacking satisfaction.

'You're a social worker?' I should have guessed. With her flat, sensible shoes and big, dangly earrings, she had the word 'busybody' stamped all over her. 'What the hell do you need a social worker for?'

'Sonia?' Jeremy gestured at her to enlighten us.

'Jeremy explained to us at the Disability Living Department that there are very real dangers faced by this vulnerable young adult,' Sonia volunteered tautly. 'He felt it imperative that one of us accompany him to court to take details of the case.'

'What?' I said, thunderstruck.

'I know it's been hard raising Merlin, and you've done an incredible job, Lucy. Do you mind if I call you Lucy? But maybe this is the right time to hand the boy over to his father. Jeremy is extending the hand of parental responsibility,' she said, in a cheering tone, as if she were offering me a warm scone. 'And I think you should take it. If only to give yourself a well-earned break.'

Jeremy gave Sonia his casual movie-star smile, followed by a quick glance deep into her eyes, then away, as though dazzled by her extraordinary perspicacity. 'Thank you, Sonia,' he said.

She flushed with pleasure.

'Are you *insane*? I would never, ever give up my son, least of all to *him*. Merlin needs constant care, love and kindness. I'd rather cut out my own ovaries with an ice pick than let him live with that narcissistic psychopath.'

Jeremy shook his head and exchanged a glance of complicity with the social worker. 'Controlling,' he said. 'She's always had issues. It's one of the reasons we broke up.'

'Cut the crap, Jeremy,' I retorted, 'or you'll be having "issues", too – with oxygen deprivation.'

Sonia speared me with a reproachful glare, then adopted the compulsory thin-as-string, pursed, sour-lemon lips of social workers worldwide. She produced a notepad and started jotting down her observations.

'Write *this* down,' I ordered furiously. 'Jeremy and I had been married for four years before he decided to tell me that he was no longer in love with me . . . Coincidentally, he realized this after screwing a size-zero, double-jointed, ex-catwalk model.'

The big wooden door creaked open at the back of the courtroom and Merlin and Phoebe entered tentatively. For our day in court, Phoebe had scraped her hair into a sensible ponytail. It boinged back and forth like a blonde metronome as she hurried towards us.

'Is everything okay?' she asked. 'When you didn't come out with everyone else for the break, we got worried.'

'You must be Merlin,' Sonia the social worker said to my son, in a voice more appropriate for speaking to a six-year-old.

Merlin perched on the pew behind me. I swivelled to smile reassuringly at him but Sonia insinuated herself into the space between us and bent down to examine him more closely. Her voluminous tent dress gathered in an elephant's bottom of grey in my face.

'What the hell's going on?' Phoebe whispered. 'I smell a very large rodent.'

'Jeremy wants custody. He's brought a social worker with him.'

'What? That's bonkers.'

'He's just told the magistrate that I've prevented him from seeing Merlin and from being a loving father.'

'Loving father?' Phoebe gasped incredulously, 'Hey, social-worker woman, Jeremy's only parenting technique was to suggest playing hide-and-seek with his son. Merlin would hide and then Jeremy would bugger off to the Caribbean with his latest bimbo.'

Jeremy shook his head with mock-sadness. 'Issues,' he mouthed to Sonia.

The social worker's smile narrowed between twin brackets of disapproval as she looked over her glasses and down her nose at these two troublesome sisters.

Phoebe drew me to one side. 'Farrrkk, Lucy. This is all my fault. I can't believe I was stupid enough to think he'd changed.' My sister tugged at a tendril of yellow hair, that tell-tale signal that she was deep in thought and probably mid-plot. 'There's nothing else for it – you're going to have to put Merlin in the witness box to give evidence.'

I glanced over at my son, who was sitting rigidly upright. He was grasping the pew so hard it looked as if he were trying to squeeze blood from the wood. As a boy, he'd been probed, prodded, pinched, stethoscoped, measured, weighed, syringed and blinded with flashlights. The poor kid had endured so many tests he must have thought he was being drafted into an elite SAS squad. The bureaucratic atmosphere of the courtroom clearly conjured up the worst of memories for him. 'No way, Phoebe. I can't put him through that, it'll trigger an anxiety attack,' I said.

'The court needs to hear from him. Merlin can explain how you only got into this position by trying to help him. And that his father is a fuckwit . . . It's the only way, Lu-Lu.'

If only we were airborne and my flight-attendant sister were taking me through the emergency options – *The exits are situated here, here and here* – but right here, right now, there was no way out.

And so it was that my poor, anxious boy, whose suit looked as though it was wearing him, instead of the other way around, took to the witness box. The court officer swore him in: 'Repeat after me. I swear to tell the truth, the whole truth and nothing but the truth . . .'

As if he knew how *not* to. It was Merlin's mantra. Asking Merlin to tell the truth was like asking a haemophiliac for a pint of blood. The kid's honesty meant that, socially, I often found myself perspiring more than a Bulgarian weightlifter taking a drugs test. Conversing with Merlin in public was the greatest laxative known to motherkind. And so it was with great trepidation that I asked him to give his full name to the court.

'But you know my name,' he replied, puzzled.

'Well, tell me it anyway.'

Molasses-slow minutes oozed by. The magistrate clasped his hands together then peered over his spectacles at my son in a clichéd judge manoeuvre. He cleared his throat and asked Merlin if he was all right.

Silence erupted again. Was I the first person to assume the crash position in a court of law? I wondered.

Finally, Merlin turned towards the magistrate to reply to his query. 'These august surroundings demand one's best composure, and Mum always says that the trouble with answering too quickly is that you may say something you haven't thought of yet . . . My name is Merlin. Having an unusual name can be such an asset if you're going into the law or any other aspect of showbusiness, but it can prove burdensome when you are differently abled,' he explained.

The magistrate's eyebrows, which resembled toothbrush bristles, scoured his forehead briefly. 'I see,' he said, a little flummoxed. Something in me broke open; I just couldn't bear to put Merlin through any more. I sat down abruptly, prompting the magistrate to give the nod to the prosecution lawyer to begin his questioning.

'Can you tell the court where you were on the night of May the sixth?' the prosecutor probed.

I watched as my son conjured up a well-practised facial expression guaranteed to make him appear attentive. This involved frowning slightly and tilting his head as though calculating the square root of the hypotenuse.

'We live in a very confusing society,' Merlin said. 'You neuro-typical people think Aspies like me are weird. Well, we think *you're* weird. You ask, "How are you?" but you don't want to know the answer. Television is called entertainment, but it isn't. McDonald's is confused with food. Donald Trump is confused with a political leader. Russia pretends to be a democracy. There are flotation devices under the seats of planes instead of parachutes . . . and my father is suddenly going in for the Concerned Father lark.'

'So when did you last see your father?' the magistrate inquired.

Merlin looked at him as though he were intellectually impaired. 'Today. In the foyer.'

'No, I mean before today.'

'I last saw him with my grandma on the sixteenth of February 2011, at three p.m. A Thursday. It was sunny and she was wearing a mauve dress, which is really just pink trying to be purple.'

'So will you tell the court why you didn't attend your

grandma's funeral earlier this year?' the prosecutor piped up. 'Was it because your mother wouldn't let you?'

'No.' Once more, Merlin looked with pity upon this solemn representative of the British judiciary. 'It was because my grandma wouldn't be there. Obviously.'

The magistrate glanced up from under wizened brows. 'Merlin, I know courtrooms can be quite intimidating places. I mean, the whole process can be terribly overwhelming . . . Before we get back to the night in question, would you like to ask *me* anything?'

'Well, yes, I would.' He had that look of a mischievous cherub again, and the impression was only enhanced by what he then asked: 'What's been on your mind lately? Would you say you have the ideal marriage? Are you a New Weak Man or a Lost Warrior? True love asks for nothing, but tell me, today are you living for tomorrow? Statistically, the probability of any of us being here is so small that you'd think the mere fact of existing would keep us in a contented dazzlement of surprise, but why then does ennui eat away at us all? Especially me.'

A snicker ran around the courtroom, but the magistrate raised a chastening finger. 'Do you know why you are here today? Your mother was arrested for breaking the law. Do you understand why?'

'Yes. May I ask you one more question?'

The magistrate gave a tentative nod.

'How big is your penis?'

It was pretty clear from the magistrate's ensuing splutter that this was not a question he'd ever been asked before in a court of law.

'It's just that it would be a great relief to know if mine is normal and what I'm supposed to do with it. With your bedraggled demeanour and long-suffering majesty, you have the air of an intelligent but ill-treated polar bear,' he then told the incredulous magistrate. 'You're wearing a wedding ring. So if *you* can find love, why can't *I*?'

'Polar bear?' the magistrate repeated, startled.

'I'm sorry, Your Honour,' I deciphered placatingly. 'Merlin gives animal totems to everyone. It's one of his quirks.'

'Really? And what is your mother?' the magistrate asked Merlin.

'Well, she's part owl, as she reads so much. Part meerkat, as she's always popping her head up to see how and where I am. But predominantly a silvery, majestic unicorn, because she's loving, unique and magical . . . Her sister, Phoebe, is a prancing Shetland pony, tossing her mane.'

'And your father?' the magistrate inquired gently.

Five seconds crawled past on their hands and knees, gasping for water, before Merlin finally replied, 'Constrictor formosissimus.'

The magistrate's brow furrowed. He glanced around the courtroom for elucidation.

Once more, Merlin was perplexed by the lack of intellectual acumen in London's law courts. 'Of the Boidae family,' he elaborated.

The magistrate threw up his hands in a gesture of incomprehension.

Merlin sighed wearily. 'A boa constrictor . . . And snakes and unicorns should never mate. I, personally, have unicorn tendencies, as I'm so exotic, but I often curl up like a petrified pangolin . . . Do you think that one day polar bears will be able to fly and meerkats will live at sea? I would feel exquisite rapture and sublime joy if Mum and I could go home now.'

Others may laugh at the way Merlin speaks, but to me his voice dripped honesty, like clear honey.

In his summation, the judge said to me, 'You have a duty of care to your son, and that is to look after his moral welfare – not, as you might think, to initiate him into the ways of sex with a prostitute. You are hereby convicted of kerb-crawling. But I have noted your excellent written character references from fellow teachers and students, and I do not believe that you meant any harm to your son. I therefore grant you a twelve-month conditional discharge. You must be of good behaviour or you could be back before me and facing prison.'

I had barely had a chance to thank him when Jeremy's social worker jumped up and asked about Merlin's 'residence'. Could the decision be referred to the Court of Protection? Merlin was out of education, unemployed and drifting . . .

'What *are* your plans, young man?' the magistrate asked Merlin kindly.

With the perfect timing of an American talk-show comic, my phone buzzed. I checked the message. One of the voluntary jobs I'd applied for on Merlin's behalf had said he could start work with them.

'He's volunteering for Oxfam. The Shoreditch store,' I interjected.

The polar bear nodded approvingly, then asked whether or not I could afford to pay the court costs. When I shook my head, he said, 'Is there nobody who could help you? Your ex-husband, for example, who seems so dedicated to his son and yet is also so far behind with his child-maintenance payments?'

Jeremy spluttered. 'I'm a bit strapped for cash right now. An investment deal went belly up. And my mother's estate, well, it's not quite settled . . .'

My mind jumped to a snapshot of the grand, aloof-looking country manor where Jeremy had grown up. It was just as cold and inhospitable as the Beaufort clan itself. I shuddered at the memory of all the misery I'd endured there during our brief marriage.

The polar bear levelled a look at Jeremy – the look of a top-order predator, clearly meant to remind him exactly where he was in the judicial food chain. Jeremy immediately acquiesced, then slithered out of court, Sonia in sycophantic tow to the Constrictor formosissimus.

The petrified pangolin and the meerkat-owl-unicorn then sauntered hand in hand out on to the street to join the Shetland pony, who was smoking a celebratory fag. As we stood on the busy road in the bright sunshine, I had the blinking, disorientated countenance of a prisoner who has somehow, quite miraculously, managed to tunnel to freedom.

7

Parenthood, or, Why Mothers Drink Gin

The newspaper report in *The Times* the next day read:

> A mother appeared in court yesterday after having attempted to hire a prostitute to initiate her twenty-year-old son into the ways of sex. The woman took the young man to a red-light district in the vicinity of Liverpool Street Station and encouraged him to select a prostitute for this purpose. In the event, the woman he chose was in fact an undercover police officer working for the city's vice squad. The young man fled the scene and his forty-six-year-old mother was arrested. The woman, who cannot be named because it would reveal the identity of her vulnerable son, admitted trying to solicit a woman to have sex with her autistic child, but was given a conditional discharge.

The relief at not losing my job was immense. Even better, Merlin now had a voluntary job, and started there the day before his twenty-first birthday. Luckily, the headmaster at my school was away on a training course that morning, so I didn't have to pretend that I'd come down with the bubonic plague in order to accompany my son on his first day.

Shoreditch looks like a film set for a Sherlock Holmes movie. As we stepped off the bus into a cobbled lane, I half expected a frock-coated, cackling Moriarty to sweep past, hotly pursued by a man in an Inverness cape smoking a calabash pipe. The rain splashed and hissed from bursting gutters, and the wind moaned around the corners like an animal. Despite the unseasonal chill, misery rose up off Merlin like steam. He was all closed up and dark, like a holiday cottage in the dead of winter.

'You might make new friends. Maybe even find a girl-friend . . . It'll be exciting.' My words ran into each other like raindrops down a windowpane. Both of us knew I was lying. What girl would ever accept his non-negotiable flaws? Doctors and their stethoscopic minds had never been able to diagnose my son. Asperger's was the closest they could get but, really, he simply had Merlin Syndrome. And there was no cure.

'Do I have to go? I can't be sociable all the time.' His eyes were tiny crescents of despair. 'And even when I do trans-mit, no girl ever picks up my signal.'

It was true. He might as well have been relaying transmis-sions from Alpha Centauri. And his social alienation was only enhanced by the fact that he was wearing an iridescent, lime-green, all-in-one Joker jumpsuit with matching green bowler hat, both of which were emblazoned in question marks. I'd tried to talk him out of the sartorial ensemble over breakfast, arguing that there was no such thing as 'lucky clothes', but he'd stood firm.

'If I'm the question, some girl may provide the answer,' he'd explained hopefully.

I sighed. Raising Merlin was the equivalent of having ten children in one. With his mood swings and anxieties and endless questions, I had to hook myself up intravenously to an encyclopaedia for even the quickest of chats. There was no time left over for friends, for fun, for love. Phoebe was right about my man drought. If it weren't for bra fittings in the local lingerie department, I wouldn't have any sex life at all. I doubted that I'd ever again have my fingers tangled in a man's hair and my bare arse pressed against a wall. Never again would there be another morning where I woke up happy but unable to walk straight. I sagged into myself like a post-party balloon. No. No. Merlin *had* to gain some independence so that I could, too.

I turned to him now in the busy street and said, 'But you can't sit at home all day. You need to get a life. Not just for you. It's exhausting for me, too.' I took a deep breath, rallied and forced my lips to beam encouragingly. 'Just give this a try. Okay, sweetie?'

Merlin bristled. 'Why must you be so happy all the time?' he yelled at me, so loudly that passers-by glared and stared. 'It wears me down! Your positivity is positively killing me!'

Most children seek psychiatric help because their parents are abusive, neglectful, destructive. My son wanted to see a shrink because his mother was too happy. Mind you, after half an hour of being berated for being too happy, I was pretty fucking depressed, let me tell you.

The sun came out from behind a grey bank of cloud, sparkled joyfully for a moment, then dived straight back under cover as though disillusioned by the gloom it had glimpsed.

'I'm sorry I'm such a disappointment as a son.' Merlin's voice was clipped and precise, like that of a brave but doomed pilot in a British war movie. 'I want to try to be a better son for you.'

A sudden stabbing sweetness caught me off guard. I gazed at him for a moment, paralysed by love. 'Darling, you're a wonderful son.' I wanted to anoint his anxiety with compliments, but could only come up with: 1) 'It's good to be different'; 2) 'You're so clever'; and 3) 'I love you.' They weren't much, but I said them anyway and hugged him hard.

The charity shop was tucked up a crooked sidestreet. A bell tinkled as I opened the door. A musty, fusty, friendly chaos of clothes and toys and towers of books leant precariously this way and that. I scanned the room for the most senior-looking person. A bearded bloke in white Croc bistro clogs sauntered over with an outstretched hand, his arm clanking with chunky silver bracelets.

'Hello. I'm Merlin's mother,' I admitted, as though this were a crime. 'He's starting voluntary work with you today.'

'Grrrrreat,' the beardy bloke said with geezerish bonhomie. 'Surrrre. How *are* you?'

'Oh, you know. Living the dream.'

When he laughed, I smiled, and it felt like the front door of an old house creaking open on rusty hinges.

'Attention, people!' Mr Croc Bistro Clogs clapped his hands. A motley crew of punks, rockers, mods and old hippies emerged from dusty corners. 'This is Merlin. He's going to be volunteering with us for work experience. Isn't that grrrrreat?'

This news clearly underwhelmed the staff, who gave my son a nonchalant once-over. I saw Merlin selecting 'Keen and Interested' from his mental Filofax of Neuro-typical Facial Expressions. Watching Merlin trying to act normal – well, it was like watching a Maori trying to Morris dance.

'Hello,' he said experimentally. When nobody answered, he pushed on heroically. 'Well, you're a very exotic bunch. Now I understand exactly how Darwin must have felt arriving on the Galápagos Islands and encountering so many esoteric creatures. Perhaps I'm really a zoologist sent to live among you to observe your behaviour and habitat? I'd say, on first observation, that you're quite colourful, rare and eccentric specimens.'

The fact that Merlin was uttering this thought while wearing his iridescent, lime-green Joker jumpsuit with matching green bowler hat made his comment unintentionally hilarious. I glanced around to enjoy some comic camaraderie but my laugh was cut short when I noticed the other volunteers exchanging eye-rolls. Sadness pressed down on me like a low ceiling.

'You're a big, strapping lad, aren't you?' The Beardy-Croc-Bistro-Clog-Wearer addressed my son in a voice that would be more appropriate used to a non-English-speaker. 'Why don't we find you some nice little jobs out the back?'

My eyes darted around the shop apprehensively, searching for anybody who might prove an ally, and snagged on the girl slouched over the till. With dyed blonde hair flamboyantly streaked with candyfloss pink, thick black eyeliner and tattoos, she reminded me of the baddie in a school teen movie – the one who chews gum, swaggers about in a dress so short you can see her ovaries, beats up female rivals, and bullies and bitches the geeky girl until she hangs herself. She was incredibly pretty, except for uneven, crooked, yellowish teeth – teeth which had clearly never seen a dentist. They looked like a little row of tombstones. I only know this because, when I smiled at her, she gnashed them. I had thought about enlisting her help to aid Merlin's assimilation but I got the distinct impression that this would be futile. And this impression was confirmed when I said, 'Excuse me, please,' to which she snarled in reply, 'Fuck, a posh cunt.'

I was just about to warn Merlin to steer clear when he popped up by the till and looked down at her with a shy, delicate glance.

'What choo lookin' at?' The girl had the slinky grace of a lynx, which was clashingly at odds with her whiny norf-ern accent. 'What brung *you* here?'

My teacherly toes curled but I thought it prudent to refrain from grammar instruction for once.

Merlin gave the girl a puzzled smile. He rubbed his forehead, dazed, as if he'd been in a fight. 'What brought me here was an internationally recognized global icon – the red double-decker bus, making me just one of the six million passengers who use the British bus service on over seven hundred different routes each day, confirming it as the most extensive bus service in Europe.'

I ached to save him from exile to Social Siberia yet again but felt as useful as a traffic policeman in the Sahara Desert. The teenage till operator blew a bubble of pink gum, said, 'Yer proper bent, you,' then looked away.

Merlin persevered courageously. 'So,' he ventured, 'how's the catwalk contract going? You're so beautiful, you would look good even if you were bald. What perfume are you wearing? I detect ambergris.'

'What thuh fuck's that?'

'Actually, it's whale bile that becomes poo.'

'What yer on about?'

'The whale gets an ulcer, probably from eating crab, then eventually excretes it. This hard, black substance is a popular base for perfumes. I find the juxtaposition of something so base with something so beautiful quite captivatingly incongruous, don't you?'

No, would be my guess, judging by the scowl on her young face.

My poor son. My heart did a flip in sympathy for him. It flopped like a pole vaulter on to a mattress as I waited for the inevitable spiteful cruelty to come.

'*Oi! Freak Squad Alert!*' Till-Girl bellowed. 'Beardy Wackjob says we haveta be nice to yer. But I doan fucken think so, freak-face.'

Merlin gave a smile full of big teeth and innocence. He was used to concealing heartbreak beneath cheery stoicism in public. But it took the effort of every muscle in my body to keep from ripping the girl's brain out through her nose with my bare hands.

I wrapped an arm around his shoulder and led him away. 'Stay away from her, Merlin. That girl has a mean streak.'

'I know in my heart that the day will come when I will have a lovely, funny female companion who can do jazz hands with me,' he said to me in a sad, tiny voice. 'Won't I, Mum?'

I executed a little jazz-hands display of my own to avoid answering. Finally, after explaining in excruciating detail what to do in case of a flash flood/earthquake/meteor storm (over-protective? *Moi?*), I reluctantly left the shop, leaving Merlin explaining the finer details of how a particle accelerator works to a bewildered customer who'd come in for a second-hand CD.

As I trudged back under a sullen sky towards the bus stop, a skittish wind pulled at my cardigan, which hit the backs of my legs and then swept around to slap my face – a deserved slap. Why had I held out any hope that this charity-shop experience would be any different from all the other humiliations Merlin had endured? Why had I made him do it? It was obviously going to be torture for him. Clearly, it was time to paper my office with Mensa rejection forms. And when this job failed, as it invariably would, what would come next? He'd be lost, like a pebble in a pond; the surface of daily life would simply close over him until the water looked smooth again and nobody would ever know he was even here.

On impulse, I turned on my heel and pushed back into the charity store. I thrust all the money I had – about £180 – into the hands of the Beardy Croc-Clogged One.

'Listen,' I whispered. 'It's my son's twenty-first birthday tomorrow. After work tonight, will you take him and all the staff down to the pub for a celebratory pint? And can you just pretend that it was their idea?'

'Surrrrre!' he said. Then, turning around to face the shop-floor, he boomed, 'Merlin, we'd like to take you out after work to say welcome. My treat. Would you like that, mate?'

My son's eyes lit up with nervous excitement and he ran his hand through his floppy fringe. Why could nobody notice the rainbow colours I saw in the kid? Because they were filtered through the prism of love, obviously. Sadly, I might be the only person on the planet ever to see the boy in all his Technicolor glory. Happy Birthday, Merlin, I thought dismally.

The offer of a free night down the pub even cheered Cruella de Vil of the Till. She gave a crooked little smile.

But maybe life was looking up? I thought hopefully as I set off to the bus stop once more. Sure . . . and Paris Hilton is actually an incredibly shy recluse who will go to any extremes to avoid publicity, I concluded sourly, as I built down my hopes once more.

8

Portrait of the Autist as a Young Man

Not wanting a C minus from the head teacher for attend-
ance, with possibly a long stint in career detention, I stayed
late at school to make up for my morning's absenteeism.

Walking into my empty street all alone that evening, I felt
as dull as the grey day. The blustery weather had escalated
into a fairly intense blizzard, or what the English know as
'high summer'. A sudden gust snatched at the scarf around
my throat and tugged on my larynx, but I was already
choked up with emotion. On the eve of his twenty-first
birthday, I'd bribed a bunch of strangers to take my son out
on the town to pretend to celebrate his coming of age. Oh,
where was my mothering medal?

'I've got a chicken to roast, a bottle of vino and the mak-
ings of a rather exotic salad.' It was my sister's voice. I'd been
too self-absorbed to notice her waiting in her car outside my
house. She hugged me in the driveway with her only free

hand. 'Oh, and some pretzels, chocolate-chip cookies and peanut brittle I brought back from New York. Let's get inside! It's about to bucket down!'

'I thought you were rostered away all week in South America?'

'I've momentarily removed the word "globe trotter" from my passport. It's my nephew's twenty-first birthday, for God's sake. I wanted to be around to make sure I retain position of Favourite Aunt.'

'You're his only aunt,' I reminded her, turning the key in the lock.

'Also, I don't like the pilot I was rostered on with,' she said, striding past me down the hallway. 'Of course, the best indication that your pilot is useless is if you find your-self deep in the Amazonian jungle eating his flesh. But why wait to find that out?'

She plonked her grocery bags down on the counter and washed her hands. 'Besides, with Mum away, I thought you might need company. The kids are over with Danny, otherwise known as my Lying Scumbag Suddenly Gone Gay Ex-Husband, which means I need to take the cork out of din-ner, swing from the chandelier and drink to Merlin's health.'

'By ruining our own?' I asked, unpacking thick, white crusty bread and full-fat, cardiac-arrest-inducing creamy blue cheese from one of the bags.

'Exactly. It's the only way to make me forget how quickly my kids have just forgiven their father for friggin' abandoning us.'

I admonished her with a baguette, waving it in her face. 'Don't make your kids take sides, Phoebe.'

'Of course they should take sides . . . *Mine*. Didn't we take sides when our dad buggered off?'

'But we shouldn't have. When Dad died, mid-bonk with his barmaid, my guilt-gland throbbed. I never really spoke to him again after he left Mum—'

'Which is ironic, as Dad always complained that the women in our family could talk with a mouth full of marbles under wet cement. He reckoned we got that motor-mouth gene from Mum.'

'Where *is* our bohemian materfamilias now, by the way? I've lost track. Rowing the Atlantic? Racing to the magnetic North Pole? Parachuting? Shark diving? Tap-dancing? Turin-shroud-authenticating?' I deadpanned.

Phoebe laughed. We adore our mother but, since she hit the menopause, most of our conversations with our only living parent begin with her saying, 'I'm just back from . . .' or 'I'm just off to . . .' and end with 'Sorry, darling, but I don't have a weekend free till late next Millennium.'

'Let me find her latest communiqué to us. Hang on.' Phoebe rummaged in her voluminous handbag, extracted a beach-and-palm-tree-themed postcard and read aloud: '"Hi kids! Setting sail from Mexico for Cuba. Prepare for tales of hurricane-dodging, Day of the Dead epiphanies and swim-ming with pigs. Hoping to snaffle myself an able-bodied sailor en route, if only for the opportunity to make semen puns."'

I stifled a brief pang of jealousy. Because of Merlin, my life would never have a second act. At times, I wasn't even sure I'd make it to the interval – let alone ever feel the thrill of a man arching hungrily over me, mouthing my breasts as though they were sweet meringues. Aghast at the utter need melting my insides, I distracted myself by moving across the kitchen to mix cocktails as Phoebe read on.

'"And Happy B'day, Merlin, sweetie. Prezzie to come. Love

from your doting Glam-ma! Meanwhile, girls, have a bottle or ten for *moi*!"' Phoebe then put the postcard under a fridge magnet for Merlin to read later.

Two hours later, my sister and I, obeying maternal orders, were on our third pitcher of martinis and about two sips away from streaking naked down the street or mortgaging the house to buy into a Ponzi scheme, then mail-ordering a few gigolos with the proceeds.

I'd just started to clear away the chicken carcass when Phoebe stopped me. 'Hey, not so fast, sis.'

She retrieved the wishbone, curled a pinky around one side and offered the other bonsai bone to me. I gazed at it forlornly for a moment. Ask most women what they most want in the world, their ultimate genie-in-a-bottle wish, and it would probably be along the lines of the undying love of a poetic, gourmet-cooking, vaginally obsessed, philanthropic billionaire who finds fellatio oppressive and just adores your kooky, undomesticated ways, including loving you best unshaven and with no make-up. But every birthday candle and chicken bone wish *I'd* made for the past twenty-one years was for my son to be happy.

I hooked my finger around the wishbone and closed my eyes. 'I wish for Merlin to find love,' I prayed silently. 'And to have a happy birthday.'

The bone broke – in Phoebe's favour. 'Jesus. And I was actually trying to let you win! Life really is a major pain in the butt for you at the moment, isn't it, Lu-Lu?'

'If I could isolate the pain just to my butt, it would be manageable.' I sighed.

'Well, running the risk of sounding sentimental, you really are an amazing mum, Lucy. I mean, it hasn't been easy.'

'Easy? Mothering Merlin has given me the same kind of ride a bucking bronco would give a cowgirl. With no saddle, reins or helmet . . . Oh God, and then whenever I go to work I have to put up with some school mum weeping and wailing about how their wayward kid is not taking to his Latin lessons.'

'Ad absurdum.'

'Exactly. I just feel this grinding hollowness. I try not to give in to the sour taste of envy, but there are some days when a gloating parent's smug pride in a perfect child makes me want to run them over repeatedly in my car until they're crushed to death.'

'Even me?' my sister asked in a small voice.

'Good God, no.' I cuddled her close. 'I adore you and Dylan and Julia. No. It's just that – well, a few more years and your kids will fly the nest, and you'll be free. Whereas unless Merlin finds someone to love him – which, let's face it, is about as likely as Vladimir Putin joining the Peace Corps – he'll always be umbilically attached to me.'

'You don't know that for sure . . .'

'Yes, I do. Our isolated evenings will be heavily noodle-focused and probably involve a lot of cats. I'll spend my life bribing people to be his friends . . . And then, Christ! What happens when I die? Whose name will Merlin write in the "In case of emergency, please notify" section on official forms? It breaks my heart, Phoebe.'

'My kids can take over when we croak. They are his cousins, for Christ's sake.'

'You know they find him too embarrassing to be around.'

'No, they don't.'

'Yes, they do. And you can't blame them. I mean, Merlin does say the most alarming things at times . . . Just today he told me that having a penis is like having a funfair in your underpants, that his toenails smell like a volcano, a nice lava smell, that lions mate over fifty times a day and that a pig's orgasm lasts for thirty minutes.'

'Not if he's a chauvinist pig! I love the stuff Merlin tells me. Like how the female praying mantis initiates sex by ripping the male's head off. Hi honey, I'm home!'

'But not everyone sees the funny side like you do. No. I'll die, and then he'll retreat into himself, friendless, misunderstood, then eventually he'll be framed for a crime he didn't commit because he doesn't have the social skills to deny it and the neighbours will start giving interviews to the tabloids about him always having been a "troubled loner".'

'I wish I were around more. You need more help with him. Some respite.'

'Getting help is too expensive.'

'Well, what about Jeremy? Why don't we hire a lawyer to fight for retrospective child-maintenance payments?'

'You know how hard I tried to get him to pay his share. But he always manages to win. His declarable income is zero, due to his offshore-company trusts. I just don't want to waste any more money or emotional energy going after the sleaze-bag.'

'I just want you to be happy, sis.'

'The secret to happiness, Pheebs, is limbo-low expectations.'

My sister looked at me in astonishment. 'When did my big, brave sis become so mousey? If you don't watch out, someone will catch you with a bit of cheese then feed you to a boa constrictor.'

'Yep. That just about sums up my marriage.' Phoebe yawned elaborately and stretched like a cat. 'Sorry. I'd love to bitch more about our bad taste in husbands but I'm so jet-lagged.'

'Let's leave the dishes until tomorrow. Why don't you stay here and go up to bed? My baby boy's turning twenty-one! I need to use my body as a repository for alcohol for a while longer.'

My sister kissed me on the forehead and tottered up the stairs to the spare room. I refilled my martini glass and sat by the living-room window, pretending not to peer down the street looking for Merlin. He was officially an adult now and I had to start treating him like one. My mind flew to all the nature documentaries I'd watched with him. Baby animals become independent so young and yet *we're* supposed to be the highest life form? Crabs squirt a few hundred thousand eggs into the water, then simply scarper back home and let the little nippers fend for themselves. Malleefowl babies hatch, then after a couple of hours' rest, waddle off into the bush to find food and, twenty-four hours later, start flying. Surface-dwelling rodents like guinea pigs and agoutis can run as soon as they're born. Wildebeest calves, born while the herd is mid-migration, can stand up and trot after their mother within fifteen frigging minutes. And yet here was I, still tying my twenty-one-year-old son's shoelaces.

My thoughts turned to my happy, hedonistic, man-hunting mother. She'd started over. And so could I. It was time to stop mollycoddling my son and to go and get a man of my own. I had to do something soon; things were getting desperate. I'd recently started to have romantic thoughts about my mobile phone when it was on vibrate. I made a vow to myself there and then that from today on I'd let go of the parental reins.

. . . But rain was peppering at the glass and all I could think about was whether or not Merlin had taken his coat. I rang his phone and left a voice message reminding him to get a taxi home. I re-texted the mini-cab number. I circled the living room like a spoon in a bowl. Clearly, I'd need a twelve-step programme to break the over-mothering habit. Finally, I flicked on the telly and tried to distract myself by watching reruns of the medical drama *House* – which, nine out of ten doctors agree, can cause hypochondria. The show's medical emergencies only made me fret about Merlin more. Restless with worry, I flicked off the TV and roamed around the living room once more. I roamed so much I grew concerned about wearing a hole in the carpet.

I opened the window to scan the road for a sight of him and stood listening to the forlorn cry of distant car horns. I so wanted the world to welcome my son, to respect and value my darling boy, but it was clearly never going to happen. The unfairness of it hit me like a slap. Cold-shouldered, excluded, belittled, bullied, shin-kicked, sucker-punched, lost and lonely – this was to be his life. He would live forever in my basement, possibly passing the time with a little light whittling ... or accidentally launching a NASA rocket from his bedroom computer.

All I could do was concentrate on loving him.

Blindsided by a queasy swell of emotion, I gave in to a brittle sob of exhaustion, slumped down on the couch, my head buried in the cushions, and cried my eyes out, my heartbreak and I sinking deeper and deeper together to the bottom of the well.

I jolted awake some time later in a blind panic. The dank smell of wet pavement wafted through the open window. My brain scrambled. What time was it? Where was Merlin? Was he alive? Throwing on the light switch, I saw his shoes, kicked off in the hall. Relief flooded through me. Wrung out, I closed the window, bolted the door and climbed the stairs to bed, lost in my own private sadness, the heavy blackness of despair letting no light in or out.

9

Coming, Ready or Not

Late on the morning of my son's twenty-first birthday, I climbed the stairs with a tray of tea and Vegemite toast (triangular, not square – square toast is only to be eaten on Wednesdays; and marmalade only on Mondays). It was nearly lunchtime and my sister was in the kitchen wrapping presents and laying out the Scrabble board. That was to be Merlin's big birthday – playing word games with his mum and aunt. Good God, the boy might as well have 'social leper' tattooed on his forehead. Still, I lectured myself, I must rally my spirits to ensure he had a happy day. But it was with a heavy heart and a fake smile that I creaked open his bedroom door.

As my eyes adjusted to the dark, I detected a flash of milky skin and a tangle of sheets and legs . . . Four legs . . . Four arms . . . Two heads. Through the shadows, a single blade of sun pierced the blind and struck the mirror, casting prisms that flickered and shifted – which is why it took me a while to discern the blazing hair on Merlin's pillow. Pink-and-gold hair. A great pink puff of candyfloss hair.

My son was in bed with a woman. The tray wobbled in my hands and tea slurped out of the cup. How the hell had this happened? At that precise moment, it would have been easier for me to spontaneously grasp the theory of sub-atomic particles and quantum gravity. In the mirror above Merlin's bed, my own eyes stared back at me, as bare and round as light bulbs. I had goose pimples on my goose pimples. The bare xylophone of a woman's spine curved towards me. She gave a feline stretch, then turned on to her back, breasts bobbing above the duvet like two poached eggs, and said to me, 'I've proper got the munchies.'

I tried to slow down my breath so that my heart would stop knocking about in my chest and I could regain my senses. I felt as though I'd been pushed on stage in a play where I didn't know the lines. 'I'm Lucy,' I said in a rush, after much too long a silence. 'Here's some toast . . . Can I get you anything else?' I offered, thinking, a medal? Jewellery? Or perhaps a gold-plated pumpkin carriage to parade you around town? Because I was so, so grateful to this sexual Cinderella I could burst with joy.

Merlin sat up, his eyes twinkling with amazement. He was effervescent with excitement, as though he'd just had a B12 shot.

'I mean, can I get you any breakfast?' I asked, as nonchalantly as an imminent cardiac arrest would allow.

'That's a splendid idea, Mother!' Merlin exclaimed.

'Great. Okay. See you downstairs, then,' I said, as though

this were an everyday occurrence and not a miracle on a par with Jesus changing water into wine. I left the tray on the bed, barrelled down the stairs two at a time and burst back into the kitchen, where Phoebe was jiggling tea bags in two cups.

'There's a girl!'

'Where?'

'In Merlin's bed!'

'What?'

'There's a girl. Naked. In Merlin's bed!' I fizzed, in a fire-cracker burst of phosphorescent joy.

Phoebe gawped at me, opening her mouth in pantomime astonishment, her hands frozen mid-jiggle.

'I know. Other mothers are over the moon when their sons get into Harvard or climb Mount Everest. But I'm euphoric because my son got laid! And on his twenty-first birthday. What a present. I will love that girl for ever!'

Drops fell from the motionless teabags, *splosh, splosh, splosh* . . .

'Jeeeesus. What? Really?' my sister finally said.

'Yes! Aren't you excited?'

'Are you kidding?! I'm more excited than when the Berlin Wall came down and the Cold War ended. Who? Who is it?'

'I think it's the pretty girl with the bad attitude and terrible teeth. From the charity shop. They're total English teeth, you know? All haphazard and unkempt. But with a straight face and no smiling, the girl could be a model. She's all willowy and pale and frail . . . you know? And she's just slept with my son! Which makes her the most beautiful girl in the world.'

'Wow! I mean, I'm just so glad I brought champagne!'

'Forget champagne. Merlin! In bed with a woman! I feel I

should – I don't know – throw a virgin sacrifice into a volcano, or dance with the whirling dervishes 'neath a harvest
moon, or ride a horse naked through the town centre or
something.'

Phoebe flung the teabags sinkwards, screamed with
amazement and hugged me, a demented grin plastered to
her pretty, lightly freckled face. Our amazed, delighted
laughter crackled like popcorn.

We were giggling so loudly we didn't hear Merlin's foot-
fall on the stairs. He didn't so much burst into the room as
spurt into it. He leapt up on to us both like a labrador puppy.
His face was vivid with joy. He was so happy he seemed to
be in Technicolor. His smile filled the hollows of my bones
with bliss.

Then he took a step backwards, raked the tousled blond
hair out of his eyes and said sombrely, 'Mum, I have an electric penis. Is it normal for a cock to get rock hard?'

'Ah, well, erm . . . yes, yes it is, dear.'

'Oh, good. Because I just rammed my hard cock into her
key lime pie.'

'Darling! I don't think you should over-share.' I tried to
interrupt, but words were crowding out of him like traffic,
colliding, crashing, zooming around the room in a Grand
Prix of superlatives and elation. Phoebe discreetly retreated
to the sink to sip her tea.

'And did you know that all women have chocolate caramel soufflé inside them? It's delicious!'

'Okay, okay – waaaaay too much information,' I said, as
once more tea shot out of my sister's nose. This was getting
to become a family trait – a trait which could see us barred
from a gathering at Highgrove.

'But don't you find it intriguing that all women have chocolate-caramel vaginas?'

My sister and I played facial semaphore for a moment before I replied sternly, 'Merlin, these things are private. You really should never discuss them.'

'Really? Why?' he asked, bewildered. He then gave me a look of giddy and gleeful abandon. 'I thought I was going to be the world's oldest virgin!' His body was pure energy; it was as though he were made up of solidified light. He was positively shimmering with exhilaration. 'Kayleigh is the most dazzling star in all of the fantastical firmament,' he sighed.

And with that, he bounded back out of the room, only a cartoon plume of exhaust smoke left behind as he evaporated upstairs.

'Okay,' I said to my sister. 'On the one hand, I'm thrilled to have raised a boy who loves cunnilingus, but on the other hand – paging Dr Freud to Reception.'

'Do you think it's too early for alcohol?'

'Definitely not.'

We'd only had time to down one vodka shot when Merlin and his paramour entered the kitchen. He had carried Kayleigh downstairs, which is why I greeted her bottom first. It was pert and clad in a mini skirt which appeared to be made from imitation synthetic leopardskin, if there is such a thing.

Next came her legs: two-tone legs, mostly orange from fake tan but with Arctic-white creases behind the knees and at the backs of her ankles. Then came the breasts, scooped into a push-up bra and strapped up under her chin someplace. Twining its way up her neck was a tattooed climbing rose, complete with thorns, and above that a delicate, pretty face with two nose rings and ten earrings weighing down each lobe. Her blur of gold-and-pink hair had been Gorgoned by a night of fitful sleep. Merlin placed her down on the floor with the delicacy of a Sotheby's auctioneer handling a rare Imperial Fabergé egg.

I took a good look at her in the light. The till operator from the charity shop was pretty but worn, like a Cindy doll that's been chewed on by a dog for a week. That furtive, suspicious, measured look she wore reminded me of an urban fox on the scavenge – in other words: not to be approached without a net and a tranquillizer dart.

Phoebe and I watched as she lit up a cigarette, took a prolonged inhalation, leant back on the wall with one thin leg up behind her like a flamingo, and bloomed smoke. 'Jeez . . . This is a fuckin' mansion,' she said with serene insouciance.

My sister and I played eye-tennis for a moment before I remembered to speak. 'Hello again. Um . . . This is my sister, Phoebe.'

'And *this* is Kayleigh,' Merlin said reverentially. His eyes were limpid with love. 'My goddess,' he added, falling to his knees to kiss her hand, then peering adoringly up at her through his silky fringe. There was hope all over him. He was positively perfumed by it. He stood back up and brushed his lips across her mouth. 'Kissing you conjures up the richness of aromatic coffee beans with a redolence of amaretto and tiramisu – a smoky, burnt flavour which is totally intoxicating.'

'Wha'ever.' Kayleigh yawned. 'I've got a hangover like a fucken haemorrhage.' Her honeysuckle timbre and

Cupid's-bow mouth were glaringly at odds with the words that came out of it. 'Feelin' proper crap. I were off me face last night. Where's me phone? That massive dick who dissed me down the pub . . . If that cunt took me phone, I'm gonna kill him, I fucken swear.'

My sister kept elbowing me as if we were watching a live concert where the acts couldn't sing.

Merlin's eyes were summery with delight. 'Here it is, *ma chérie*. It fell off the bed when you were asleep and I was watching over you.' He retrieved it from his pyjama-top pocket. 'Have you ever wondered why people say they "slept like a baby", when babies wake up and cry every one or two hours? It's one of life's many conundrums.'

Ignoring this typical Merlinism, Kayleigh snatched the phone and started scrolling through her messages. Her pink nails were long enough to impale a porcupine.

'Would you like some poached eggs?' I asked politely. 'Or scrambled?'

'Wha'ever,' Kayleigh replied, bent over her phone like a lion over its kill in the Serengeti.

'Don't panic,' my sister whispered to me as we made breakfast. 'It's not as though he's marrying her.'

'Hell, I'm so happy *I'd* marry her! My son got laid!' I reiterated *sotto voce*. 'Nothing can rain on my happiness parade, not even those dropped t's and n's and gruesome grammar.'

Kayleigh didn't glance up again until the steaming plate of lightly whisked eggs, tomatoes and bacon was placed down on the table before her.

'Posh telly. What's it worf, then?' she asked, scraping back a chair. 'Nice gaff, too. Yer well minted, ain't cha? I mean, *ker-ching*!'

It was then I noticed that Merlin was wearing a pair of my mother's Qantas pajamas with FIRST CLASS emblazoned across the pocket. She'd kept them from the one trip where she'd been upgraded. The PJs, and the large-screen TV I was still paying off, and the big, old rambling house which was mortgaged to within a cement-rendered inch of its semi-detached life were perhaps helping to give a false impression of our financial well-being.

'Good garden an' all. Great place to bring up sprogs, innit?'

'*Sprogs?*' Phoebe sent me an SOS via her eyebrows. 'You know that happiness parade of yours?' she whispered. 'Well, quick weather warning: I'm feeling a light drizzle approaching.'

Kayleigh hunched down to her food to shorten the journey between plate and mouth. Merlin watched her with adoration. He was unable to eat anything, mainly because he was nearly choking on his own elation.

'Always wanted sprogs,' Kayleigh volunteered. 'Jeez, I know that bein' a mum ain't easy. It's, like, a huge responsibility an' that . . . At least a free-to-four-year-type commitment fing, right? Till they start nurs'ry an' that.'

My sister caught my eye again, with a look of alarm. '*Three to four years?*' she mouthed, eyebrows now halfway up her flawless forehead.

As Phoebe had predicted, my happiness parade suddenly became inundated by a cold, grey deluge.

When Kayleigh lit up another cigarette I suggested Merlin take her to smoke outside. As soon as they'd left for the garden, I erupted with volcanic intensity.

'Oh my God. I'm going to be a grandma, aren't I?!'

'No, you're not. Now calm down.'

'But I didn't provide him with any condoms before he went out. Nor did I reiterate the contraception lecture I gave him before we went kerb-crawling. And you know how Merlin forgets things. I just thought, if he ever *did* get into a relationship, we'd revise the whole safe-sex talk then.'

'Lucy, relax. You're—'

'Relax? How can I relax when I'm going to be a granny . . . And the granny of an autistic grandchild, because it's genetic. And God knows what pond scum the grammar-challenged Kayleigh has in her shallow little gene pool!'

I was pacing the kitchen now, like a stereotypical expectant father in a fifties sitcom. Phoebe passed me another shot of vodka as I lurched by. I downed it in one gulp. As she did hers.

'Don't get ahead of yourself—'

'Kayleigh will get up the duff then bugger off to leave me to raise the baby . . . which means I'll just have to start all over again – fighting for the kid to get an education, fighting for funding, fighting off bullies, decoding the world for him, day in, day out, trying to get him laid on his twenty-first birthday . . . Ugh. It will be even *more* embarrassing being arrested by the police trying to pick up a prostitute when I'm a withered old pensioner! Oh, how the papers will laugh at my expense. "Retired teacher caught putting the 'sex' into 'sexagenarian'."'

Phoebe refilled my shot glass and I once more mainlined it in one go, even though it was only brunch time. My sister followed suit.

'I'm sure Merlin will have used a condom,' she reassured me. 'You have shown him how, right?'

'Yes, of course. But the kid can't even put on a washing-up glove correctly. Honestly, you'd think I was asking him to put together a nuclear reactor . . . He probably put the condom on his nose, for God's sake.'

'Don't be silly. He—'

'And *oh!* What if Merlin gets herpes? Or Aids? I mean, it's not as though Kayleigh's been living in a convent, now is it?'

'You mollycoddle him, Lu-Lu! In an ideal world, you'd only want Merlin to go out with girls who wear a hygiene sash reading "Sanitized for your protection".'

'If only!'

'Girls are very street-smart these days. I'm sure *she'll* have used protection, even if *he* didn't.'

'But how can I be sure?' The alcohol surged through my bloodstream. 'Oh, Christ. I'm going to have to insist that he tells me everything a mother should never hear just so I can make sure he's got that lifeguard by his gene pool. Then I can give him tips on how to stay safe.'

'*Really?* You're so out of practice, getting sex tips from *you* will be like getting, I dunno, diplomacy lessons from Jeremy Clarkson.'

'Well, help me, then. What other advice should I give him? Clearly, he can't talk to his dad, so it's going to have to be me.'

'I dunno,' my sister slurred. 'Oh, I'm suddenly feeling a tad jarred.'

'Come on, Pheebs! You're so much more experienced than me! Since Danny left you, you've had sex with everyone . . . bar the Pope and Graham Norton.'

'Well, okay. If you really wanna know . . .' She hiccoughed tipsily. 'My top tip to a fella? Never do anything to a clitoris with your teeth that you wouldn't do to vintage Porsche upholstery.'

'That's it?'

'Always meet them for a c–c–cocktail first, as that gives you the opporrrrtunity to re-evaluate and maybe just go back to your r–r–room and masturbate . . .'

'Okaaay . . .'

'And definitely check the s–s–sex of your date before you get naked?

'Good point.'

'Oh, and never s–s–stick your genitals into anything you're not certain they'll come out of . . .'

'Rrriiight . . .'

'Plus, if you happen to have special needs, *then adopt celibacy, 'cause sex is complicated enough even for normal people.*'

Those harsh words brought me abruptly to my senses. I sobered up immediately. 'Celibacy? Are you mad? I don't know what I'm complaining about. Oh my God! Let's get a grip. I'm going to look on Kayleigh as a bank error in my favour – I just need to make sure there are more withdrawals than deposits,' I punned.

'Wait. You're not actually going to encourage this relationship?' Now it was Phoebe's turn to sober up.

'Of course I am.'

'Well, you clearly have Stevie Wonder's eye for detail, dah-ling.'

'What do you mean?'

'If you weren't blinded by love for Merlin, you'd be able to see that the girl's just taking him for a ride.'

'Well, exactly! And isn't that the point? Jesus, I got arrested trying to give him that very thing. I just need to make sure that they're safe.'

Merlin came streaming back into the kitchen like a

sunbeam. 'My divine diva had to depart. I wish I could catch this moment somehow and seal it in a jar, like a firefly, with holes in the top so the feeling can breathe happily forever more. I don't ever want to lose this moment, Mum.'

'Merlin, darling, I don't mean to pry, but I just need to know, did you use a condom?'

'Oh, don't worry,' he replied matter-of-factly. 'The sperm didn't leave the sperm bank at that particular time.'

'Oh.'

'Yes, Kayleigh bites the top of the lid of the penis really well.'

Out of my vast vocabulary, '*Oh!*' was the only word which presented itself to me.

'Nobody will take her away from me, will they, Mum?' My son was so happy even the air around him seemed freshly laundered. 'I want the sublime joy and exquisite rapture I feel right now to become a person, so I can walk it down the aisle and marry it!' he exclaimed, before bounding up to his bedroom to get dressed.

'You see?' I said to my dubious sister. 'This girl is the best thing that's ever happened to him. Nose rings, tattoos, candyfloss-pink hair, stunted vocab ... who cares? I've never seen him so happy. I'll do anything to make it work out for him. Safely, of course ... *Happy birthday, Merlin!*' I yelled up the stairs, simultaneously making a mental note to dash out to buy his present – a rubber plantation's worth of condoms. 'It'll be fine. You'll see,' I told Phoebe.

Outside the kitchen window, the grey day had cleared to a mackerel sky with patches of blue brightness. I decided to take it as a good omen.

PART TWO

10

A Date with Destiny

And so it was that I got my first girlfriend. Yes, I might be a middle-aged heterosexual mother of one, but that didn't mean I wasn't wooing a girl every night, showering her with gifts and generally charming the bejaysus out of the pink-haired poppet.

My first task was surreptitiously to discover all Kayleigh's interests – skate-boarding, football, car racing, death metal – then organize outings. I researched her favourite foods and filled the fridge with the correct tasty morsels. I stocked up on her preferred films, music and magazines. I basically made my home, and hence, by association, my son, as desirable as possible.

To sweeten the deal, I bought tickets I couldn't really afford to events she might like – Beyoncé, Rihanna and Metallica concerts, plays featuring celebrities such as David

Tennant, Lindsay Lohan or Chandler from *Friends* . . . Basically, I began to date my son's date.

'Jesus, Lucy. When Kayleigh breaks it off, you're going to be more devastated than Merlin!' Phoebe wisecracked as she watched me grill the life out of four lamb chops because Kayleigh liked them practically Cajun. 'You'll be all *Oh God! How could she leave me? Wasn't I good enough? Where did I go wrong?* You'll be racked with jealousy – *Which son and mum is she seeing now?*, you'll sob . . . before stalking them both in a fit of envy.'

'Hey, my quirky boy has found a girlfriend, against all the autistic odds. I will do *anything* to keep them together,' I said, squirting tomato sauce over everything edible within a two-mile radius because Kayleigh likes condiments.

In short, over the next few weeks, I did everything to make my home attractive to her, bar filling the bath with vodka and putting in a full-length heated pool and a petting zoo.

In an effort to make the whole package as appealing as possible, I was endlessly kind and attentive: washing and ironing her clothes, ferrying her to and from the tube station – even, on a couple of occasions, dog-sitting her flatulent, fleabitten Alsatian. Nor did I correct her grammar once, no matter that to experience Kayleigh wrestling with the mother tongue was like seeing a Ming vase in the hands of a toddler. Even though speech was clearly not her native tongue, I adopted some of her flippin', mingin' norf-ern vernacular to make her feel at home. Essentially, I bent over so far backwards a career with the Beijing acrobatic team clearly beckoned.

I also started accepting all kinds of invitations I would

normally have binned. My highly sociable and sought-after arty-farty mum was always being invited to fundraisers, which were invariably hosted by the kind of celebrities Phoebe and I would pay money *not* to meet.

'Prince Harry?!' Kayleigh salivated as I sorted through my absentee mother's post. The invitation which had caught her eye was a gala to benefit kids orphaned by the Aids epidemic in Lesotho. 'Aids? How excitin'! Can yer take me? I'd be proper chuffed.'

I was about to explain that I'd happily send a donation but would rather be abducted by aliens and force-fed live frogspawn than run the risk of contracting a chronic case of A-Listeria at such a sycophantic Sleb-fest, but instead heard myself uttering a cheery 'Sure! No worries! With pleasure!'

Merlin has no interest in fame. 'A celebrity is nothing more than a nonentity who is well-known for their well-known-ness,' he concluded, bowing out to stay home and bone up on the Juno spacecraft's 1.7 billion mile trek to Jupiter and its probe's precise approach into orbit around the gas giant (as you do).

I endured the royal cocktail party, even though I found it only marginally more enjoyable than, say, a DIY lobotomy. But Kayleigh begged for more.

My mother's volunteer work for various charities also meant that she often got asked to high-profile perfume launches and Parisian-themed fashion shows. Even though events like this were not remotely up my boulevard, to entertain my son's girlfriend, I now RSVPed with alacrity, accepting every offer that came our way.

A feminist organization my mum supported was hosting an evening with the activist Eve Ensler at which survivors would address the grim issue of domestic violence. I was going to decline, as I didn't think the subject would remotely interest Kayleigh, but when she discovered that Angelina Jolie was rumoured to be speaking she leapt at the opportunity to go like a drug addict into a glue factory.

In truth, I found myself really looking forward to the high-calibre discourse and call to action. It was so unlike me to have a social life. My world had been all about Merlin for so long I'd forgotten what it felt like to dress up and chat socially with adults who weren't solely concerned about exam results or nit outbreaks during torturous parent–teacher nights.

As Kayleigh was late, I left her ticket at the Southbank box office and made my way into the fluorescent-lit hall to join the ranks of seated women in sombre suits and sensible shoes. Fifteen minutes into the lecture, Merlin's girlfriend arrived, with cartoonish inevitability, in sky-scraper, follow-me-home-and-fuck-me high heels and a guacamole-green mini dress revealing so much cleavage I couldn't believe the fire department hadn't closed down her Wonderbra due to overcrowding. Wait. Did I say 'dress'? It was more of a Post-it note. When she tottered in, mid-speech, clackity-clacking over the wooden floor, everyone in the hall swivelled their heads in her direction with the choreographed unison of a synchronized-swimming team.

'Heal her, oh Lord, for she is injured in the taste buds,' I muttered to myself, ducking low in my seat. As survivors shared their harrowing tales on stage, Kayleigh, completely oblivious to the pathos and poignancy, stomped up and down the aisle, peering into every row in search of her cinematic heroine.

To make up for Angelina's no-show, I next took Kayleigh to a War on Want fundraising event my absentee mother had helped to promote in the pavilion at the Houses of Parliament. But as Emma Watson spoke in disturbing detail about the Somalian famine, all I could hear was Kayleigh munching crisps. The packet in her paws rustled like something alive right through the talk. At the reception afterwards, the sensitivity of the subject meant that nobody felt the slightest pang of hunger for the hors d'oeuvres – except Kayleigh, who ate with the appetite of a sixteenth-century peasant fortifying herself for a day slaving in the fields.

After Serena Williams had made a very moving speech on the plight of Africans, Kayleigh went up and introduced herself. I cowered in embarrassment as, moments later, racist insults about the 'stoopid Pakis' she grew up with in Rotherham began burping out of her mouth. I tried to keep my gaze absolutely neutral, absolutely unperturbed ... absolutely not giving away the fact that I was groping beneath my seat for an emergency ejector button.

A few days later, I was due to attend a Buckingham Palace garden party for an awards ceremony to give literary prizes to disadvantaged secondary-school children. One of my A-star students had been shortlisted for a prize.

I'd ummed and aahed about daring to take Kayleigh as my plus one, but she'd solemnly promised to be discreet and on her best behaviour and, of course, I so wanted to please her. But within minutes of our arrival I yet again deeply regretted her presence, as I watched her ask a bewildered Benedict Cumberbatch for a selfie, ''cause Sherlock gives me a flippin' wide-on, despite the fact that he's a bit of a, yer know, spaz.'

My A-star student was looking at me, wide-eyed. 'Why is your friend taking a Trump?' my clever pupil asked.

'A Trump?'

'Yes. The act of excreting cruel, fascist, racist, sexist or politically incorrect rhetoric from one's oral sphincter.'

I concluded, mortified, that emigration to New Zealand was clearly my only possible option.

After every outing, I'd go to bed determined that it would be best for Merlin to undergo an immediate Kayleigh-ectomy, however painful, especially after her appalling 'spaz' comment, but then I'd see my son's beaming face in the morning and it would suddenly all be worth it. The kid was haloed in happiness. Overflowing with vim and verve, he babbled away to Kayleigh about asteroids and planets and time continuums. It was as though he were presenting a one-man show on Broadway. All that was missing was the tap-dancing and the curtain call.

'Kayleigh's kiss is a tang of apricots, honey and truffles,' he confided one day, shimmering with excitement. 'Birdsong bursts from her skin under the magical pressure of my lips.'

I touched his face, amazed. 'If Kayleigh makes you so happy, darling, then she's okay by me.' I pressed my face into his messy puff of hair and kissed the top of his warm, sweet-smelling head. 'As long as you're practising safe sex.'

'She is a moon shimmer on a grey horizon.' He sighed contentedly. 'She bathes me in silvery light. She is the big, broad band of the Milky Way – a dazzlement which rings my world with joy.'

'Well, that's one way of putting it, dear . . . as long as you put it in a condom,' I emphasized pointedly.

Whenever Kayleigh irritated me, which was excruciatingly often, I only had to think of Merlin's laughter and a smile stayed in my eyes for the rest of the day, even during the coma-inducing tedium of school assemblies and the Mount Everest piles of assignment marking. It had been so long since I'd heard him laugh like this.

Phoebe wanted to be pleased . . . but doubts continued to creep into her mind, like a thief.

'Kayleigh's like one of those roses you buy at a service station – stunning, but no fragrance,' my sister said as we prepared Saturday lunch one summer's day in early July.

'Whatever happened to the optimistic, positive Pollyanna who used to be my little sister?' I sighed. 'Since Danny left, you've become all BTC.' (Our code for Bitter, Cynical and Twisted.)

'Come on, Lucy. You have to admit that there's something sly – even a bit cruel – about the slant of the girl's eyes.'

'Look, it's hard enough for any of us to meet the right person,' I replied, chopping salad vegetables. 'The timing's always a little skew-whiff. She's married; he's single. She's a masochist; he's a masochist . . . Or in Merlin's case, she's an earthling; he's an alien.'

Phoebe started grating Parmesan. 'I know, but—'

'No buts, Phoebe.' I diced the veggies more vigorously. 'Normally, when Merlin is quiet in his room, doing nothing, that's a sign to ring the White House because he's accidentally rerouted an American satellite into Soviet airspace, but these days silence just indicates that he's horizontal. I mean, look at him over there.' I gestured through the glass doors separating the kitchen from the living room to where the contented couple were coiled, all cosy and post-coital, on the couch, watching TV. 'I can't thank Kayleigh enough. In fact, I'm going to buy her another present to say thank you. What kind of gift should I – sorry, should *Merlin* – get to impress her, do you think?'

'Gee, let me think. A month's supply of morning-after pills? Ouch!' My sister yelped as she accidentally grated her fingertip into the cheese.

'Serves you right!' I chided.

'It just worries me that she's so unfriendly. I mean, I try my best to be nice, but that girl couldn't crack a smile at a joke festival.'

'That's just because she's embarrassed about her teeth. I doubt she's ever even been to the dentist. Not once. But, apart from the tooth decay, you do have to admit that Kayleigh did hit the genetic jackpot.'

'Yes . . .' My sister raised a combative brow. 'If only she didn't have that ruthless, hardened-criminal look so common to manipulative man-eaters, the girl could be a swimwear model.'

'BCT,' I retaliated, and shook my head in despair at her cynicism.

'And then there's the mess.' With hesitant, pincered fingers Phoebe picked up a pair of Kayleigh's scrunched-up knickers from under the kitchen table. 'I really don't want to think about how they got there,' she cringed.

I'd become used to the fact that Kayleigh left a trail of clothing like fairy-tale breadcrumbs all over my house. 'Well, they do spend a lot of time in the kitchen, because Kayleigh likes to cook. Cakes, mostly. All inspired by *The Great British Bake Off*. Isn't that sweet?' I passed Phoebe a batch of biscuits Kayleigh had knocked up that morning. 'I was saving these for dessert, but you can be my taste-tester. What do you think?'

Phoebe took a tentative bite and, much to her chagrin, found no fault with the flavour. 'But leaving a cake tin to soak is not washing up, is it?' She gestured to the overladen sink before turning on the taps and sloshing her hands into the soapy water. 'Why don't you ask her to help clean up occasionally?'

'I have. But really, it'd be faster to move things telekinetically. She's like a snail with attitude.'

'Which makes *you* Kayleigh's personal maid and laundress . . . Basically, you're an indentured servant, Lu-Lu. Serf's up! *Is everything to Madam's satisfaction? Would you like your waterbed filled with champagne for added carnal comfort?*'

Her criticisms were abruptly drowned out as the house shook with the measured insistence of a bass drum: *doomf doomf doomf.*

Phoebe, mid-munch on a biscuit, swallowed it whole at the shock of decibels, before covering her ears. 'What the hell . . . ?'

'I'M AFRAID KAYLEIGH'S PREFERRED MUSICAL TASTE IS DEATH METAL. IN PARTICULAR, THE BANDS ANTHRAX, NAPALM DEATH AND CRADLE OF FILTH,' I yelled.

'CHARMING.'

'I'M GETTING A TASTE FOR IT, ACTUALLY,' I lied, nodding my head in time with the migraine-inducing beat. For Merlin's sake, I would put up with this discordant torture until my ears bled. In between beats, I detected the shrill trill of the bell and the front door opening and closing.

Phoebe took a disgruntled bite of another biscuit before

peering around the corner of the kitchen into the sitting room. 'AND WHO THE HELL ARE ALL THESE PEOPLE ARRIVING?' she fog-horned over her shoulder at me.

'KAYLEIGH'S COTERIE,' I hollered back.

'OH, MARVELLOUS. YOUR HOUSE IS NOW A DROP-IN CENTRE FOR DROP-OUTS.'

'IT'S NICE SHE BRINGS HER PALS AROUND. I MEAN, MERLIN'S NEVER HAD FRIENDS BEFORE.'

Raucous voices sounded above the ear-lacerating music. 'JESUS. AND WHAT'S ALL THE SHOUTING ABOUT?'

'THAT'S JUST KAYLEIGH-SPEAK FOR "GO AND GET ME MORE CRISPS."'

'WHAT?'

I cupped my hand to my sister's ear so she could hear me. 'But we can't judge the poor girl. I mean, think how she must have been raised.'

'EXACTLY.' My sister yanked me into the utility room and closed the door so we could talk without shredding our vocal cords. 'Do you know anything at all about her parents?'

'She's an orphan, poor poppet.'

'God, how very *Jane Eyre*. So she's just like the pathetic heroine from a dusty Victorian novel . . . only Kayleigh doesn't turn out to have been swapped at birth and is secretly rich in the end. Am I right?'

'Don't be glib, Pheebs. Imagine how hard it's been for the kid. Her dad was Russian, mum English. Born up north. Then raised in foster homes after her parents died. Sadly, this is the normal outcome when young people lack any supervision. She and her friends just need sympathy and understanding—'

'Yes ... or a ten-year stint in reform school,' Phoebe declared, devouring another biscuit. 'Or even a paying job. I imagine that you're forking out for everything. I mean, what are her skills?'

'As far as I can make out, flirting, frottage and Advanced Lip Gloss Addiction, but I'm hoping I can encourage her into a career. Obviously, the poor girl's had little education and no parental guidance, which means it's impossible to tell what talents might be lying dormant—'

'Yes, judging by the success she's made of her life so far, the next step will no doubt be to branch out into neuroscience.'

Years of practice in dealing with irksome airline passengers mean that my sister has perfected the sardonic eye-roll. She now rolled her eyes so far back into her head she must have been able to see her synapses zinging around her cranium.

'Look, the girl's volunteering at Oxfam, so she can't be all bad—'

I stopped talking as the utility door swung open to reveal Kayleigh, who was wearing saucer-sized pink sunglasses and a lime-green bikini.

'Oi! Are youse two talkin' about *me* in there?'

'I was just saying how commendable it is that you volunteer at Oxfam.'

'Volunteerin'? I ain't volunteerin'. That charity shop's proper mingin'. I doan wanna do it, I gotta.'

'Why?' Phoebe probed, licking biscuit crumbs from her fingertips.

"Cause I doan wanna go away.'

'Away? On holiday?' I asked hopefully.

'No. *Away* away. Holloway.'

'Holloway? In north London? That's not far to go for a holiday.'

'Na. Holloway. Yer know. Flippin' 'Olloway Prison.'

My head spun to see her staring at us as though we were profoundly deficient in the IQ department.

'Got done, din I? For shopliftin'. Fuckers. But I neva done owt! I was off me face is all. It was well annoyin'. An' now I gotta do community service an' that.'

Phoebe suddenly lurched forward. 'Oh God. I don't feel well.'

I steered her out of the laundry room and into a chair. 'Is it jet-lag?'

'I don't know. The room's spinning and everything's a bit blurry—'

'Proper brilliant cookies, in't they? Me speciality. You gotta get the recipe jest right. Especially the hash dose.'

'Hash?!'

'Yeah. J'want one?' Kayleigh thrust the plate at me. 'Only one though, 'cause they're proper strong.'

'One?' my sister moaned. 'I ate half the plate.'

'Flippin' heck. That's proper nasty. Yer off yer 'ead, you!' Kayleigh laughed.

And with that she sashayed outside to sunbathe topless on the lawn, giving the Polish builders next door a collective cardiac arrest.

My sister immediately started giggling and guffawing, repeating 'proper nasty' before lurching off into a rambling tirade about how all philandering, deserting husbands need to be locked on a decommissioned submarine then towed out to the deepest part of the sea and torpedoed repeatedly, after, of course, watching their own testicles being removed by triumphant wives wielding rusty salad tongs.

As I piloted my giddy, now sobbing sister upstairs for a lie-down, I decided that, as far as Kayleigh was concerned, it was probably best to just dread one second at a time.

11

If Symptoms Persist, Contact Your Doctor

As a teacher, I'm always up for learning new things. And putting up with Kayleigh taught me one very good lesson – namely, that you don't have to fight in a war to get post-traumatic stress disorder. No. All you have to do is try to mother someone with autism when he starts dating a convicted felon who promptly poisons your sister.

When Phoebe finally woke from her drug haze that evening, she shuffled groggily into my bedroom, where I was folding some clothes, and flumped down on my bed, eyes narrowed.

'That's it – she's gotta go . . . I mean, OhMyGod. What if I'd been due to fly? What if I'd got on board stoned and shagged a passenger on the drinks trolley?'

'Now that's what I'd call in-flight service.' My pathetic attempt at Tension Diffusion fell flat as Phoebe seized my hand and said emphatically, 'I'm serious, Lucy. You need to call off their relationship. Today. Otherwise, from here on in, I predict a downhill slalom into insanity – or, possibly, a prison cell.' My sister levelled her gaze at me earnestly. 'I doubt hash is the only drug Kayleigh's doing. I mean, the girl's so manic she makes the Energizer bunny look lethargic.'

'She's young. She's just got lots of get up and go.'

My sister hitched an eyebrow. 'Yes, she gets up to go and see her coke dealer.'

'Stop it! You have no proof she's snorting coke.'

'Don't I? "I just gotta go to the loo"' – Phoebe imitated Kayleigh's whiny voice – '"And so do Cindy, Sarah, Blake and Jake."'

'Look, Phoebe, I'd like nothing more than for Merlin to bring home a girl who's employed, has no tattoos or visible piercings and is in the possession of an extensive vocabulary. But he hasn't. He's brought home Kayleigh.'

'Yes – an orphaned, unemployed, bludging, half-Russian, drug-addicted convicted criminal.'

'The one word I'm really worried about in that sentence is "Russian",' I joshed. 'But seriously, Kayleigh may be rough, but kids in care are six times more likely to end up with a criminal record. People are allowed a second chance. She seems to genuinely like Merlin. And he's crazy about her.'

'*You're* the crazy one. Sincerity in a girl like that is as rare as – I dunno – a monogamous husband,' my sister concluded bitterly.

'Well, whatever, we just have to make the best of it, sis. We don't get to choose Merlin's girlfriend. Kayleigh has just come into our lives—'

'Yeah, been tossed in like a hand grenade.'

'But she's *Merlin's* hand grenade and it's our job to welcome her. He's really fallen for her—'

'Yes. Like a condemned building.'

'—and we just need to concentrate on the positive. There
must be something you like about the girl. I mean, she does
have nice hair.'

'Hmmm? What's that noise? Oh, it's just the sound of the
bottom of a barrel being scraped.'

'She's really no trouble,' I said, laboriously picking lint off
each item of clothing because Kayleigh had left a tissue in her
jeans pocket. 'Falling in love is exactly the same as gaming at
a casino table. You play the hand you're dealt.'

'Really? Have you forgotten her saying how much she
wants children? Despite the fact that she's the type to eat
her own young. Is that *really* the hand you want to play?'

'They're taking precautions. You're just still foggy from
all those chemicals coursing through your veins.'

'Well, if I were you, I'd be on the internet investigating
how to bring on early menopause. Or maybe we could just
drug her and tie her tubes in her sleep? Or at least just put
in a bit of a – you know – slip knot. Have you thought about
giving Merlin a vasectomy?'

'*No!* Who do you think I am – Hitler? Can't you just try to
concentrate on the girl's good features?'

'Yeah, you're right. Which of her distinguishing features
should I concentrate on first? Her locust-like ability to
strip-mine the weekly food shop? The "lick me" tattoo on her
abdomen? Her communication skills, which mimic those of
a shrub? Hell, if you put Kayleigh in the sun, she'd photo-
synthesize. Or perhaps the scars left after her attempt to
scrub the Satanic "666" off her forehead?'

'You know what, Phoebe? Your husband has run off with your gay best friend and your kids aren't talking to you because you won't talk to *him*. So I think taking advice from you on life right now is – I dunno – like asking a Kalahari Desert camel herder how to cope with an iceberg.'

My sister sagged like a day-old soufflé. I immediately regretted my harsh words. If only I could claw them back. I wouldn't hurt my darling sister for all the world, but her pessimism was becoming corrosive.

'Okay, point taken,' Phoebe said sadly, 'but can you at least lay down some house rules? For starters: no more hash cookies. Ever.'

'Okay.'

'Other commandments: thou shalt flush, especially if thou art over ten and have the use of both arms.'

'Okay.'

'Thou shalt not stand in front of the refrigerator door waiting for a meal to materialize.'

'Okay.'

'Thou shalt remember the electricity bill and rejoice in natural light now and then.'

'Okay.'

'Thou shalt honour thy boyfriend's mother's sister's ear drums and not turn the music above five decibels.'

'Okay.'

'And thou shalt not disrespect Merlin's mother ... I don't want to see you being walked over. It's just not you, Lucy.'

My protective sister was right. I used to be a vibrant, funny, fun, strong woman, accelerating through life, but of late I'd become little more than Merlin and Kayleigh's sidecar. It was as though I'd been taking Pathetic Pills. And it definitely *was* out of character. Finding the balance between helping Merlin to keep his HMS *Relationship* afloat but at the same time not scuppering my own self-esteem was the equivalent of manoeuvring a supertanker at high speed through a paddling pool. But I determinedly vowed, then and there, to try.

'Okay, okay, I'll make some rules,' I said, pairing Kayleigh's linty socks. 'I promise . . . as long as you promise to start talking to your ex-husband, okay?'

On cue, Phoebe's phone rang.

'It's Danny,' she gasped. 'How spooky is that?'

'Well, answer it. And be nice.'

She spoke into the phone monosyllabically for a moment or two, then rang off.

'Well?'

'He wanted to make arrangements for the kids to attend his wedding in September.'

'Oh darling, well done. You showed admirable restraint.'

'Yeah, well, "admirable restraint" is what abandoned wives exercise . . . right up until the moment we shoot our lousy, cheating, fucking husbands.'

I knew just how she felt. 'Admirable restraint' became my mantra over the next few weeks, because every time I was tempted to tell Kayleigh off for some misdemeanour, Merlin would leap into view, an ecstatic grin splitting his face, to tell me that 'love was roaring like a tiger inside him', or 'thundering like an avalanche' – and I'd bite my tongue.

When Kayleigh started making Merlin wear his hair as though it had been styled by an egg whisk, my complaint was cut short when he grabbed me in a bear hug and enthused, 'Hooray! Joy to the world! She's a cosmic girl from another galaxy and she's transmitting on my frequency' – and I bit my tongue.

When I found my son with an unlit cigarette bobbing in his mouth, I was about to read the riot act to his girlfriend when he interjected, 'I didn't think any woman would ever spend the night on Planet Merlin. But somehow this goddess is now in my amorous orbit. I love her to the moon and back, via Jupiter' – and, again, I bit my tongue.

In truth, I bit my tongue so much over the next week I nearly put my teeth right through it. Especially when Kayleigh kept turning up with more and more of her undesirable pals in boisterous tow. An endless stream of stick-thin girls wobbled down my hallway on spike heels, holding themselves aloft with the nervous trepidation of untrained waiters desperately balancing overloaded cocktail trays. The boys clumped together on the sofa and shouted over each other in guttural, rapid-fire slang, only occasionally pin-balling off the furniture, on the hunt for more booze.

Manoeuvring my way through the living room to the front door was like trying to get through a rugby scrum, but when I tentatively suggested a Kayleigh-free weekend, Merlin physically baulked. I was hugging him at the time and he flung me away from him like a flamenco dancer.

'The warm spicy scent of her skin makes my senses spectacularly enhanced. Her love is a caress of lavender. I lie awake at night to listen to her soft breathing. When her sleeping face is turned to the window, starlight dances on her long, lovely eyelashes. I cannot forgo one sublime night in her magical embrace.'

But, fed up with the noise and the mess, I marched off to the kitchen to interrupt Kayleigh's fridge-raiding and asked her straight out to go home for a few days and to take her vulgar pals with her.

Her lower lip trembled. 'Yer right. I were out of line. Yer proper nice, you. For not kickin' off and goin' ape-shit about the mess an' that. I'm proper sorry.' She immediately started putting food back into the fridge. 'It's just the way we was treated in the care home. I had some proper dark times in that shithole. But I'm tryin' not to be like them lot . . . If only I'd had a ma like you . . . to show me the way an' that.'

She rolled up her sleeves and started running hot water into the sink.

'It's just so tragic that your parents died so young, Kayleigh,' I sympathized. 'Don't you have a foster parent or a social worker or anyone to take care of you?' I started stacking dirty dishes on the counter to help her.

'Social worker, yeah . . . but I find her well annoyin', if I'm honest. Social Services are a bunch of thick, lazy-arse fuckers. It's all blah-de-blah. People – let-downs, the lot of 'em . . . except for Merlin. Which is why I proper love him.'

I paused, crusty plates in hand. 'You do?'

'He's such a funny fucker! Lucky he never hooked up with one of them trampy little weasels from the charity shop. Those skanks'd never get him. But I do. I swear on me ma's grave, I proper love 'im. I never done owt with a boy that I've loved before.' She sloshed suds around with her hand. 'I never cared for anyone as much as him. Not since me ma died.' Her pretty face crumbled. 'So thanks for lettin' me, yer know, crash at yours. Me and me mates – well, nobody's got a job, nobody's got no money, nobody's got owt. And if you do have owt it gets nicked by all the smackheads down the squats an' that. Yer the first person who's ever been kind to me. And to me mates. They proper like Merlin, too.'

'They do?'

She blew a halo of soapsuds off a cup before inverting it on the draining board. 'Million per cent. Swear on me ma's grave. I'm always honest, me. And takin' me in an' that . . . well, it's well mint of yer.' And then she gave me that crooked little smile of tombstone teeth and part of me melted for the poor little foundling, so I made her a cup of soothing tea, offered her friends some cake and took over the washing up.

When Phoebe came to collect me for book club the next night, she eyed my house with horror. 'There seems to be an adolescent pestilent outbreak in your living room. Who *are* all these people? It's like a meeting of Losers Anonymous.'

'Kayleigh's friends . . . A lot of them seem to be ex-boyfriends. They've all had such shitty lives that I'm just trying to be accepting. But it's a lot like running a wild-animal park. And it's always feeding time at the zoo.'

'Jeepers. How many boyfriends has she had? Although I suspect the correct term for Kayleigh's male friends is "clients". I mean, *look* at them.' Phoebe drew me towards the glass-panelled doors so we could take a surreptitious peek in at the party. An acned boy with a buzz cut who was wallpapered in tats and another who resembled a photo from an infectious-diseases medical textbook chose that moment to crush their beer cans against their foreheads. Another teen, muscled like a fighting dog, his eyes as sharp as sword points, was absent-mindedly playing with a flick-knife.

'Knives! Oh great. And *your* only defence is a sharp

tongue,' my sister gasped. 'Hmmmm. Do you think a cutting one-liner will be enough to repel a vicious attack?'

'Calm down, Phoebe, please. Okay, they may be a bit rough around the edges, but they like Merlin. He's never had friends before. He makes them laugh.'

'Oh Lucy, they're not laughing with him, they're laughing *at* him. Merlin's vocabulary and way with words must sound hysterical to their ears. A bit like Chaucer's "Thou art my liege"-type speech sounds to your belligerent school pupils.'

'Kayleigh wouldn't allow that. She's quite protective.' Kayleigh was now shimmying around Merlin's legs like a slinky alley cat. 'She's mad about him. She told me so.' I knocked on the glass and waved at the couple. Kayleigh flashed me the crooked geometry of her graveyard smile.

'Oh, really? It would take Kayleigh exactly one spliff and a half-bottle of vodka to get over Merlin. When a boy with a bigger house and a more gullible mother comes along, she'll break his heart as insouciantly as she breaks a nail.'

'When did my lovely, kind sister get beamed up and replaced with this cynical Pod Person? You should hear the lovely things Kayleigh says about Merlin. And it's not as though there's a million other girls beating down his door.'

'Oh God, not another sermon on how any girl is better than no girl.'

'Of course not. No more sermons, though verily I say unto you that perhaps you should rejoice in the fact that your antisocial autistic nephew has found a girl to love who loves him back? Here endeth the lesson. Now go forth and drink some communion wine,' I preached, before handing my sister a big glass of Chardonnay.

*

Compassion for Kayleigh's hard life and joy at Merlin's new status as Beloved Boyfriend meant that I simply refused to heed my sister's warnings – not even when objects started disappearing from around the house: a silver photo frame one day, an iPad the next. When money went missing from Merlin's bank account, as far as Phoebe was concerned, it was time for Kayleigh to freeze-and-assume-the-position, shortly followed by a long custodial sentence. But I thought back to what Kayleigh had said about people constantly letting her down and mistrusting her.

'You have no proof Kayleigh's taken anything. Besides, she hasn't even been here the last few days.'

'Lucy, you may think that Kayleigh has a kicked-dog, stray-cat quality, but she's actually a man-eating, mammalian carnivore,' my sister cautioned me, as she pored over my son's bank statement. The money Merlin had saved from his disability living allowance, accumulated birthday gifts and odd-job payments from his doting grandma had vanished. 'It's nearly four thousand pounds!' Phoebe calculated. 'And clearly, it's Kayleigh who's stolen it.'

'This newly acquired misanthropy of yours – does it come with its own noose?'

'Oh, ha ha.'

'It could just be a bank error, you know. Or fraud. I'll go down tomorrow and sort it out.'

Though the words were coming out of my mouth, even to my own ears they sounded like the biggest leap of faith since Neville Chamberlain announced his peace pact with Hitler.

'Face facts, Lucy. Kayleigh is pure vampire. Merlin's account is her blood bank, and she's sucked his savings dry.'

'Where's your evidence? The girl's still wearing Primark,

not Prada. She's still eating fried chicken and chips, not caviar. She's still *here*.'

My eyes were drawn to the glass doors, through which I could see Kayleigh dancing in a hip-thrusting dervish for Merlin's delectation. I watched a smile spread all the way across my son's cheeks until it nearly burst them, as it was just way too big for his face. Since Kayleigh had come on the scene, my son seemed so light, his life buoyant with possibilities. Wasn't this exactly what I'd always wished for?

'You just don't seem able to see what's staring you in the face. I love that about brain damage,' my sister chided sarcastically.

In truth, I *was* worried, but whenever I thought my toothpaste tube of patience and positivity and trust was all squeezed out, there would come another dollop. 'You and I are always judging people who are judgemental of Merlin, are we not?'

'Yes, of course.'

'So we mustn't now be equally judgemental of Kayleigh. We hardly know her. Just because she's had a rough childhood doesn't mean she can't turn into a nice adult.'

Kayleigh then pushed open the glass doors and sashayed into the kitchen to get a beer and a vodka chaser. Her hair, wet with sweat, was brushed straight back, heightening her resemblance to a mafia hitwoman.

I was about to say hello when I was suddenly blinded by a neon flash of brightness. It was Kayleigh's smile – a white picket fence of freshly straightened, capped white teeth – at least four thousand pounds' worth – and I could bite my tongue no longer, as the Kayleigh scales finally dropped from my eyes.

12

Today is the First Day of the Rest of Your Life Savings

There really is no good way to tell your besotted son that he's swapping bodily fluids with a manipulative sociopath. At first I tried gentle cross-examination. As soon as the house was empty, I confiscated Merlin's credit card, made him a hot chocolate and asked him how Kayleigh had paid for her dental upgrade.

'She used my credit card.'

'Did you know that she'd taken your credit card?'

'Oh, yes.'

'Why didn't you stop her?'

'Well, I couldn't.'

'Why?'

'Due to casual bondage.'

I gulped like a fish. 'Casual bondage?'

'Yes. While you were at work. Kayleigh said it was normal to be tied to the bed and left there while she took my

wallet and then went out with someone more attractive . . .
I'm not sure what it all meant but I prefer vanilla sex – where
you have ice cream afterwards.'

Oh dear Lord. As usual, my protective instinct was
lioness-like. My claws, always curled inside, ready to strike
out, immediately unfurled. When I'd first met Kayleigh,
I'd presumed she had the intellect of a dust mite. Her
friends made me rethink Darwin – I couldn't believe
they didn't get carpet burns on their knuckles when they
walked across my living room. But it turned out that what
the girl missed out in cleverness, she made up for in cunning. How to explain this to my love-struck and innocent
offspring?

'Merlin, darling, you know you must never give your pin
number to anyone. You also know that I would never lie to
you,' I said, in my most gentle, hypnotically soothing voice.
'And you know that I have your best interests at heart. Well,
the truth is, Kayleigh's not the right girl for you.'

But my words just wafted away like notes from a piano.
Merlin was standing with his back to the door, one foot turned
out like a dancer, as if ready to pirouette out of the room.

'Kayleigh is majestic and sublime and makes my heart
sing.'

He spoke in a childish lilt which tore at my heartstrings.

'Okay.' I picked my words as carefully as an explosives
expert defuses a bomb. 'But there are plenty of other girls in
the world who could make you feel that way, too.'

'But I love her,' he replied mulishly. Merlin's sneakered foot jacked up and down, working an invisible
pump. 'Being with her is as happy as a holiday. I bask in the
tropical warmth of her charismatic affection.'

To me, Kayleigh now seemed to have the warmth and affection of a steel bollard. 'But sweetheart, you two are so different, it will never work.'

'Love is like music. Luminous unity is achieved when separate, disparate elements melt together to arrive at a glorious harmony, usually by way of discords.'

'But Merlin, darling, do you really think she's smart enough for you? When you were telling her about the solar system, I heard her ask if Pluto was the furthest dog from Earth.'

'The brain is an over-rated organ. It's not only mushy and grey, it clearly doesn't offer as much pleasure as other parts of the anatomy.'

I pictured Kayleigh in that lime-green bikini she'd been wearing all summer – a bikini that would have been too small for a Barbie doll. Yes, the girl was gorgeous; the only trouble was that her sun-protection factor was higher than her emotional IQ. Kayleigh possessed such a cartoonish 'baddie' character that I half expected word balloons to keep forming above her head.

'I–wor–ship–her,' Merlin said in a sighing staccato. 'When I hear her name I feel snowflakes on my face.'

While Kayleigh was clearly raised by wolves, my son had the killer instincts of a cocker spaniel. 'Oh, Merlin!' I put my head in my hands, suddenly overcome with exhaustion. 'It's been a hell of a day. Do you think you could make me a cup of tea, please, love?'

He looked at me, his big blue eyes wide with wonder. 'Why should I?'

His answer took me aback. 'Well, just think of all the things I've done for you.'

He dwelt on this thought for a moment, before finally concluding, 'But you haven't done anything for me today.'

'But think of all the things I've done for you on other days!' I replied incredulously. 'The holidays and trips I saved up for . . . the scrimping and saving to pay for tennis and guitar lessons . . . You are so, so lucky,' I finished crossly.

He thought about this again for a moment. 'Yes, but you've never taken me skiing,' he said, with the exasperating, literal, autistic logic that leaves devoted mums agog at the ingratitude. 'And now I must away to my empyrean empress.'

And I was left talking to his slipstream, every peevish protestation dying on my lips.

All I could do was go for the time-honoured, traditional option for under-appreciated mums the world over and dive head-first into a vat of wine, taking a packet of chocolate biscuits in with me.

Slurping and munching despondently, I pondered my next move. The problem was, my son was now a complete Kayleigh addict. The poor kid was so hooked he needed to go to Kayleigh Anonymous meetings to be weaned off her. Over the next few days, at the merest suggestion of going Kayleigh Cold Turkey, Merlin would erupt into meltdown. We soon had more wars breaking out per day than there are in the Middle East.

Then there was the fact that, as far as sharing information with Merlin that you wouldn't ever want repeated goes – well, you'd be better off confiding in Edward Snowden or Guy Burgess.

'So, Merlin says yer think I'm a lyin', cheatin' skank.'

Kayleigh's mouth was lipsticked bright orange and snarled with outraged bravado.

It was now Monday night and I was at the kitchen table writing end-of-year reports, which was proving so tedious I was fighting the overwhelming desire to sharpen a pencil, stab myself in the aorta and be done with it. I looked up from my work to see Kayleigh standing before me in a sequinned miniskirt, eyebrows flared. She looked like a disgruntled mannequin, her plastic pelvis thrust out, shoulders flung back, an ugly, belligerent expression marring her pretty face.

'I know you stole Merlin's money to pay for your high-end dentition, Kayleigh.'

'Me teef? What? It were a gift!' She blinked slowly – the calculating, cold blink of a predatory carnivore. Her greasy green eyeshadow only enhanced her resemblance to a crocodile. 'Chill, Lu-Lu. I know it must be well annoyin' that yer mummy's boy no longer loves *you* the most. But there's room for two of us, yer know . . . Merlin?!'

My son darted into the kitchen then, and I reached for his hand, but he squirted past me to get to Kayleigh's side. Think moth, think flame, I ruminated gloomily.

'Yer ma thinks I'm usin' ya. Yer know that ain't true, right?'

'Right!' he echoed.

Yeah, *right*, I thought dismally. And Elton John has his own hair.

She kissed him then – well, when I say 'kiss', it was more like she was dental-flossing his teeth with her tongue. When Merlin surfaced he gave a smile so luminous you could have read by it at night.

131

'Yer love me new teef I got for yer, right?'

'Right!' Merlin enthused, pouting up once more.

Kayleigh held him at arm's length for a moment. 'Well, yer ma's kickin' off. If yer gonna kiss me, yer want it to be like the best kiss ever, yeah?' Merlin nodded. 'So tell 'er the truth, 'cause I doan want 'er tryin' to break us up over it. I only done it for *you*, babe.'

Merlin spoke to me but didn't take his eyes off his beloved. 'There is veracity in her utterance, Mother. As I kiss her so much, Kayleigh said she needed to make hers the most beautiful mouth ever.'

'I didn't nick owt from him. It's doin' me 'ead in that you'd think I'd do somethin' so proper nasty. Right, Merlin?'

'Right!' he parroted, transfixed.

I squeezed the pen in my hand so hard that ink bled on to my fingers. If I'd been marking myself in a mothering exam right then, I'd have scored an F minus. But where was my lesson plan? Single-parenting a kid with Asperger's takes the combined skills of Nietzsche, a nuclear physicist, a trapeze artist, a magician and an animal behaviourist. Hell, it was tougher than an SAS endurance course.

'Merlin, I need to talk to you alone,' I said seriously. But he just brushed me off like an annoying insect, as usual.

From that moment on, Merlin seemed to have an 'I find my mother contemptible' clause written into his contract. My son and I had never been the type to sit around exchanging pleasantries about the asparagus. Our conversations had always been deep, tangential, surprising, coruscating. But now he became positively sullen in my

132

presence. Put it this way: a Trappist monk would be more chatty.

One rule I learnt straight away was that the family that eats together . . . gets indigestion. Meals became a torturous nightmare. The room was full of so many undercurrents it felt more treacherous than swimming on the roughest, remotest beach on the Horn of Africa. I needed markers to distinguish the socially safe areas. Conversationally, I just kept trying to swim between the flags.

'Do help set the table, Merlin, will you, love? Forks on the left, knives on the right.' *Or, preferably, stabbed into your girlfriend's jugular*, I thought darkly.

When the Zara clothes vouchers I'd given him for his birthday went missing from his bedside-table drawer, I asked her straight out if she had taken them.

Kayleigh twitched like a spider on the sofa, long pale legs akimbo. 'You have trust issues, j'know that? Yer proper passive-aggressive, you . . . After all the shit I've been frew an' that, it's proper painful to abuse me hooman rights.'

'Let me guess. You're plagiarizing Nelson Mandela again, aren't you?'

She popped open a Diet Coke and took a leisurely sip. The girl was imperturbable, beyond the reach of sarcasm.

When my car was stolen a day later and the spare car keys were found to be missing from the hall table, I asked the police to question her. Kayleigh's reply – 'I know nowt about it' – sounded as straight as Rupert Everett in a tiara.

I'd seen a mouse in the kitchen and had walked to the shops

to buy a trap. As I carted the shopping home on foot, I found myself wishing there was a Rent-a-Kill for irritating, pesky, two-legged pests. Actually, it struck me that mice, cockroaches and Kayleigh have a lot in common: they skulk in the shadows, eat everything in sight and are impossible to get rid of.

When money went missing from *my* wallet the next day, Merlin owned up right away.

'Oh yes, we needed it to go to a nightclub. Our debauched merriment would make a Tudor feast look like a vegan retreat.'

'Are you kidding me? Kayleigh's now got you stealing on her behalf? That's *it*. I'm banning her from this house. The girl is not allowed to set foot on my property ever again. Is that clear?'

Merlin, unused to my Authoritative Parent voice, winced and withdrew, which is why I thought he'd understood my edict. But later that night I woke to the jarring signature cadence of Kayleigh's high heels *cloppity-cloppity-clopp*ing up the staircase to Merlin's room.

I scrambled out of bed, bounded up one flight of stairs and burst in on them, my white nightgown billowing around me like a sail. 'I thought I'd made it clear that Kayleigh's no longer welcome here,' I said as I dragged Merlin away from her embrace.

Kayleigh's face dropped melodramatically. 'It doan matter. I'm used to bein' treated like shit. I'll just go live in the squat on the estate. It's always like this. Just when I fink I can trust someone they flippin' knife me. But not Merlin. You believe in me, doncha babe?'

My son slipped past me like a fish into the harbour of her arms. They closed around him like a net. 'If you leave, can

I come, too?' My son turned to me. 'Where my goddess goes, there go I.'

'You sure that's what ya want, babe? To live in the squat with me?' There was a disconcertingly smug note of certainty in Kayleigh's voice. Merlin nodded. The girl had colonized my son as if he were a remote island in the Indian Ocean, ripe for exploitation.

A wave of panic rolled in and pulled me under. Every follicle, every cell, every pore of my skin prickled with dislike. I was reminded of the time I'd discovered a leech on my leg by one of the Hampstead ponds. I'd felt a similar surge of repugnance and revulsion.

'Oh, an' he really needs his credit card back, too, doncha, pet?' she said. 'To help you live an independent life an' that.'

'Yes, Mother,' Merlin addressed me formally. 'I feel it's imperative that you reinstate my fiscal independence.'

'Else, he might call the cops an' say his ma nicked his credit card.' She laughed, flashing those tailored teeth, to show that she was joking, but there was a veiled threat in her voice.

Momentarily out-manoeuvred, I lied that the card had demagnetized and that a replacement was in the post. I also told Kayleigh that she could stay for now, before beating a hasty retreat to my bedroom. I then did the only thing a woman on the brink of a nervous breakdown could do – Skype her sister.

'When are you back from Dubai?'

'Tomorrow.'

'I'll be drinking battery acid on the rocks. Care to join me?'

'Um, yes, it'll go nicely with the ricin sandwich in my

135

handbag, which I'm craving, having just received an invitation to my husband's wedding.'

'At least we know what to give them for a present. His and his hand towels, right?'

'I was thinking along the lines of a chihuahua called Haemorrhoid. Despite my kids voting, shaving and driving, Danny explained his relationship to Trevor using doll analogies. Did I tell you? It's a Ken and Ken situation, apparently . . . With Barbie left weeping at the bar in her Dorito-stained party frock . . . So, where's Kayleigh now?'

'Oh, I don't know. Probably sitting around in the house somewhere setting fire to her eye make-up while smoking crack.'

'Crikey, can I join her?'

When Phoebe walked into my kitchen the next evening she voiced what I already knew, namely, that as Merlin was totally smitten and has an obsessive nature, I had as much chance of controlling him as I would have in a hot-air balloon in a hurricane.

'Well, I did warn you, Lu-Lu. But now we need to think strategically. Even though it seems that Merlin has picked this Princess Bitch-Face up from some maximum-security nail salon, if you announce that Kayleigh seems so much like a wanted felon you're tempted to send her photo to Interpol for identification purposes, he'll probably marry her.'

'Oh God.' I put my head in my hands.

'If he does, you can always turn to heroin,' Phoebe placated, just as Kayleigh turned up the bass on the heavy death metal music playing in the living room. 'Although, on second thoughts, WILL IT BE STRONG ENOUGH?!'

We took our wine out to the garden, where we could talk undisturbed. I felt an overwhelming desire to bang my head on the wooden garden table. If only it came with emergency airbags to lessen the blow.

'I didn't listen to you before but I bloody am now . . . So what do you suggest?'

'Be innovative.'

'How?'

'Well, an innovative mother must resort to more creative means to deter a kid's hideous beau from moving in. Take up the descant recorder . . . the bagpipes . . . belly-dancing. When that fails, start talking loudly and in minute detail about your peri-menopausal symptoms. Leave the TV tuned to *Antiques Roadshow* and hide the remote. Fill the fridge with urine samples and serve mung beans on toast for tea. Play the Bee Gees full blast—'

'But for how long?' I moaned.

'As long as it takes for her to get sick of it. I don't know. But, for now, you just have to go with the flow.'

'Flow? I wouldn't call it a flow. I'd call it surging rapids racing towards a Niagara Falls-type cliff face with no paddle.'

'Don't worry. Once she gets an earful of *Midsomer Murders* at full volume and a taste of tofu, she'll go screaming back to the ghetto. Especially if you keep saying his new bank card hasn't arrived and hide all your own.'

I kissed my sister on the crown of her head. 'What would I do without you?'

'I wish my own kids thought that. Right now, their opinion of me is lower than Donald Trump's IQ.'

I nodded in sympathy. 'It seems to me that the hardest thing about being a parent is that you know all the answers, but nobody bothers asking you the questions.'

'So true, sis.'

Later, as I was marking some essays, a few Q&As of my own sprang to mind.

Q: What is parenthood?
A: Feeding the mouth that bites you.

Q: What is parenthood like?
A: It's like juggling chainsaws and at the same time wondering why it's so loud, why your shoulders are aching and why you seem to be short a limb or two.

Q: What are parents?
A: The last people on the planet who should have children, especially ones with special needs.

13

The Kayleighectomy

As instructed, from then on, I left the TV tuned to *Antiques Roadshow* and hid the remote. I filled the fridge with urine samples and served mung-bean burgers only. Whenever Kayleigh appeared, I arranged my face just so – not smiling, not sad, just attentive. I kept busy in the kitchen so I could overhear everything, doling out the vegetarian tofu risotto with a lock-jawed smile and all the time feeling Kayleigh's cool, pale eyes on my back. I made endless courgette cakes, my whisk beating against the glass bowl: tap, tap, tap. Kayleigh just kept watching me with slant-eyed hostility. Her small, tight smile was as sharp as a razor blade. Determined not to arouse her wrath, I patted her gingerly on the back, as you would a stray dog that might bite off your fingers. 'More coriander-and-kale cake, Kayleigh?'

When Kayleigh brought her friends home – we're talking

yobs straight out of Central Casting, playing every thug you've ever seen in a gritty crime thriller – at first, I wouldn't let them in. But Merlin confronted me with the following uncharacteristically hurtful words:

'I presumed my deficiency in the friends department was my fault. But Kayleigh says you want me socially marooned, like an urban Robinson Crusoe, to keep you company on Mum Island. Perhaps it's time I sailed into the sunset on HMS *Kayleigh*?'

Dreading the thought of him moving out with her, I had no choice but to let her friends in, making sure to stay upwind. When this crème de la scum played their eardrum-splitting music by bands with names like Nostril Phlegm and Toe Grunge, I employed ambassadorial diplomacy by simply leaving, offering to do a food shop.

At the supermarket, I noted the car spaces close to the store designated for mums with babies, but what about providing a car space for frazzled mothers of special-needs sons dating undesirable girlfriends who've probably stolen the family car, which is why said Mum is now driving some mucky mustard 'courtesy' car with orange upholstery?

Driving back to feed the hoards on quinoa granola, I noticed how my house wore its steep, gabled roof pulled over its ears like a red hat, as though it, too, couldn't stand to hear the bass music thumping from the living room below.

When Kayleigh made racist or sexist comments, a spasm of irritation darted raggedly through my temples, but I repressed all my instincts and said nothing. Now I knew how Switzerland felt in the war, staying silent and neutral while chaos erupted on every side. I felt desperately, claustrophobically helpless; it was like being stuck in an elevator with a Mormon recruitment officer. The whole house was on tenterhooks. Even my furniture looked suddenly spindly, poised on nervous tiptoe, ready to sprint out of the door at a moment's notice.

Dear God, it took a lot of patience to play the Long Game. When it all got too much, I anesthetized myself with alcohol and shuffled aimlessly around like Liza Minnelli on a Vegas comeback tour. I tried to keep calm and positive. I found it reassuring to dwell on the thought that far, far away, butterflies flitted peacefully among alpine wild flowers and children frolicked in remote Costa Rican rainforests, blissfully unaware of the darker dangers in the world.

I lost the ability to sleep, drifting off only at four a.m., which meant I was constantly late to school. One thing I discovered in those deranged days is that your boss is the person who is always late when you're early and invariably early when you're late. Work files and folders sat unopened on my desk, mutely accusing. Missed meetings led to nudging and winks from other teachers in the staffroom. The headmaster's disapproval started to weigh on me like a thick blanket.

To make matters worse, a call came from the charity shop one lunchtime informing me that Merlin was being sacked for theft. Apparently, a twenty-two-carat-gold necklace had been stolen while Merlin was alone on the shopfloor.

'I've got to go,' I told my staffroom colleagues, abandoning my half-eaten sandwich. 'If the head asks where I am, tell him it was an emergency.'

'What kind of emergency?' asked my line manager dubiously.

'Just say that the wavy line on the terminal by my bed

started flat-lining and fading to black,' I said bleakly, half-way out the door.

I drove straight to Shoreditch to confront Beardy-Croc-Wearer.

'Merlin would never steal anything,' I said. 'Would you, darling?' I turned to my son, who had a bewildered, lost look on his face as he shook his head. Hot anger crackled into my throat. 'Clearly, he was set up by someone more duplicitous,' I deduced, glaring at Kayleigh.

Kayleigh gave a crooked smile, as insincere as it was sour. She used a purple-painted fingernail to extract a mango fibre from between her perfect, pearl-white teeth. I suspected it was the mango I'd been saving for dessert that evening.

'Yeah, it's a proper myst'ry, innit?' Kayleigh said, her eyes glittering with amused spite.

Beardy-Croc-Wearer showed me a photo of the stolen necklace on his iPhone. 'The finger of suspicion is pointing at your disabled son, I'm afraid, which is why I'm terminating his employment with us.'

'Merlin's not disabled. He's differently abled.'

Kayleigh laughed – a sharp, contemptuous bark of a laugh. I caught sight of her making a gargoyle face behind Merlin's back to amuse the other workers. When some of the boys mocked my son by mimicking her expression, Kayleigh laughed even harder, her giggle vibrating on a high, piercing note.

Merlin drew his lips up into a baffled smile which was heartbreaking in its transparency. It was as if they were baiting a field mouse. The boys remained indifferent to my searing stare, which bored into them like a drill. But

Kayleigh, noticing me observing her cruel behaviour, was suddenly all over Merlin like a fake tan.

'Poor baby,' she soothed.

I looked my son in the eyes. 'Did you take the necklace, Merlin?'

Merlin looked mystified. 'Why would a man want jewellery?' he asked innocently, with that literal logic of his.

'You see? I suspect it was someone who already has a criminal record,' I said, eyeballing my adversary.

Kayleigh bristled with pique. 'The trouble with growin' up poor an' that is people reckon yer bad. Just 'cause I been' – she groped for the precise, politically correct vernacular – 'alternatively schooled and I'm involuntarily leisured and under-housed right now, don't mean I'd nick, I mean, resort to non-traditional shoppin'—'

'Whatever euphemisms you've picked up from your social worker, Kayleigh, it's still shoplifting. And I know you stole that necklace.'

'Are you gonna let that daft cow disrespect me like that?' Kayleigh's sudden, fierce anger pinned Merlin against the wall. My bedraggled son stared over at me sadly, like a dog that's been kicked. With his fair hair all tangled, his eyes mournful and upturned, his face seemed so sad and long it looked like it was melting.

'She's lying to you, Merlin. Can't you see that?' I pleaded.

For a moment, doubt flickered into my son's big, blue eyes, but then Kayleigh aimed her glossed lips at his mouth. As they kissed, silence fell like dust over a house no longer lived in.

'I neva took owt. I swear on me ma's grave. Come on, Merlin. Let's get away from this, like, totally negative atmosphere.' Kayleigh stomped off through the door, narrow hips swishing, and Merlin followed in overawed obedience.

'Darling, please don't go.' I seized his arm. 'That girl is no good. You must trust me.'

'But Mum, without love, your life is like a book with the best pages ripped out.'

What he said was true – only the romantic comedy he thought he was part of had turned into a chilling noir thriller.

My son then paused courteously before his ex-employer. 'I would like to thank you for the sublime experience of locating new homes for all your pre-loved, orphaned items. I hope you have a fulfilling and mesmerizing future.' Then he hightailed it out of the door in passionate pursuit of his paramour.

I would have chased after them, but I was late for my afternoon lessons. Before rushing back to school I turned to Beardy Croc Bloke. 'Even though you sacked my son with no evidence, I feel no bitterness towards you and your co-horts, who are a bunch of hypercritical twats,' I said, before dashing back to my car, just as a parking attendant was writing me a ticket.

'Are you okay, Miss?' one of my Year 9 pupils asked as I crashed breathlessly into the classroom twenty minutes after the bell had gone. I slumped dejectedly into my chair and cast a listless eye over the lesson notes I'd prepared on Dylan Thomas.

'I'd like to make a public-service announcement on behalf of the More Vowels for Wales lobby. Please send any clean, unused or new vowels to Ms SClwlly St Prwddyl . . . Poles need not apply,' I replied.

Thirty-six sets of bemused eyes darted my way. I appointed one child to start reading aloud from *Under Milk Wood*, then texted my sister in Bahrain: 'Why's Kayleigh still hanging around? Merlin's bank account's empty and I've confiscated his bank card. There must be some other reason.'

'Maybe she's just doing it 2 torture u?' Phoebe texted back. Followed by a 'Keep on yr toes.'

'Hey, if I were any more on my toes, I'd be in the corps de ballet,' I typed back.

There was nothing else for it – I started spying on my son. The summer holidays started two days later, which gave me extra sleuthing time. Whenever Merlin was out I searched his room forensically. I ransacked his backpack and bottom drawers. With Inspector Morse-like tenacity, I studied the browsing history on his computer. I crawled under his bed and upended his sneakers. I checked for hollowed-out books. I left no nook nor cranny unriffled. Basically, I made the Stasi, Mossad and the KGB look restrained. When my undercover surveillance of Merlin turned up nothing new, I took to spying on Kayleigh. Whenever she was in the shower or soaking in the bath, I'd check her phone and search her bag.

When I finally found the envelope with a cellophane window revealing Merlin's name and address scrunched up in the back pocket of her jeans, my heart shrank like a raisin. As I ironed out the creases with my palm and read the official letter addressed to Mr Merlin Beaufort, my face took on the pallor of someone who's just realized, mid-bungee-jump, that the safety harness has snapped.

Jeremy's mother's face had become a little indistinct in my memory, but I could visualize her nose perfectly – perhaps because a lot of the time I spent with her, she was looking at me down it. When Mrs Beaufort had realized Merlin was 'faulty', as she put it, she'd wanted to put him out with the recycling, or leave him at the orphanage with a note pinned to his PJs reading, 'Please feed and water occasionally' – anything so as not to embarrass her pinstripe-underpanted, buttock-flogged Tory-politician hubby. But it seems that the formidable, frosty matriarch had suffered some kind of guilt spasm on her deathbed. What else could explain the letter from her bank informing Merlin that his grandmother had left her house to him, in trust – and the trust fund would come into effect on his twenty-second birthday.

Kayleigh must have found it in his backpack – Merlin never opened official-looking letters, which invariably indicated some tediously grown-up matter to which he was allergic. I plonked down on the end of Merlin's bed, dumbfounded. But then another flash of insight hit me. Of course – this also explained Jeremy's sudden interest in Merlin. As the executor of his mother's will, he would know all about the trust fund, but was clearly unaware that the bank had made independent contact. My reaction on realizing that Jeremy was simply after Merlin's inheritance was the gasp of a warm body entering a chilly sea.

'That fuckwit!' I seethed, in what was either a perimenopausal outburst or a precise analysis of my ex-husband's character. A heaviness came over me quickly, like bad weather. It sat deep in my bones and chilled me to the marrow.

I pocketed the bank's letter, then locked myself in my bedroom to Skype my sister in her hotel room in New York. I held the letter up in front of my face so that only my astonished eyes were visible over the top. When my sister finally understood the true reason why Jeremy and Kayleigh were so keen on my son, she feigned huge astonishment – staggering backwards a few feet, her hand to her forehead in the manner of a silent-movie actress about to be tied to a railway track. 'Kayleigh's just using him? No! Shock! Horror!'

'And what about Jeremy? That lowly worm. That man only ever holds out an olive branch in order to clobber you over the head with it.'

'Well, Jeremy, we can't do anything about. He's Teflon man. Nothing sticks. But how are we going to rescue Merlin from the gold-digging mattress-actress?'

'I don't know. Nothing's working. And if I ban Kayleigh from the house he'll just run away with the little minx. The only answer is to get him besotted by another girl.'

'Oh God. Can you just try not to get arrested for kerb-crawling this time?'

'I'd like to be a perfect mother, I really would, but I just seem to be too frantically preoccupied bringing up my son,' I said dryly.

I was back exactly where I'd begun two months earlier. Operation Get Merlin Laid – Take Two. It was time to make Kayleigh erotica non-grata.

14

Divine Intervention

'Wrinkled with problems? Well, let us give you a faith lift,' the denim-clad vicar enthused over the microphone from the stage. Poised behind their synthesizers and guitars, the rock band – or rather, rock bland, judging by their ironed jeans and bright white trainers – smiled and nodded enthusiastically. 'Crack the Bible,' their mentor continued, 'and get high on life.'

The young congregation showed appreciation of their vicar's Wildean wit with a chorus of 'Praise the Lord!'s.

He responded by shaking his long, freshly washed locks as though he were starring in a shampoo ad. Even his wisteria sideburns looked as though they'd been lovingly conditioned and coiffured. 'Let us now ask for forgiveness,' he intoned.

The slim, fresh-faced girl seated next to Merlin lowered her head in prayer, her chocolatey hair falling in waves around her delicate face.

'I'd rather ask for an employment opportunity, having been recently randomly retrenched for the most spurious reasons,' Merlin told her.

I braced myself for a disapproving rebuke, but the pretty girl just smiled angelically up at him. 'I'm between jobs, too,' she said sympathetically.

'My only question is, if work is such a desirable option, wouldn't those really rich people lazing on their yachts keep more of it for themselves?' said Merlin, which made her laugh.

It was nine o'clock on a Sunday morning and Merlin, Phoebe and I were in an ornately decorated Edwardian church in Paddington, happy-clapping along to a modern service which served up rock music during, and muffins after. It was all Phoebe's idea – step one in Operation New and Improved Girlfriend, as we now both agreed that Kayleigh fell several thousand feet below AGS (Acceptable Girlfriend Standard).

'If Merlin's going to have a Kayleighectomy, he needs to meet other females,' she'd told me while we were grocery shopping together a few days before. 'The thing is, dating for normal types is a minefield, what with transgender people, non-gendered people, transitioning, transitioned, the androgynous and those with gender fluidity. But for Merlin? Yikes. How the hell does the poor boy get his head around all that?'

Which is why Phoebe's solution was to find him a nice Christian girl. 'Christian girls are kind, compassionate, tolerant, patient, and, best of all, they don't have sex before marriage, so no unwanted pregnancies! It's a win–win!'

To say I was dubious was a little like saying that Kim Jong-un is only a little bat-shit crazy.

'You've got to be kidding, right? The only time I took Merlin to church as a little boy he used the collection plate as a Frisbee and told the vicar he looked like a dangly alpaca.'

'Yes, but that was before he grew up and got all hormonal. Believe me, churches are full of young, beautiful, *kind* women. Women who want to do good. Women who see the best in people—'

'Women who can wean him off Princess Bitch-Face.'

'Exactly, and who knows? *You* may even meet some sexual Good Samaritan who takes pity on your celibate state and makes you call out, "Oh God! *Oh God*! OH GOD!!!" on a daily basis.'

'You're sick – do you know that? Seriously ill.' I giggled.

'No. You are. And you need to take the Phallic Cure to get over it. Let Dr Love take your temperature with his fleshy thermometer. I prescribe some men-icillin.'

'Don't be ridiculous. Any sexual frustrations I have are easily controlled, simply by lying alone in my bed and screaming into my pillow for a few hours each night.'

My sister patted my hand affectionately. Hers was the only touch I experienced these days. And yes, I yearned for a man, but what red-blooded bloke would ever accept the excess emotional baggage of Merlin in their lives?

But still, despite sun worship being my preferred religion, I got up that Sunday morning, donned my most respectable clothes and dragooned my son to morning service.

The vicar now lifted his bouncy, blow-dried head and

flashed his gleaming dentition in the direction of his faith-
ful followers. 'God is watching us,' he beamed.

Merlin suddenly sat still as a statue, ear cocked to the
silence, as though taking the pulse of the universe. Then, as
soon as the rock band struck their next chords, he leapt to
standing and executed a few of his more innovative dance
manoeuvres, including the Typewriter, Angel Wings, the
Jumping Bean and the Chopping Board.

'What are you doing?' I hissed, the moment he took a
short break from his eccentric choreography.

'Well, if God is watching us, surely we should try to be as
entertaining as possible, which means not dancing in a
restrained or overly Caucasian way.'

I shrank to a state of pale discomfort and picked up my
handbag in preparation to leave, but the smiley girl next to
Merlin flicked her sweet, apple-scented hair over one shoulder and enthused, 'You're so right.' She then stood and
led Merlin by the hand into the aisle, where they could
dance with more abandon. Others rose and joined them, or
stood, swaying, eyes closed, palms extended towards the
heavens.

Phoebe elbowed me in the ribs, then cupped her hand to
my ear and whispered, 'I'm sure you won't mind if I allow
myself momentarily to exceed the Daily Recommended
Amount of Smug Gloating.'

I watched on, amazed. Maybe miracles really did happen? Turning water into wine, walking on water, rising up
from the dead, parting seas – these miracles were nothing
compared to Merlin's immediate acceptance by a bunch of
beautiful, charming and well-educated females.

With renewed optimism, I now clapped along to each

song of worship, leaping to my feet like a gazelle on the hills of Maharashtra with every 'Hallelujah!'

An hour later, hands numb from happy-clapping, I watched in rapture as Merlin was swept up into the surge of young people moving to the back of the hall for tea and muffins. I looked heavenward and offered up a silent prayer of thanks. As Phoebe and I sipped our Styrofoam cups of tea, I felt so overcome with gratitude I was on the point of converting to Christianity by diving head-first into the font, but then I heard a loud sob. I turned towards the tea urn to see the chocolate-haired girl's face distorted into a red gargoyle mask of fury.

'Don't you want to get into heaven?' I heard her ask my son through thinned lips.

'Heaven is an artificial construct designed to assuage man's feelings of guilt and fear of death,' Merlin explained rationally.

'Why do you come to church if you're an atheist?' another of the girls who were gathered around my son now demanded.

The vicar, who was chatting to a group of mums way up near the altar, glanced down the aisle to ascertain why his female flock was all a-flap and bleating madly.

'If God decides everything, then how do you know that it wasn't God's choice that I became an atheist?' I heard my son ask with plaintive sincerity.

If looks could pulverize, Merlin would have been pâté. My son knew he was in trouble but didn't understand why. Unnerved and anxious, he now loudly scattergunned his angst-riddled thoughts around the church.

'The worst aspect of atheism is the lack of holidays.

Perhaps atheists should agitate for a day where we get to stay home from school and work to not worship anything at all?' he ventured conversationally, in an attempt to be congenial.

Silence erupted.

'Have I said too much, too early?' Merlin panicked. 'As we retreat from religion, our ancient opiate, there are bound to be withdrawal symptoms—'

Another young parishioner let out an angry gasp and called for the vicar. He approached at speed, as though invisible wheels were hidden under his ironed flares.

'My point is that if there *is* a God, he must take a lot of rather long naps. How else do you explain war, cancer, famine and female biological inconveniences? I feel it's imperative that the women of the world join forces to file a class-action suit against God for period cramps, childbirth pain, pelvic-floor disintegration and vaginal dryness. I overheard my grandmother discussing her lack of mucous viscosity on Skype with my mum. It's a real worry, apparently.'

'Oh God,' I muttered.

'I don't think God's taking your call right now, Lucy,' Phoebe pointed out, head in hands, just as the vicar suggested through tightened lips that we might like to take our leave asap . . . but I was already steering my bemused son towards the church door.

'Why do you make me spend time with people?!' Merlin demanded in high-pitched agitation as soon as we emerged into the cool morning air. 'You know I'm not good at socializing.' In an effort to soothe his frayed nerves, he stopped stock-still to smell his fingers, an action that sometimes grounded him. But not today. Still perturbed, he began to rock back and forth on his heels.

'I'm sorry, Merlin. I just thought it might be a nice place to meet a new girlfriend.'

'I have a girlfriend! The divine girl of my dreams!' He began swaying more violently while emitting a nervous hum of anxiety. 'My slinky white snow leopard – crepuscular, secretive and extremely endangered. It's my job to protect her!'

A snow leopard? That was Kayleigh's totem? Oh great, I sighed – a hunter which can kill an animal four times its own weight with one bite to the neck. Especially with those nice new teeth.

'Okay, okay. Let's just get into the car.'

Merlin cursed and raged at me the whole way home. He was as scratchy as sandpaper.

'You're tired, darling. I'm sorry. I got you up too early. Why don't you go back to bed for a while and rest?' I suggested, dropping him outside our house. 'Aunt Phoebe and I are just going for coffee. Have you got your key?'

'I'm hoping "coffee" is a euphemism for "alcohol",' Phoebe sighed as soon as Merlin had slammed the car door shut behind him. 'I think today requires a liquid lunch.' She checked her watch. 'It is wine o'clock yet?'

'Hey, in Australia it's already five p.m., so let's just flatten our vowels and get on with it, no worries, mate,' I drawled.

Moments later, we were eyeing the drinks menu in Sloshed.

'Don't despair, Lu-Lu. There are plenty of other options. Rock choir, birdwatching, the local theatre group, a movie club, art classes ... they're all filled with females. Plus, there's another church fellowship my friend's daughter goes to. They're having a weekend away camping in Hastings—'

'But you heard Merlin.' I suddenly felt as dejected as the limp lemon slice a previous customer had dropped on the floor beneath my chair. 'He's lonely, but he likes being alone. It's the autistic conundrum. He'll never hit it off with any woman until he learns to be more sociable – and there's no way that's ever going to happen, because he doesn't like people.'

Phoebe leant forward conspiratorially. 'Well, there is one way.'

'No, there isn't.'

'Actually, yes, there is.'

'What?'

'Ecstasy,' she whispered.

'*Ecstasy?!*' I looked at her, bug-eyed with disbelief.

'Shhhh!' She glanced around nervously. 'Gee, do you think there could be a base of scientists in the Arctic who didn't hear you say that?'

'Sorry, sis, but you're clearly jet-lagged. That's insane.'

'No, it's not. Ecstasy is good for autistic people, apparently.'

I shot a sceptical gaze in my sister's direction but lowered my voice. 'I don't suppose you want to spoil that bit of information with any research.'

'They're doing trials with autistic people in the US. I was in a holding pattern coming into Gatwick the other morning so had time to flick through all the magazines. That's when I came across this medical article saying that Ecstasy's called the Love Drug because it pumps you full of serotonin and dopamine, making you much more sociable.

It's still in the experimental stage but scientists have had excellent results so far—'

'Wait a minute. Let me get this right. You're suggesting we score some drugs and get my son high?'

'High on happiness, yes.'

'Oh, well, that's a brilliant plan. Pure genius, Phoebe. Your Nobel Prize is clearly long overdue. I'll write to those bearded blokes in Sweden immediately.'

'Well, what's *your* plan, then, Sherlock? Just to leave him in Kayleigh's evil, clawed clutches?'

'Something will turn up,' I shrugged half-heartedly.

'Like what? Divine intervention? Yeah, that worked so well this morning, didn't it?'

'The only thing I have faith in now is that there's nothing to have faith in.' I sighed wearily.

'Well, now there is! Ecstasy. You just said yourself that he desperately needs help in the socializing department.'

'But exactly how sociable will these pills make him? Doesn't Ecstasy make you feel you love everyone?'

'Well, yes, but—'

'I don't want him getting arrested for rogering the rhododendron and shagging the shagpile.'

'Ecstasy makes normal people feel abnormally euphoric, but it makes autistic people – well, it just makes them feel normal, apparently. You know, sociable, affable, happy—'

'You're serious, aren't you? Christ, Phoebe. I can't believe you're even suggesting this. I mean, Ecstasy is dangerous. What does the manufacturer's warning say? *This drug destroys brain cells and leads to psychosis, heart palpitations and death . . . Otherwise, this high comes highly recommended!?'*

'It's not like taking acid. He's not going to hallucinate or anything.'

'How the hell do you know? It's kinda difficult to be sociable when you're being chased down the road by a banshee with nine eyes breathing fire out of her fanny.'

'Ecstasy won't make him see things that aren't there. Hell, the things that *are* there are scary enough, right? I mean, just take a look around your living room!'

'But even if I thought it really was a good idea – which I don't – where the hell would we score Ecstasy?'

'I dunno . . . Can't you ask some of the kids at school?'

'Oh, yes, that's a great idea. Then I'll just conduct all my lessons from prison. *So, class, what is the missing punctuation in this graffiti: "Die police scum"? Today, we are learning about maths – will number 459 please step forward?*'

'Okay, okay.' She silenced me with her hand. 'Maybe Kayleigh will just magically turn into a kind, caring person and stop using Merlin for the money he's going to inherit from his ginormous trust fund . . . Why do you never take my advice?' Resentment radiated from her in waves that I could almost see.

'Gee, I dunno. Let me think for a minute. Could it be because your kids are about to write the sequel to *Mommie Dearest*?'

My words wounded her and I regretted them instantly.

'I'm sorry, Pheebs. Please forgive me . . . Let's regroup. Take a deep breath. Maybe we're going about this the wrong way. People aren't born evil. Kayleigh's been orphaned, abandoned, fostered. The teeth, the stolen money, the missing necklace, clinging to the promise of Merlin's trust fund – it's a cry for help. I'm going to talk to her rationally and calmly and explain that using Merlin is wrong. I'm a teacher, for God's sake. I firmly believe that, with under-standing, all kids can bloom—'

'Jesus.' My sister eye-rolled. 'Was *I* this annoying when I was all optimistic and Pollyanna-esque? You're like an embroidered pillow with a blow-dry.'

'You'll see.'

And by God, we soon did . . .

'Yer frigid daft cow!' were the first words hurled my way when I turned my key in the lock of my own home an hour later.

Phoebe turned to me. 'I think you just got totally stitched up by your embroidered pillow.'

Merlin was standing, frozen, in the hallway behind his girlfriend. His smile flickered on and off like a faulty light bulb, as he looked from Kayleigh to me, then back again.

'Are you going to allow your "girlfriend" to talk to me that way, Merlin?'

'Um . . . Kayleigh, to describe my mother as a cow when you've never seen her being milked or eyed up by a carniv-orous barbecue fanatic is libellous and irrational,' he volunteered.

She ignored him and pressed on. 'Yer took Merlin to meet those skanky church chicks, to get him a new girlfriend. That's yer plan, innit? Or did yer mingin' bitch sister come up wiv it?!'

'Are you going to let her talk to your favourite aunty in that hostile fashion?' Phoebe asked Merlin, following my lead.

'Um . . . to describe Aunt Phoebe as a bitch when you've never seen her lurking in alleyways, possibly on heat, howling at the moon, is also clearly inaccurate and possibly defamatory,' he explained patiently to his agitated paramour.

'Flippin' heck. Yer precious son could win a place in the Barkin' Mad Hall of Fame, but I put up wiv his shit, doan I? And then youse diss me.'

I felt my anger rising with a geyser's gush.

'The only reason you "put up with his shit', Kayleigh, is because you found out about his trust fund.'

'What trust fund?' Merlin asked, trustingly.

Caught out, Kayleigh just smiled, showcasing those flawless white veneers. Her great golden mane of pink-tinged, teased hair, which I'd always admired, suddenly reminded me of a cobra's hood.

'You've used him for his money from the start. Then, when you intercepted the letter from the bank, you must have thought you'd hit the jackpot.' I turned to Merlin and said sombrely, 'I'm sorry to be so blunt, Merlin, but she doesn't love you.' I tried to rephrase in Merlin-speak. 'Snow leopards are opportunistic feeders who like to ambush defenceless, innocent creatures.'

Kayleigh whispered a few sharp words to my son, words that made his shoulders go up around his ears. 'Go on,' she cajoled irritably.

Merlin was rocking again, the anxious hum vibrating from him like an electric current. 'Kayleigh says you should . . . that you should . . .'

'Say it!' she insisted.

' . . . Fuck off,' he muttered.

I steeled myself in an effort to let his words bounce off me. I reminded myself that autistics are obsessive. His obsession meant he treated everything his girlfriend said like an edict from the Vatican. But it took every molecule of willpower I possessed not to take those painful words personally.

'Well, goading a son into talking to his mother so disrespectfully just proves Kayleigh's not a nice person.'

'What yer on about? Merlin, I swear on me ma's grave to tell the troof, the whole troof and nowt but the troof, I love yer so much. But yer ma's jest jealous. Can't ya see that?'

Merlin flailed an arm in front of his face as if under attack from wasps. 'I love you, too, with passion undaunted,' he said to Kayleigh, but I could hear hysteria bubbling beneath the surface of his words.

'Merlin, I want you to break up with Kayleigh, right now, once and for all,' I insisted urgently.

At this suggestion, a werewolf-like transformation came over my son. Okay, he didn't sprout foaming fangs, grow claws and start howling at an imaginary moon, but his eyes went dark, then narrowed into bloodshot slits of rage. 'Mum, no!' His voice was thick-lipped, juddering. 'Would you melt my soul? I'd rather terminate my existence.'

Kayleigh gave an acid chuckle, seized his hand and yanked him into the hallway. They crashed their way upstairs and the whole house shook when they slammed his bedroom door.

Phoebe and I stood, shell-shocked, for a moment. 'Gee, that whole "I'm going to give her another chance" thing went well, didn't it?' Phoebe finally said. 'What were you saying about how all kids, given the right encouragement, can bloom?'

'Okay, okay, don't lecture me.'

'Why don't you just call the police and let them handle it?'

'Because I'm frightened Merlin will never speak to me again. You heard him!' And oh, how I longed for the miraculous comfort of his smile right now.

'Jesus Christ. Shall we drown our sorrows?'

'I would . . . if only I could hold her head under for long enough.'

Phoebe then announced that she needed to smoke – a *lot* – so we took our tea into the garden. We sat there until it got dark, hunched over my laptop, busily enrolling Merlin into local rock choirs and theatrical companies and art lessons and any other vaguely girl-orientated activity, including – I kid you not – needlepoint and quilt-making classes. The boy would be ovulating by the time we'd finished with him.

As we trawled the Net, Phoebe painted my nails pink and put up my hair, just as we did when we shared a bedroom all those years ago.

'You actually scrub up really well, Lu-Lu. You could easily get a man if you'd just make an effort—'

'Stop it. You're making me feel like some ready meal left on the shelf, ticking away towards the expiry date stamped on my packaging.'

'Tick tock,' she said. 'Tick tock.'

To distract myself from my sister's nagging, I turned back to my laptop. I was soon so engrossed in our electronic matchmaking endeavours, and Phoebe in my mandatory make-over, that we didn't realize Merlin had run away until about nine that evening.

Having cooled off, I swallowed my pride (it was all I'd eaten for dinner) and trudged upstairs to make amends – at least until I could come up with a foolproof plan to release the snow leopard back into the wilderness of the remote Kazakhstan alpine ranges – only to find Merlin's room empty. The bed was cold and his backpack was gone . . . And he'd forgotten his condoms.

I barrelled back down the stairs, calling for my sister. 'He's run away to her squat. Plus, he hasn't taken his rubbers . . . which means that I'm slightly wrestling with the idea of my grandchildren being raised by Marine Le Pen.'

'Okay. Let's go. Panic stations!' Phoebe exclaimed, grabbing her handbag. 'This is not a drill. Repeat: This is not a drill.'

Mothering Merlin was a lot like canoeing in a cyclone – and things were clearly about to go up a category.

15

Emergency Stations! This is Not a Drill. Repeat: This is Not a Drill

My sister's car jounced through Vauxhall at a loose clip.

'Can you please go faster?' I fretted.

'Jesus! I'm driving so fast I'm leaving a roadkill of pedestrian purée along the pavement.'

The sticky neon night rushed past the car window. We veered on to Stockwell High Street on two wheels to find ourselves wedged into a horn-tooting traffic jam, with nobody getting anywhere yet everybody driving like hell.

We finally skidded to a halt in a dank cul-de-sac. As the GPS announced that we'd reached our final destination, I looked up at a grim tombstone of a tower block. The council estate where Kayleigh had told me she'd been squatting was called the Chomsky Estate and I wondered who exactly this guy had infuriated to have such a horrible, depressing place named after him.

One nice thing about finding yourself in such a rough

neighbourhood is that you can drink as much alcohol and eat as many carbs and smoke as many cigarettes as you like. Why? Well, it takes a lot off your mind when the average life expectancy is, oh, about thirty-five seconds. Especially if you're a couple of middle-aged, blow-dried mums with freshly painted pink fingernails wearing pretty floral frocks you put on to go to church that morning. Walking across the asphalt car park, we stuck out like an Amish butter churner at a nudist camp.

We may have looked like easy pickings, but my sister and I have hidden skills and secret weapons. As a flight attendant, Phoebe can tackle an entire drunken football team to the floor and wrap them up in duct tape faster than you can say 'Doors to manual.' As a teacher, I was used to wrangling with the most dangerous and unpredictable creature of all – the reluctant pupil. Now, spying a group of skateboarders, we edged towards them, utilizing the pincer-like movements of a pride of African lionesses. Employing my most authoritative 'Do as I Say or It's Detention' voice, I collared two of the boys and extracted directions to Kayleigh's squat.

Despite grave misgivings, and a vigorous tirade of expletives in the lift-well from some crack addicts, our arrival at the designated dingy tower block didn't cause much alarm – until, that is, we located the storey that had been taken over by squatters.

I eased open a door which was already yawning on its hinges. The first thing I saw was a pile of fuzzy pizza boxes playing host to an exuberant cockroach colony. The flat also clearly had a rodent infestation – either that, or they were very small squatters. The squat was so filthy even the rats were probably wearing rubber gloves. It was a gloomy place of bare or broken bulbs. A film of grime, grit, sewage fumes and dope haze seemed to coat everything. The peeling paint made it look as though the walls had eczema.

'John Lewis, eat your heart out,' my sister said, using flippancy to mask her fears.

'So where was *this* place when I was cooking crystal meth?' I joshed, resorting to the same nerve-fortifying technique.

Various walls had been knocked through, creating a ragged rabbit warren. We heard laughter and headed towards it, alarm bells clanging in my cranium. To pick our way over the debris and dog shit, my fastidious sister and I walked like two dressage horses. We followed the raucous snorting until it led us into an eerie inner sanctum. In the corner was a sofa which looked like an elephant that had been dead for quite a while, all grey and lumpy with its stuffing coming out. Dirty yellow sponge spilled out like a jaundiced liver from a rotting gut. Upon this couch carcass perched Kayleigh. She was wearing my missing suede coat and my only pair of designer shoes. My mild misgivings morphed into something solid and sinister.

Foreboding sliced through me. I prickled with dread as I saw that Kayleigh was surrounded by a coterie of druggies wearing knowing smirks. As my eyes adjusted to the gloom, I saw what they were smirking at.

There, in the fluttering halo of a lamp, stood my angelic boy. He had a glazed, fish-eye look and one side of his face was swollen, testifying to an eventful date with his beau and her creepy cronies. The pockets of his jeans were jerked inside out. He was red-faced, sweating, distressed . . . and about to eat a writhing maggot.

A burning sensation skittered across my stomach. Anger slammed through me and an involuntary shiver gripped my spine. 'Merlin. Stop! What the hell are you doing?'

'I'm proving my love in an Odysseus-type quest,' he panted. 'So far, I have eaten a chilli, drunk a glass of raw eggs and digested a cockroach. My next heroic task is to consume this live maggot.'

It was no longer a small alarm bell ringing in my head; loud, sonorous bells bigger than Big Ben were now tolling urgently. I exhibited an improbable athleticism by leaping across the room in one bound, knocking the maggot out of Merlin's hand and scooping my son into a protective embrace. I could smell the confusion on him, a sour tang like mildew and freshly turned earth.

'Who put you up to this?' I said – as if I needed to ask.

'I'm second rate, you see, Mum. Damaged goods. Factory seconds. That's why it's important – no, vital – that I prove I'm worthy of love in extreme ways. Just like Odysseus in Homer's *Iliad*, I must be set challenges.' His smile was painful in its nakedness. He no longer seemed to have a presence; he was like the outline of a person, an absence rather than a fully-fledged human being. He was disappearing slowly, like a snowman melting. All that would be left soon was a pool of sad, cold water.

A steel vice wrapped around my chest and squeezed tight until I couldn't breathe. 'Merlin, darling, there's nothing second rate about you!'

'It's my autism.' His voice trembled. 'I must be punished and corrected.'

Although vibrating with anger like some kind of malignant tuning fork, I somehow repressed the urge to tear

Kayleigh's heart out of her chest with my pretty pink nails. 'What kind of monster are you?'

Kayleigh was majestically uninterested in my concerns. She fluttered her hands aimlessly, then drummed her fingers on the side of her beer can. Without thinking, my arm swept out like a cat flashing its claws and raked her face.

'Mum! *No!*' Merlin cried, eeling out of my grasp and collapsing on to the couch beside her, cradling her face in his hands.

When a dark comma of blood appeared on Kayleigh's cheek, her cohorts sprang up, ninja-like, fists clenched.

Kayleigh uncoiled on her couch like a boa constrictor. She kicked off one high-heeled shoe and slipped her foot into Merlin's lap. Merlin's eyes went wide. 'J'love me?' she said in an unconvincing monotone.

Merlin nodded so hard I'm amazed his neck didn't snap like a twig.

'Then tell yer ma to stop babyin' ya, the old slapper.'

I saw Merlin's shoulders slacken. He deflated like a poolside lilo.

'*Tell 'er!*'

Merlin's face crumbled at her barked command. His cheeks were on fire with misery.

'Tell that slut that yer not a mummy's boy! *Tell 'er!*'

Merlin, ravaged with despair, leapt up, gripped me fiercely and parroted, 'I'm not a mummy's boy, you, you . . . you slut!'

Silence lay between us like a bruise. I felt translucent, like a hand held over a lamp's light.

'Merlin, don't ever use that word to me or to any other woman,' I finally said.

'Why not?' he asked, perplexed. 'What does it mean?'

'It means a woman who sleeps with a lot of men.'

Merlin considered this for a moment, then replied, 'What's wrong with that? Isn't it a compliment?'

The menagerie of misfits and castaways Kayleigh had collected around her erupted into cruel laughter.

I made an angry move towards them, but my sister restrained me. 'Hey, I'd love to take them all on, too, but I kinda like my facial features in their current configuration, you know? Let's just get out of here.'

It suddenly crossed what was left of my mind that, as a teacher, the only injury I'd ever sustained was a tongue-lashing from my irate headmaster. 'Okay. You're right. Let's go. Come on, my darling.'

Merlin shook his head. An awkward membrane had grown around him, separating us.

'Merlin, we need to leave. Now,' I insisted.

'No. Not without my beloved. I refuse to be wrenched untimely from her side.'

Kayleigh cast a scornful eye over me and then laughed right in my face. The almighty towering injustice of it tore at my heart like a contraction. I fixed my eyes on the dangling light bulb with its aureole of insects and willed myself not to cry. We all just stood there, in an aching, tourniqueted silence, for what seemed an eternity.

'Just say yes,' my sister murmured into my ear. 'The important thing is to get him, and us, the hell out of here.'

I looked down on Kayleigh with loathing. I felt like a gunslinger with an empty holster.

'Okay,' I mumbled, my voice raw with anger.

Kayleigh zapped Merlin with a smile – a smile he'd paid for.

'I'll just get my bag,' she smirked. Only it was *my* bag. The missing leather designer handbag Mum and Phoebe had given me for my fortieth birthday. And then I noticed the necklace glinting at her throat – the stolen gold necklace from the charity store that Beardy Bistro-Croc-Wearer had shown me on his iPhone.

Forget snow leopards. If zoologists were guessing at Kayleigh's species, I suspect they'd probably start with broad categories such as 'werewolf' and 'vampire'. Yet despite the fact that I didn't have a licence to keep ferocious creatures in captivity and would be in breach of the Dangerous Wild Animals Act, I had little choice but to take her home.

16

Grammar for Beginners – Never End a Proposition with a Sentence

The first thing my sister did when we walked into a bar in Brixton in order to score drugs was to point at the buttocks of a big, burly man bent over a pool table in low-riding jeans and say, 'There's our man. I mean, *he's* clearly peddling a commercial quantity of crack.'

'You seriously think this is a time to joke?' I said. 'I just want to hurry home and have a nice cup of tea and watch a Poirot. Or maybe some *Midsomer Murders.*'

It was the night after I'd found Kayleigh force-feeding my son a maggot. We'd waited until they'd gone upstairs, then caught an Uber to Brixton. We were on the hunt for Ecstasy tabs – a leisure pursuit we'd most probably omit from our list of hobbies in our *Who's Who* entry.

My sister had heard from a rock 'n' roll passenger in business class about a certain punk, poxy, run-down pub that operated as a drug den. We skulked in, ordered two gin and tonics, then sat in a dank corner, as nonchalantly as two middle-aged mums can when way, way out of their comfort zones, and cased the place for obvious-looking dealers.

'But what am I looking for?' I asked, squinting around at the other patrons, perplexed.

'How the hell would I know? But from what I've seen on telly, I think dealers have a clothing code. Like, one jeans leg rolled up, or a sideways baseball cap or something.'

'What, like sartorial semaphore?'

'I believe so.'

'Oh, shit, then what are *we* saying?' I glanced down at our attire. I'd tried to look 'street', changing into torn jeans and high-heeled boots, but had only achieved a kind of 'pathetically disguised undercover cop' look.

Phoebe gave me the once-over. 'I'd say your attire clearly screams "Desperate and Deranged Heartbroken Mother of Autistic Boy Trying to Score Ecstasy to Enable Him to Become Sociable Enough to Attend a Church Fellowship Weekend and Get a Normal Girlfriend" . . . Wouldn't you?'

'One thing's for sure, we're definitely the only ones wearing natural fibres in a two-mile radius . . . So what should we do?'

'Hmmm. I think I'm just going to find the youngest member of staff, slip them twenty quid and then ask who's selling,' my sister suggested.

'And God knows what they *are* selling. I'll have to bloody well swallow a tab first, you do realize. Just to make sure there are no terrible side effects.'

'Good idea! Some Ecstasy might even encourage you to let go and actually, like, talk to a man. And – God knows! – maybe even go on a date!'

'Well, the drugs certainly can't hurt my grey matter, as I'm clearly already brain damaged to have let you talk me into this ridiculous idea in the first friggin' place.'

'What about *him*?' My sister nodded towards a shadowy, sly-looking guy hunkered down in a corner nook.

His fidgety hands were jammed deeply into his jeans pockets. His eyes were half closed, as though squinting to keep out the gritty light, and his mouth was so tightly shut it looked zipped. He was sitting with a girl who was thin enough to be employed as his swizzle stick.

'Well, I doubt he's an accountant,' I conceded.

My palms were suddenly sweaty. 'Let's just go home before it's too late.' I leapt to my feet. 'I don't know what's happened to my life. Until recently, the most illegal thing I'd ever done was to recycle a yoghurt pot without washing it first.'

But to prevent me following through on my decision to leave, my sister gave me a shove – the kind of push you'd give a parachutist making their first leap out of an aeroplane – and I found myself standing before them.

'Hello,' I ventured.

The furtive couple turned their faces up to me in unison, their mouths matching thin slits, then examined me with hard, anthracite eyes.

'Thuh fuck you want?' the man said eloquently. He gave the distinct impression that he spent a large part of his leisure time bludgeoning stray dogs to death.

'Um ... I was hoping to secure some Ecstasy tabs.' It was not a sentence I'd ever expected to hear come out of my mouth. But before he could tell me into exactly which orifice it would be best for me to stuff my request, I blurted out the true story. 'You see, scientists have proven in medical trials that Ecstasy helps autistic people to become more sociable, which would enable my son to charm a nice, normal girl in the Church Fellowship and get rid of his current psycho girlfriend, who recently tried to make him eat a live maggot.'

After a beat or two, the dealer's girlfriend adjudicated: 'Jeeezus. That shit's too weird to be a lie.'

The dealer gave me a long, slow, lazy look in which he summed up my worth to the nearest decimal point. 'Twenty quid a tab,' he concluded.

'What? It's usually ten. I checked online,' I started to complain, but my sister materialized by my side and jabbed me in the ribs.

'We'll take it,' she said.

We tailed the man out of the pub into a maze of blinking neon, then down a fume-filled alley. I'd been in a hot sweat since entering the pub, but the cool night air revived me. The city glittered in the distance, all meringue domes, towers and brachiosaurus-like building cranes. Despite the Brexit recession, sky-scrapers in London were still being thrown up faster than Ikea bookshelves.

The dealer scuttled left ahead of us into a battered, pocket-handkerchief-sized park filled with a moonscape of rubble. I tried to orientate myself in the dark, then saw him windmilling his arms for us to follow. It was only now that it crossed my mind that he had perhaps merely lured us here to take the measurements for our body bags before a kidnap and eventual dual beheading.

In a secluded corner of the eerily dark park the dealer showed me the drugs, now in the palm of his hand. There were eight big yellow pills, all wearing happy, smiley expressions.

My sister jabbed me in the ribs again. 'Pay him.'

I was concentrating so hard on counting money into the dealer's grubby paw that I only half noticed the rustling in the shrubs behind me. Some remote part of my brain dismissed it as an urban fox growling at the shadows, but the pill-pusher suddenly shot me a wild-eyed look, thrust the pills at me while enunciating a gaseous torrent of obscenities, then bolted over a fence, directly into a brutish flow of traffic. I glanced over at my sister. She'd gone all crouching tiger, hidden dragon, then she abruptly leapt up as though electrocuted, crying, 'Run!'

I swivelled to see a giant shadow melting along a dark wall and instantly regretted not filling out my organ donor card. I locked eyes on the Frankensteinesque heavy black boots of the policeman before I saw his face. Even if he'd been undercover, I would have known he was an officer of the law by his marine's stance.

'Ma'am, I'm Constable O'Carroll. I have reasonable cause to suspect that an offence has occurred. Can you show me what it is that you have in your hand?'

I obediently unfurled my fingers to reveal the pills stamped with smiley faces clutched in my trembling palm. The officer took possession of the drugs, then asked me for ID. Having taken the precaution of leaving my wallet at home, a rummage in my handbag revealed my only identification – a library card – clearly cementing my reputation as a ruthless criminal.

The policeman placed the drugs in an exhibit bag. He then began, in a dreary monotone, to read me my rights. As he recited the long, baleful list of facts, my stomach churned sourly. How could this be happening – again? What was I?

A police magnet? Did I have a big neon sign saying 'Felon' on my forehead? All the unsolved evil crimes in the big bad city, and yet *I* was the one constantly being arrested?

'You do not have to say anything' – I zoned out in shock for a moment – 'but anything you do say may be given in evidence.'

'But, Officer, it's not what it looks like . . . The drugs aren't for me. They're for someone else.'

The officer cocked a brow, then said slowly, 'Ma'am, I'm going to caution you again now – you do not have to say or do anything . . . do you understand that?'

'Yes, but let me explain . . .'

The officer was agreeable enough, but small talk did not seem the order of the day so I cut straight to the conversational chase. 'I'm not a drug user. I was only purchasing them for my son.'

The light under the forlorn trees thickened and turned malevolent.

'Ma'am, you don't seem to understand that buying such a small amount is a minor offence. It's called "possessing a prohibited drug". But now you're telling me you're not just using, you're *supplying*?'

Whoops! seemed the most inappropriate response to the situation, but I said it anyway.

'Will you stay there for me for a moment, please? I'm just going to conduct some background checks.' He spoke into his radio, then turned to me with a knowing look.

'Due to information I've just received, I have to inform you that you are now under arrest. I'm taking you to the police station, where we will conduct further inquiries.'

'Oh God.' The suspended sentence. I'd forgotten all about

it. Being an English teacher taught you nothing about the School of Life, particularly not how to avoid ending every proposition with a sentence.

And so, once more, it was into a police car for a ride to the station.

'You may want legal representation,' the officer volunteered ominously.

'A lawyer?!' As far as I was concerned, a lawyer is the person you hire when you've killed your son's girlfriend for ruining his life and you want it explained to the jury in the best possible light. I didn't need a lawyer. I just needed a new girlfriend for my son. Was that such a crime?

Living with Merlin had always been an eventful ride – the psychological version of the Big Dipper. But that ride had now mutated into the Terrifying Spiral Hell Drop Tower of Death – no hard hat provided. The bloodcurdling yelp I was emitting inside my own head rivalled, in panic-stricken decibels, the scream in the shower scene in *Psycho*.

17

Planet Grim

'We've got to stop meeting like this,' the custody sergeant drawled, glancing up from his desk as I walked by, my elbow firmly in the grip of Constable O'Carroll. It was the same custody sergeant who'd sent my case to the Crown Prosecution Service, the muscled hunk with the world-weary eyes whom I'd peevishly insulted as 'ugly', 'beer-bellied' and 'boring' after my arrest for kerb-crawling. I blushed hotly at the memory of it because a) the outburst had got me into so much trouble and b) the man mountain now checking me out was clearly the antithesis of that damning description. 'It's Lucy, isn't it? Lucy the lunatic. So, what brings you back here, dare I bloody well ask?'

'Oh, clearly, your charm, wit and animal magnetism.'

I trudged on through the tenth circle of hell to take my place at the back of the queue in front of his desk. I'd just dodged one man's projectile vomit, only to step immediately into a pile of human excrement. To my left was a drunk head-butting a chair, while to my right another man started smearing the above-mentioned shit on the wall. A fat, sweaty bloke directly in front of me suddenly stripped naked, bent over and spread his cheeks. 'Ya wanna do a cavity search, Officer?' he asked as we tried to pass.

A forty-year-old woman in denim shorts and a tatty T-shirt yelled out to the crowd, 'They arrested me when I was in bed wiv me old man, and I was *that* close. Ruined me whole fuckin' day.'

The vomiter wiped his mouth on his sleeve before help-fully responding, 'Can I finish you off, love?'

'Whatja reckon about this?' A skinny girl darted into my path and slapped her scrawny abdomen. 'Ya wouldn't think that I've spat six kids out, now wouldja? A sex kitten like me!'

The sharp, hot smell of urine assailed my nostrils as the sex kitten unexpectedly wet her pants. Hidden from view far behind the custody sergeant's desk, prisoners could be heard banging on their cell doors and screaming.

Yep. An inner-city London police station is basically just like downtown Haiti, only without the glamour. The lino-leum floors were overlaid with antiseptic, but it didn't mask the stench of despair soaked into every corner. The fluores-cent furry light bathed us all in a sickly, sleazy yellow. Numb with shock, I joined the others from Planet Grim and obediently waited in line until collapsing into the seat I was told to take, directly before the custody sergeant.

'Name, address, star sign . . . ? he said.

'Star sign?'

'Hey, a man has to amuse himself. Do you suffer from asthma, diabetes, heart disease or epilepsy?' he went on, filling out the obligatory health-and-welfare form. 'Are you currently on any medication? Have you ever tried to take your own life?'

'No, but I'm thinking about it today,' I replied.

'Really?' The custody sergeant glanced up from his paperwork. 'And why would you want to do that?' he rasped, in a been-around-the-block tone.

'Why? Gee, let me think. A vulnerable son being exploited by his evil girlfriend; a scheming, lying ex-husband, and a looming prison sentence for drug possession – and people say you can't have it all! Would you mind lending me your gun so I can kill myself?'

He took a long, slow look at me and, if I wasn't imagining it, kind of smirked. 'Let's just get the form finished first, okay? Any history of mental illness in the family?' he asked.

'Well, my father ran off with a Polish barmaid-cum-masseuse and part-time Druid priestess and died doing the horizontal tango, and my mother took up t'ai chi late in life. Does that count?'

This time the custody sergeant rocked back in his chair, balancing on two of its legs, and looked me over properly – a long, slow, whole-body scan. And I saw it without a doubt this time – an amused smirk.

Emboldened, I risked a wan smile in the direction of Constable O'Carroll, who was leaning on the desk waiting for the custody sergeant to book me in. But from the constable's sucked-on-lemon scowl it was clear he was taking a rather dim view of the discovery of Ecstasy pills in the handbag of a secondary-school teacher. After giving his account of events, the constable marched off to take photos of the drugs and enter them as exhibits.

The gravel-voiced custody sergeant shoved a plate of biscuits towards me, then looked at me with what I hoped was a hint of pity. 'Okay,' he sighed resignedly. 'If my age, looks and bulk don't offend you too much, do you want to walk me through this particular quagmire and general shit-fest?'

'Well, the good news is that my son did finally get a girlfriend. The bad news is that she's a vindictive psychopath.'

I went on to explain that, while Posh and Becks and Jools and Jamie Oliver and all those other Perfect Parents who name their kids after subcontinents or pieces of fruit were probably having a challenging time trying to help their offspring choose between studying medicine or nuclear science, or whether to take their gap year going down the Amazon or up the Himalayas, or maybe just joining the Space Programme, I'd been trying to rescue my son from the She-bitch from Hell.

When I'd completed my surreal tale, the custody sergeant just stared at me in silence. I felt like an ant under a magnifying glass. He finally slid his untouched cup of tea across the desk. I took this as a good sign. I also took a grateful sip, even though it had stood too long and tasted like fish.

'So lemme get this right. Your son is going out with an undesirable and you would prefer him to fraternize with a nice church-going girl?' He scrunched his eyes closed and smacked the heel of his hand against his forehead. 'And you thought scoring Ecstasy was the best solution to achieve this end?'

'Well, it seemed like a good idea at the time.' Feeling faint, I took a bite of one of the biscuits he'd given me, only to find that it would be better employed paving a road.

'You have been arrested for being in possession of Ecstasy. You do understand that there is a difference between possessing drugs and intending to supply drugs?'

'Supplying?' I spat out some road paving. 'I wasn't supplying! I don't believe in drugs! Taking drugs could leave you in a vegetative state, in which case you could spend the rest of your life selling real estate or fundraising for the Tory party, which would then cut money from vital services *like our beloved police force.*'

I dished up an endearing smile, but the officer chose to ignore my pathetic attempt at ironic sycophancy.

'You're under conditional discharge. Breaching that means you could go to prison for your kerb-crawling antics, as well as serving many years on top of that for supplying class-A drugs.'

A Hindsight Warning Alarm Signal suddenly went off on my mental dashboard, quickly followed by a *Wake up! You're having a nightmare! This is NOT happening* psychological siren.

'Do you think the judge will believe that I wasn't scoring drugs for personal reasons, but rather trying to keep them out of the hands of our nation's underage schoolchildren?' I hazarded.

'Don't make me taser you,' the custody sergeant reproached. 'I've just started work and I haven't had my cuppa yet. You're in the big league now, love. You'll be going to Crown Court for this one. What were you bloody well thinking?'

What I was *thinking* was how on earth I could get out of here. I racked my brains for a good excuse to leave. Was I too old to go into labour? I wondered desperately.

'Please, Sergeant. You can't charge me. What good will making me a client of a correctional institution do my vulnerable son? Who will look after him then? I teach class A, I don't *deal* it, and yes, I may complain about my job sometimes – I mean, why bother teaching literature? Books these days are just something people use to pass the time until the television, internet or computer repair man comes. But it's my vocation. And a secondary-school-teaching, middle-class mum like me has no more business in an orange Day-Glo jumpsuit than a – I don't know – a panda in a tutu. You must know that. And who will take care of Merlin if I'm in prison? Anxiety about my son's welfare is constant, like tinnitus, but imagine the anxiety *he*'ll feel, left all alone in the world, with his mum behind bars?'

The sergeant gave me a Resigned Police Officer look. 'Jesus. I thought lawyers could waffle on – I mean, a lawyer can take an entire week to get through one sentence – but *you*? What I was going to ask, if you'd just stop yappin' for five seconds, is whether you'd let me check your phone?'

'My phone? Why?'

'Hopefully, to prove you're not a dealer. Key in your password,' he grunted.

'Oh, right. Okay.' I extracted my iPhone, punched in the code (Merlin's birthday) and handed it over. 'And I'm sorry about the yapping. I'm actually considering an emergency operation to have my voice box removed.'

'Shhh,' he suggested.

'Okay. Okay. Sorry.'

The custody sergeant was still scrolling through my messages when Constable O'Carroll returned.

'This druggy arrest of yours?' the custody sergeant said to him. 'Well, she's a clean skin. I checked her mobile, and there's no drug chat on it, nobody asking for gear or where to get tabs, just a lot of anguished texts about her son. J'know she's got an autistic kid? Well, anyways, I reckon this supports her assertion that it was a one-off thing. I think the stress of single-parenting a disabled boy – well, it just sent her momentarily doolally.'

'So? It doesn't mean she can break the law,' Constable O'Carroll said sternly.

'You're new to the station, right? You may have noticed that we have more crazy shit going on in here than Elvis making out with aliens using Trump's comb-over as a bed-spread. This woman's story makes *that* look sane . . . but I believe her. Maybe we could just bail her at this point and release her, pending further inquiries?'

I wanted to marry the sergeant right there and then and have his love-child. Although seriously, in the state I was in, who would want me? If only he'd just get ill, so I could give him an internal organ – though not my liver obviously, as that was clearly pickled by now in Pinot Noir.

The two officers moved away from the desk to confer in hushed tones. I strained to overhear their conversation above the hubbub but suddenly felt exhausted. Life with Merlin had become so glutinous. Pushing through it was such an effort, like swimming underwater. Finally, the cus-tody sergeant returned. I tried to read his face. Was I fated to be stamping due dates in prison library books for the rest of my pathetic life?

'Having reviewed the relevant information, I've formed the opinion that this was simply a mistake on your part. I've persuaded the arresting officer not to book you in for an interview. Clearly, you're not a career criminal. But this is a final warning. One more misdemeanour and you'll be banged up. Got it?'

Despite my bone-numbing fatigue, I shot up on to my feet as though doing army callisthenics. 'Thank you! Thank you!' I clung to the custody sergeant for a moment, like, I imagine, a rescued mountaineer to a St Bernard. This was better than winning the lottery. It was better than accidentally running into a starkers Tom Hiddleston in a shower room so misty he slips and uses your naked body to break his fall.

The custody sergeant gripped my upper arms and boosted me off his body. His touch glowed briefly on my skin, like a burnt-out match. It had been so pitiably long since a man had touched me I was caught off guard.

'Now bugger off. And try to stay out of trouble this time,' he warned, with the darkest of smiles.

'I will. I'm thinking of never going out again, except maybe to a feminist women's club or book group.'

'A feminist women's club, eh? That could be fun. Especially the pole-dancing class they have on Tuesdays,' he wisecracked. 'Now shove off already, Loony Lucy.'

A moment later, and I was striding back through the station towards freedom. But wait? What was that thwacking noise? Oh, just the final nail for my cross.

That was the thought in my mind when I saw my son coming in through the police-station door, his hands in cuffs.

I may be an educator, but life was about to teach me a hard lesson – that fate gives with one hand while punching you in the guts with the other.

18

All Names Have Been Changed to Protect the Deranged

Dating Kayleigh was the equivalent of doing a black ski run, and Merlin and I were clearly only equipped for a little light tobogganing on the beginners' slope.

It was her voice I heard first; it rasped like a wasp trapped in a dirty jar.

'Get off me, yer tosser. Yer touched me an' shit. Doan you dare. Touch me an I'll kill yer, I fucken swear.'

And then there she was, barrelling into the police station behind my son. And with her came well-founded gloom.

I shoved, elbowed and barged my way through the crowded area around the front desk to get to my boy. 'What the hell's going on? Are you okay?' Merlin looked shaken, blurry at the edges, like a watercolour smudged by rain. I pressed my face into the angle of his shoulder and neck and breathed in his familiar scent. 'Tell me.'

Kayleigh's dark eyes glittered. 'Keep that daft bitch away

from me! She attacked me. Look!' She pointed to the scratch on her cheek before clawing the air in my direction.

The arresting officer restrained her, but the ensuing ruckus had attracted the attention of the custody sergeant, who slowly lumbered up from behind his desk. 'Jesus. What *now*?'

'This is my son,' I told him. 'And *that's* the girl I've been telling you about. What's happened?' I demanded once more of the arresting officer.

'Theft. Off-licence. Two crates of vodka nicked.'

My mind was clattering, panicking – this made no sense. 'But what on earth does Merlin have to do with that? He doesn't even drink alcohol.'

'The manager took down the number plate of the get-away car. It turned out to be a courtesy car, which we traced to the residential address' – he consulted his notes – '16 Thornbury Road . . .'

'That's my address.' My heart backflipped in my chest.

' . . . then we apprehended the suspects. The girl says Genius here was the robber and the getaway driver.' He indicated my son with a casual crook of a finger.

Seeing me attempt to teach Merlin to do anything mundane – cut a tomato or stack a dishwasher, for instance – you'd think I was giving him instructions on how to fuel a nuclear reactor. The thought of him being able to drive a car was laughably ludicrous. 'But my son doesn't drive.'

The arresting officer glanced at his notebook. 'Not according to evidence taken at the scene of the arrest.'

Merlin's face registered a look of baffled incomprehension so intense it was almost a caricature. 'If we put this unfortunate incident into cosmic perspective, I'm sure we'll come to see it as a mere blip,' my son offered up as a defence.

'I never knew he'd stolen owt from the offie,' Kayleigh said, spitting out a chewed nail. 'I fort he was just buyin' snacks an' that.'

The sharp, steely realization that Kayleigh was framing my son left me lacerated. I felt it as keenly as the cut of a new razor blade.

'Merlin,' I said, as calmly as I could, 'did you drive my hire car to the off-licence and rob it?'

My son's eyes danced on hot coals, darting and flinching around the room. 'Is life merely an experiment being carried out on a lesser planet?' he asked fretfully.

'What happened exactly?' I demanded.

Merlin just stood looking at me in a dazed way, like a pet rabbit in a python cage.

'It's imperative you tell me the truth *right now.*'

In the silence, my words crashed and flapped, rattling around the room like trapped birds in a panic. Merlin was back in spooked-deer mode, his wind-tangled hair blurring wildly around his face.

'Babycakes' – Kayleigh, her voice as cold as peppermint, placed a restraining claw on my son's arm – 'remember what we agreed an' that?'

'Kayleigh says I'm not allowed to talk to anyone,' my son said, turning to me with confused eyes. 'Although, technically, telling you that I can't talk to you *is* talking to you, of course.'

'And why would that be?' the custody sergeant asked, zapping Kayleigh with a suspicious glare.

Caught out, Kayleigh suddenly became preoccupied picking clumps of dried goo off her heavily mascara-ed lashes. I seized my moment and moved Merlin to one side.

'Okay, but Kayleigh didn't say anything about not answering questions in mime, now did she? Just nod or shake your head, okay, my love? Did you let Kayleigh and her friends drive my car?'

He nodded.

'Were you at the wheel?'

He shook his head: no.

'Did you go into the off-licence?'

Another nod.

'Did you rob the off-licence?'

Once more he shook his head: no.

'Did you know they were robbing it?'

Another negative shake.

'Oy!' Kayleigh interrupted. 'Yer know yer stole the grog.' Her sticky voice spun a spider's web around my son.

I mentally kicked myself for ever encouraging Merlin's relationship with this girl. Phoebe had been right. The price for losing his virginity was just too high. It was like: *Congratulations! You're a man! Now, go to prison, where there are no females.* Merlin had been used and abused and, once more, I hadn't been there to protect him. I felt exactly the way people describe root-canal surgery – only minus the anaesthetic.

'We didn't know he was robbin' the store. We just went in to buy smokes an' that. Isn't that right, babe?' Kayleigh's light voice was falsely cheery. Her smile, as sharp and sweet as icing, set my teeth on edge. 'But yer know, 'cause of his special needs an' that, you can't really charge us, right?' she said to the custody sergeant, spinning her nasty web more tightly. 'That's the truth, innit?' A tiny flicker in her eyes betrayed her deceit – that, and the fact that, despite the room being cold, small beads of sweat were studding her skin like diamonds. 'I was proper gutted when the Old Bill turned up at Merlin's gaff. Till then, I neva knew he'd robbed the store. I would neva do anyfink illegal again after all the proper shit I got in last time.' She shuddered theatrically, like a child being force-fed offal. 'It ain't easy, bein' an orphan,' she simpered. 'Yer can end up in the wrong company so quick an' that. But no more. I'm a good girl I am,' she Eliza Doolittled, her lips pouting in a small, innocent moue.

I turned to the custody sergeant. 'Surely you can see she's coerced him into lying. Just book her, get her interviewed and charge the minx.'

'With what?'

'Exploitation.'

'Of what? A minor? The boy's shaving, for Chrissake.'

'Where's the CCTV footage? That'll prove Merlin's innocence. It's the first time he's ever been in trouble. Unlike *some*.' I glowered at Kayleigh.

Her face blanched at the mention of security cameras. She squirmed and trembled and her plucked eyebrows collided for a worried moment. Her composure cracked and I glimpsed for the first time a frightened little girl cornered in a school playground. But then the Fate Fairy waved her wand in the orphan's favour.

"Fraid the surveillance camera's been vandalized,' the arresting officer said, and with that Kayleigh was back in control, her smile as lacquered as her nails.

My heart pounded, seemingly in time with the ticks and hisses of the geriatric plumbing of the old police station. 'So it's Kayleigh's word against my son's?' I asked.

'Yep,' the arresting officer clarified. 'And he's not speaking.'

'Well?' the seasoned custody sergeant asked me curiously. 'What do you say to all that?'

'I'm so angry I . . . I . . . I can't speak.'

'Crikey. I've never seen you *that* angry before,' he deadpanned.

Glancing at my son, I winced with dread. He stood in a defeated droop, his eyes unreadable beneath his floppy fringe. Just as I was contemplating killing Kayleigh right there and then, so saving the police the inconvenience of launching a lengthy murder investigation, the big, heavy doors to the station thwacked open and a middle-aged woman strode in. She walked with the gait of a horse wrangler – but a horse wrangler wearing a denim mini skirt and little white, rhinestone-studded boots. Her legs were thick and muscular, as though she'd had capsicums implanted in her calves. Her lined face was deep brown except for a white area stencilled around her eyes from where her sunglasses had rested all summer. Her hair was dyed a vivid chartreuse and her handbag was canary yellow.

If this were a black-and-white Raymond Chandler movie, the detective would have clutched his gun closer, lowered his hat brim and muttered darkly, 'Now, there's one helluva tough broad.' But it was an inner-city English police station, so the only comment that broke the silence was 'Oh shit. What do *you* want, yer old slapper?'

The comment came from Kayleigh. I swivelled my gaze from one to the other, trying to work out the connection. Was she a pimp? A mobster boss? A seedy solicitor? What was left of my mind was boggling.

'Old? I'm only fifty-flippin'-seven. And just so you know, I'm wearing a G-string that's shrunk in the wash, so I'm feelin' pretty put out and pissed off, so don't push me, sweet'eart,' the horse wrangler replied in a husky voice. 'So Jack' – she addressed the custody sergeant – 'you've not met my darlin' daughter, 'ave yer? What's the little scamp done this time?'

The man I now knew as Jack shrugged. 'Whatever it is, it's way above my pay grade,' he said, and busied himself with something on his desk.

'*Daughter?*' I reeled. 'I thought you were dead.'

'Come again, pet?' the woman said.

'Kayleigh told us she was an orphan.'

The big, blousy woman let out an acerbic cackle. 'Well, motherin' a tearaway like 'er, I'm a step closer to the grave every friggin' day, but I'm not quite there yet, pet. So?' She turned on a cowboy heel to face me fully. 'Fill me in. I gotta call from one of my mates – she cleans 'ouses in norf Lambeth – sayin' that she'd seen my sweet little angel gettin' carted off in a cop car. *Again.* But just gimme the crib notes, okay, not the 'ole twenty volumes.'

The arresting officer cracked open a Diet Coke, then delivered a nearly complete account of the criminal debacle, as dishonestly described by Kayleigh. I jumped in with my own version, explaining how Kayleigh had tricked Merlin into giving her my courtesy car keys so she could then drive to the off-licence to rob it, and how she was now trying to get my autistic son to take the rap, presuming his condition would work like a 'get out of jail free' card.

Kayleigh's mother squeezed out a chuckle. 'Cute,' was her succinct appraisal.

'It's not *cute*. It's totally conniving.' I looked the woman up and down. I suspected a career of dancing without underpants in discotheques, most probably in some seedy lap-dancing club featuring pudgy peroxide blondes who were no longer employable in Bulgaria.

'Hey, why don't ya crack a smile and give yer ass a break? It's amusin' 'cause it's so damn stoopid. The clueless numpty.'

'Kayleigh's like a stray dog picked up out of compassion off the cold streets and given shelter, only to turn on you and bite your hand,' I levelled with her.

Kayleigh's mother bristled. 'She ain't no stray. She belongs to me. What exactly are you insinuatin'?' She narrowed her eyes. 'You need to work on your fuckin' people skills, lady.'

Despite the chaos and cacophony of the police station, people were now looking in our direction. 'Look. Perhaps we could have a quiet word, mother to mother?' I suggested, my voice furiously measured. 'Officer, can you give us a few minutes?' I turned to the woman. 'I'm sorry, what's your name?'

'June.'

'June, I'm Lucy. Merlin, will you be okay if I leave you for a moment?'

'I'm just going to press my knuckles to my ears to keep my grey matter from seeping out,' Merlin said, which sounded quite sensible under the crazy circumstances.

I kissed his soft, sweet cheek, then steered Kayleigh's mother to a quieter corner. 'In case you didn't know, our kids have been seeing each other all summer. They met volunteering at Oxfam. I was encouraging and welcoming at first. But it turns out she's using and abusing him, and now she's set him up as the fall guy in a theft. I don't know how she was raised, but the girl's clearly gone feral.'

'Hey, I raised that kid in a warm an' 'appy 'ome.' June jabbed her finger into my chest, her arm fat swinging like heavy washing in the wind. 'She jus' got in with the wrong crowd – a bunch of ignorant fuckmuppets. But hey, who didn't turn into Attila the Teenager and run wild once upon a time, eh?'

'Me, actually.'

June looked me up and down with pity. 'No shit, Sherlock. Don't need to be Einstein to figure *that* out.'

'The point is, your daughter's using my son.'

'What for?

'His money.'

'Hey, love, they met when they were workin' for free in a charity shop. So he's not exactly Rocker-fuckin'-feller, is he?'

'But what little he has, she takes. And she's holding out for a whole lot more.'

'Well, what about what she's givin' him?'

'Venereal disease, you mean?'

June narrowed her eyes once more. 'Like I said – people skills. Yer need to fuckin' work on 'em.'

'Look, I'm sorry. But my poor son's deluded enough to think your daughter's in love with him. I want her out of his life. I'm desperate. I'll pay good money for her to go away.'

'Can't yer kid make up his own mind?'

'No! No, he can't. Because, well, an intelligent person, or even a reasonably bright fungus, can see that my son's easily manipulated.'

'Autistic, ya said? Flippin' heck. That's a bloody challenge.' The woman's sympathy was robust but unpatronizing.

'Yes, you could call mothering him a "challenge" – the

same way you could call a tornado an air current.' I sighed wearily.

'Look, I love my daughter. But sadly, she takes after her effing father. That bloke's so mean he could skin a fart. And that girl of his could milk hot piss out of an igloo.' Her laugh was like a saucepan lid dropped on a terracotta tile; the burst of it made me leap.

'Then you'll help me break them up?'

'Yeah, sure, 'cause girls that age just so love takin' advice from their freakin' mothers. Besides, believe it or not, they're adults, pet. You've gotta let 'em work it out for 'emselves. Fact.'

'Well, a little *fact* I'd be only too happy to share with the police right now is that your daughter's currently wearing the gold necklace she stole from the charity shop where they met. A theft she falsely blamed on my son.'

We faced each other like two old gunslingers in the Last Chance Saloon.

'Okay,' June conceded. 'I'll talk to 'er, though, I won't lie, she doesn't look all that friggin' delighted to see me. There could be fierce words and a restrainin' order. But I'll do my best to break 'em up. Okay?'

'Thank you.' I stifled a sob rising in my throat. 'I really am at the end of my psychological tether. But I was kind to your daughter. I do want you to know that. I did my best . . .'

Something softened in the big woman's face. 'Doan worry, pet. I promise to make this whole shit-fest just go away.'

'How?'

'Bribery and corruption . . . oh, and a bit of arse kissin'. Honey, I've kissed so much arse for my delinquent daughter

my lips are chafed. I need an arse-kissin' chapstick perma-
nently attached to me friggin' face.'

With that, June adjusted her underwear with a thumb
and a wiggle of her opulent backside before screeching,
'Kayleigh! Come 'ere, you little bugger. Tell me the names of
the weasel-headed shitnuggets who robbed the bloody
off-licence. *Now!*'

Police scattered like shingle before June's booming voice,
but Kayleigh screwed up her face in defiance. June seized
her daughter tightly by the arm. 'Tell me now, yer little ras-
cal, or I'll post on Facebook all those videos of yer with the
bad perm in the Russian peasant outfit yer grandma made
ya wear, singin' "Babushka" into yer hairbrush.' June's voice
was low and smoky; gravelly, even – gravel wrapped in
velvet.

Kayleigh cowered for a moment in horror, giving me a
glimpse of that bullied schoolgirl again, before blurting out
a list of boys' names, which the arresting officer duly noted.

What happened next was a masterclass in manipulation.
First there was humour – June's laughter, vibrant with bravado and bonhomie. 'My Russian ex-hubby, well, he was a
good-lookin', muscly bloke who worked whatever hours
suited him, picked up nightclub tabs and was good in the
sack – qualities I'm always attracted to in a Mafioso
millionaire!'

Then there was pathos. June's sob story about being a
single mother abandoned by her callous, ruthless gangster
husband was laid on so thickly she could secure immediate
employment wielding a trowel on a building site.

There was also eyelash-batting seduction. It hadn't even
crossed my mind to flirt with the police officers. Besides,

it'd been so long since I'd flirted I was like a circus animal who's forgotten all her tricks.

Finally, June burst into theatrical tears, citing menopausal hormonal distress, and fanning herself with a law magazine whose cover story most conveniently just happened to be 'How to Sue the Police', and I figured it was safe to leave her to her own devious devices and go to check on Merlin.

I got back to my son in time to hear him telling a pack of dangerous drug dealers and hard-core crims that poor people were not his 'milieu . . . Clearly, poverty is not my genre.'

Oh God. I was just about to suggest a police escort out of the building, and perhaps relocation into a witness-protection scheme in, say, Finland, when an even greater danger encroached on my horrific horizon . . .

19

Dancing in Quicksand

Jeremy's tie was a snarl of designer silk knotted too tightly around his neck. He was entering from the cells, but could only have been summoned to a Hogarthian hell-hole of a police station like this for a posh crime – one of his banker mates mugging a pensioner of her life savings, no doubt.

'Oh, look who's here!' he boomed in greeting. 'It's that heroic icon of modern motherhood! What have you been doing *this* time? Hiring more prostitutes for our son? Oh, wait. Scoring drugs, isn't it? Or so the arresting officer informed me. That's a new low. Drugs you were going to push on to my poor, innocent son, apparently.'

'So,' I retaliated, in an effort to camouflage my shock at bumping into him here, 'what have *you* been up to lately, Jeremy? Found any new groups of naïve people to exploit? Done any light raping and pillaging? Invented any new weapons of mass destruction? Or has the law simply finally caught up with you?'

'I'm here seeing a client in the cells.'

'Really? Who? Let me guess . . . Claus von Bülow? Bernie Made-off-with-the-Money? Jack the Ripper? Or maybe just the devil incarnate?'

'So,' he continued, ignoring my taunts, 'you can imagine my surprise on being told that my ex-wife was upstairs on a drugs charge. With his mother in custody, as a concerned father, I immediately rang Merlin to make sure he was all right. And that was when I discovered that he, *too*, had been arrested. I felt duty bound to contact Social Services immediately.'

He gestured across to the other side of the police station, to the woman I'd met at court. I recognized Sonia by the big, owl eyes and pinched expression. The woman was so bland I hadn't noticed her sitting quietly in the corner. Clocking us, she immediately scuttled over, tightened up the bitty sinews that passed for her lips and spoke crisply.

'Clearly, your home is not the correct environment for a boy with such complex needs,' she said, with the glacial condemnation and polite contempt which are the default position of all holier-than-thou do-gooders hired for their ability to remain stoical in the face of another's misfortunes.

Medusa-like, my livid gaze nearly turned her to stone. 'You know nothing about the complexities of our life! For starters, you don't seem to understand that I married a shyster. You appear to be wearing shyster-blinkers.'

'Paternal influence is imperative for global wellness and societal assimilation,' Sonia asserted, her face blissfully unsullied by even the rumour of irony.

'What?' Trying to talk to a social worker is like conversing with one of those computer programs that mimic human responses.

'Jeremy sincerely wants to help his son.'

'Huh! Sincerity in an ex-husband is as believable as a cheap bill from a lawyer,' I shot back. 'For God's sake, don't make the mistake of trusting this maniac, Sonia. I don't think Jeremy's even got an iron-clad alibi for what he was doing the night Azaria went missing.'

'You see what she's like?' Jeremy gave a long-suffering sigh for Sonia's benefit.

The 'impartial' social worker made a tut-tutting noise in sanctimonious agreement.

'So, has Jeremy told you about his mother's trust fund, Sonia? I suspect not.' I skewered him with a look of contempt.

Jeremy was clearly floored by the fact that I knew about the fund, but quickly recovered his chilly composure. 'As usual, I have no idea what you're talking about.' His tongue lolled like a snake as his lies slithered out on to the floor at my feet.

'Yes, rich parents are known for their long pockets and longevity,' I persevered. 'And then, when they finally *do* fall off the parental perch, they invariably leave their money to a cat sanctuary or a pet cemetery . . . or to the autistic grandson they neglected while they were alive.'

My ex-husband ran his hand through his hair in a poised gesture perfected before hundreds of mirrors and gave a self-satisfied chuckle – the chuckle of a puppeteer who knows exactly what strings he can pull.

'Don't try to dissemble, Lucinda. This is about you, not

me. What kind of mother are you? First, you're arrested for kerb-crawling in an effort to debauch our vulnerable child. Then you encourage fraternization with a bit of trailer-trash who is also a known felon, putting Merlin in considerable danger and resulting in his arrest on a theft charge while *you're* out – wait, what were you doing again?' My ex went for me like a wasp at a rotting fig. 'Oh *yes*. Trying to score illegal drugs to give to our son, leading to his possible addiction and/or a fatal overdose. Merlin clearly needs to be in a stable, loving environment, and that is what I am offering.'

'You don't love Merlin! You just want to get guardianship so you can parcel him off to some hideous care home and spend his inheritance. You're like a bottom-feeding fish, living off the scraps of your mother's leftovers.'

'You're talking gibberish. Are you actually high right now? Officer! I say, Officer? . . . Have you administered a drugs test?' he demanded bullishly.

When Jack didn't look up, Jeremy fog-horned, 'Are you the custody sergeant?'

'All day, every day,' Jack replied with a mirthless smile.

'Well, do your job properly and get this woman a tox-screen.'

Jack flinched, then very slowly looked our way. Jeremy was wearing the smugly confident look of a man who presumes his profile will eventually end up on a stamp.

'You know, I almost never shoot people, but sometimes it's just so damn tempting. Ma'am,' Jack addressed me, 'is this man harassing you?'

'I'm sorry, Officer. This is my ex. Just ignore him. The man can bullshit on about himself for, approximately, eternity . . . I suggest you just drop the act, Jeremy, because the bank sent Merlin a letter. And I have it.'

That got his attention. Jeremy blinked at me, once, twice, absorbing this unwelcome information.

'Sonia, I'm sorry. Would you kindly give us a moment?'

Sonia, who'd been mosquito-ing around us, notebook in hand, obediently buzzed back to the seat next to Merlin. He was slumped in the middle of a row of empty chairs lined up against the wall as if set out for a firing squad. My son looked up at her, his face a blur of misery. My poor boy. If *I* was finding this whole scenario discombobulating, I could only imagine how disorientating it was for him. Even on a *normal* day, Merlin felt he was in a foreign land, constantly struggling to make himself understood without speaking the lingo.

As soon as Sonia was out of earshot, Jeremy rounded on me. 'I suppose it didn't cross your puny mind that drug dealing is a breach of your twelve-month good-behaviour order? Thank goodness Merlin has another parent to take him in while you're in prison.'

'Well, thank you for your most magnanimous offer,' I said derisively, 'but there's no need for you to put yourself out, Jeremy.' I paused to savour my small moment of victory, rolling it around in my mouth like a vintage wine. 'Because I've been let off with – gosh, what's the legal language? Oh yes. That's right – a caution. Proving that not everybody is as cynical and cruel as you are.'

Jeremy's smile seeped away. He winced like a slug on a snail pellet. In a blind fury, he agitatedly punched a number into his iPhone.

'Theo, maaaate, how the hell are you? How are things

down at the *Mail*? Actually, I'm just en route to my ex-wife's latest arrest – yes, ha ha. I don't like to miss any of her court appearances.' His tone was thick and artery-cloggingly creamy. 'Well, yes, actually. I think I do have a rather good story for you . . . Salacious? Yeah, it's got everything except a naked Royal and perhaps the Pope.'

A story in the tabloids. Oh great. What more could I do to embarrass myself? Walk around naked with an incontinence pad stuck to my forehead?

'So you're interested? Thought you would be. Okay. I'll call back with the gory details.' Jeremy pocketed his phone, then said to me coolly, 'Of course, I don't have to give Britain's biggest-selling newspaper the details of the Ecstasy-dealing English teacher whose disabled son got caught stealing from an off-licence in the company of a known felon while his negligent mother was off scoring drugs to push on to her vulnerable son . . . Not if we can come to some form of compromise . . .'

I turned to look at Merlin. He was being talked at by the insipid social worker. He had a bemused air about him, as though he'd lost his glasses and was trying to read a far-away street sign. I wondered how Jeremy would seal the deal when I handed over custody of my beloved boy. Would he sign our legal contract in ink, or in the human blood of his latest victim? The Armani-suited vampire I'd once foolishly married was so evil I felt sure that even a Buddhist would be driven to murder the rotten bastard.

'Sooooo . . .' The boisterous voice of June broke into my bleak ruminations. She sashayed towards us, hips swishing. 'The cops now have the names of the real witless cock-splats who robbed the off-licence. Those little shit-weevils have prior – apparently, the acned shit-gibbons specialize in muggin' pensioners at cash machines.'

'How despicable!' Jeremy carped.

'Really? I'd say they're not unlike the wanker-banker client you came here to rescue, Jeremy, though I suspect *your* client wasn't charged. Am I right?' I deduced caustically.

'Anyway, seems like Kayleigh's little scummy, crummy posse of shit-spackled muppet-farts have graduated to usin' kids with disabilities 'cause they think nobody'd have the heart to charge 'em. A class act all friggin' round, wouldn't you say?' June elucidated. 'But anyway, now that the cops have the names of the real culprits, they've decided to let our kids go.'

Thwarted, Jeremy's face took on a thunderous countenance. He just stood silently with his hands behind his back, feet apart, eyes obscured behind dark glasses, like the dictator of some dodgy Balkan Republic tax haven.

'But let's all get the hell out of here before the Old Bill change their freakin' minds. *Comprende?*'

'Not so fast!' Jeremy thundered. 'Just because the police made the mistake of letting you and Merlin off doesn't mean I can't still sell the story. In fact, that's a story in itself. Why was the drug-dealing school teacher already on a suspended sentence let off so leniently?'

Jack, who'd been leaning on the wall behind Jeremy and observing us, sauntered past on his way back to his desk.

'Oh, by the way, Lucy,' he said casually, taking a sip of steaming tea. 'Those pills? We tested them. Just got the results back from the lab. The only side effect you'd get from that lot is a cavity.'

'I'm sorry?'

'Yep, the only high you'd get is a high dental bill. Pure

sugar. You might want to make a complaint to Consumer Affairs,' he joked.

Jeremy deflated like a pool-side lilo at the end of summer.

As the custody sergeant turned to walk away, he looked my way and winked. That's when I knew he was lying.

'Oh, and by the way, big shot,' he said to Jeremy, 'there's a cream to cure people like you – a haemorrhoid cream, 'cause you're such a pain in the arse. So, if your business here is done, may I suggest you bugger off out of my police station before I arrest you for loitering with intent? And that goes for the bloody lot of you.'

It was the best invitation I'd had all day. I lunged towards the seats, grasping Merlin's hand in mine, and burst out of that police station as though pursued by a poltergeist. Rain peppered my face. The cool, gentle touch of it nearly made me cry in relief. We only stopped running when we reached the traffic lights.

'Mum,' Merlin said, his voice very quiet and tentative, 'I keep thinking everyone around me is an actor. Have I been adopted by a movie studio? Are you my real mother?'

'I'm seriously starting to wonder that myself. Listen, darling. I don't ask for much, do I?'

He thought this over. 'Well, you did ask me to make you a cup of tea the other day.'

'I know.' I sighed. 'But besides that. The thing is, I need you to promise me something right now. You are not to see Kayleigh again.'

'Why?!' I could hear the popcorn going off between his ears. 'Kayleigh says you need psychiatric help. And maybe she's right. Your mothering techniques have been quite inadequate of late.'

'Get this straight, Merlin, if you see her again, I'm calling the police. And you don't want to go back to the police station, do you?'

He shook his head, horrified.

'And Kayleigh will be arrested and sent to prison. And you don't want that, do you?'

'*No!*' he exclaimed, distraught. 'Snow leopards must live in the wild.'

'Then I want you to promise me, on Einstein's grave, that you won't see her again.'

He shuddered but gave a tiny nod of his head.

'I'll explain it more carefully over supper, okay?' I suggested, in an effort to buy some time. 'Why don't you pop into that fast-food place there and get us a table? I'll join you in a minute.'

I turned to scan the neon-lit pavement behind me for June. The busy city street, with its spluttering exhausts, was a molten river of red and green traffic lights as far as I could see. Eventually, I spotted her striding towards me, Kayleigh's arm clenched in a vice-like grip. The pouting, pink-haired girl was in a grand sulk, hoodie up, lost in the *tschh tschh* of her headphones.

'Thank you.' I gave June a grateful look. 'I have no idea how you did that.'

'I just did a Sharon Stone and flashed a Fallopian tube.'

'Really?!'

'No, you idiot! I've known the arrestin' officer for yonks,' she said stoutly. 'Drinks at my joint. So does Jack. A lot of the boys do. I run a pub. Anyway, the arrestin' officer's "being rested" from his anti-corruption post over bribery allegations,' she chuckled.

'So . . . you bribed him?'

'Let's just say he dislikes the formalities of normal high-street banking.'

June gave me a big, juicy wink.

'The necklace,' I reminded her, gesturing at Kayleigh's throat. 'Don't forget your promise to break them up.'

'Yeah, 'cause like I said, tearaway daughters so enjoy a good old heart-to-heart with their mum!' She pointed to Kayleigh's hoodie and headphones. 'But yeah, okay, I promise. I've confiscated the little scallywag's phone, so at least he won't be able to find her, okay?'

'Thank you,' I said, and meant it.

'So.' She shrugged. ''Ave a nice life.' She strong-armed her daughter to her side, executed a one-hundred-and-eighty-degree swivel on her cowboy heel and then they were gone. For ever.

20

Love is in the Air – or Maybe it's Carbon Dioxide

I immediately whisked Merlin away on the train for a summer break, a 'cheap and cheerful' trip to a B&B in Brighton which proved to be neither. Back in London, I spent the rest of the summer dragging the poor kid around to endless job interviews for jobs he never got and enrolling him on courses he didn't want to take.

'Why is it that, just when I was getting used to yesterday, along comes today?' Merlin moaned every morning as I prodded him awake. 'And please – ugh – please don't give me that cheesy smile,' he'd wince, as though I'd thrown a vial of acid in his face. 'That cheesy smile of yours really unnerves me.'

As a vote of confidence, I gave him back his bank card, but he couldn't have been less interested. In fact, he lost interest in everything. First, he gave up doing his press-ups and sit-ups, then he stopped watching tennis, then he even

developed an aversion to his telescope. 'Without my goddess, I feel all turned inside out, my nerves cruelly exposed
to the brutal air,' he explained, when I asked him what was
wrong. 'I'm crippled inside.'

Exhausted, I decided I'd only worry about him on the
days when the sun came up.

By the time the new school year was about to start, Merlin
still had nothing to fill his days. Desperate, I'd booked
him on to a week-long retreat for autistic kids in the
countryside, in the vague hope that he'd make friends of
his own – well, of his own species. I hadn't heard from him
for five days so was cautiously optimistic that he was
happier. The house was very quiet and calm, for a change,
but I missed him. I didn't feel like an empty-nester, more
like a small hotel off-season. Still, Merlin's absence meant
I could finally concentrate on my career – a career which
had been careering into the toilet bowl for quite some
time now.

On my first day back at work I was up early, determined
to make a better impression on my disgruntled headmaster.
The post came while I was having breakfast. I'd always been
Merlin's unofficial PA, adviser, medic, shrink, social secretary and banker, so I didn't think twice about sliding my
nail across an envelope addressed to my son – especially as
it was an envelope with a cellophane window.

The letter was from the bank. I gave it a perfunctory scan
and was about to add it to my pile of papers when my eyes
snagged on the debit column. Merlin was two thousand
pounds overdrawn. I blinked in disbelief, then scrutinized
the itemized list of purchases: high-heeled shoes, bikinis,

cocktails at a bar called Venus VIP, plus tickets to see a band called Jism – and all in the last week. My heart plunged at the realization that Merlin must have been seeing Kayleigh behind my back. I felt like a skydiver with a cast-iron parachute.

I then tore open my own credit-card bill and discovered purchases I'd not made – of clothes, shoes, make-up, a facial . . . My current expression in the mirror above the dining-room table resembled that of a castaway who discovers that her uninhabited island is actually home to hungry cannibals who are ending a five-day fast and crying out for a feast.

It was the last emotional straw. I would go to court and get a restraining order. I would send Merlin on a deep-sea-diving expedition, or to a scientific camp in the Arctic, or I would enrol him on a mission to Mars – whatever it took to get him as far away from Kayleigh as possible. Steeling myself for Merlin's anger, I pressed his number on my speed dial.

A bleary voice answered.

'Merlin, it's Mum. We have to talk. After what happened at the police station, you *promised* me you wouldn't see Kayleigh again. You promised me on Einstein's grave. But I just opened your credit-card bill this morning to discover you've been secretly buying her things—'

'I'm sorry, Mum. That was wrong, and it won't happen again.'

'I know you hate me interfering in your life, but have I ever led you astray? Have I ever done anything that wasn't in your best interest? You just have to trust me when I say that I know what's best for you, darling, and this girl is evil.' I girded my loins for a fight as I delivered the ultimatum. 'If she comes near you again I'm going to have her arrested. You must break up with Kayleigh for good, and from this minute!'

'Oh, I already have,' he interrupted sleepily.

'You have?' Relief flooded through my body and I executed a 'The hills are alive' Julie Andrews twirl around the kitchen and nearly burst into song. 'Oh, that's so good, Merlin. You'll find another girlfriend soon. I know you will.'

'Oh, I already have.'

'You have?' I gulped. My stomach did a fast fandango.

'Yes, I met her recently.'

'Where? At camp?'

'In a happy collision orchestrated by the cosmos.'

'Is she autistic?'

'She's awesome.'

My euphoria was immediately checked by a sense of dread. 'Does she have a job?' I asked warily.

'Yes.'

'Does she have her own place to live?'

'Yes.'

'Has she asked you to pay her rent?'

'No.'

'Does she expect you to pay for everything else?'

'No.'

'Does she have tattoos or piercings?'

'No. Only earrings.'

'Is she into drugs?'

'No.'

'Does she drink?'

'Water, yes. Tea, yes. Beer and whisky occasionally.'

'I hate to ask you this, Merlin, but you know that you and

I are always straight with each other, and I only need to ask just to make sure that you are safe . . . Are you having sex with her yet?'

'Oh yes.'

I felt my stomach drop once more. 'Are you . . . using protection?'

'Yes, but it's okay, Mum, she doesn't want progeny.'

'Really? Oh, well, that's great. Amazing. She sounds wonderful. When can I meet her?'

'We're upstairs right now.'

'*What?* No way. Really?' I instinctively glanced at the ceiling. 'You left summer camp early? Why didn't you call me?'

'My phone ran out of battery.'

'Oh, right. Well, I didn't hear you come in last night. Why didn't you say you were upstairs earlier in this conversation, you silly sausage?'

'You didn't ask.'

'Oh. Oh, okay. Of course I didn't. My fault. Well, can I bring you up anything?' I inquired, overcome with curiosity.

'Hot chocolate would be nice.' Merlin laughed delightedly.

'Okay! Hot chocolate coming up!'

Excitement percolated through my veins. I mentally high-fived myself. I then made two cups of hot chocolate in record speed. What a morning! It was warm outside, in spite of the wind. London glittered in the early September sunlight. Merlin had undergone a relatively pain-free Kayleighectomy. He was safely upstairs, with a financially viable, independent girl with no body piercings or addictions, who didn't want babies. And just for a moment, I allowed myself the thought that this might be the moment when life made it up to me. It might be the moment when fate glanced up from the crossword puzzle, strolled over to the drawing board and had a little rethink about where to move the pieces.

Bursting with elation, I knocked on Merlin's bedroom door.

'Enter, Mother dear,' his voice boomed out.

I picked up the hot cocoa I'd rested on the windowsill and creaked open the door to see my son's jeans dumped on the floor, denim legs splayed. There was a dreamy underwater mood to the room. Sun slanted through the blinds and glided over two entwined bodies. Through the half-light I discerned a snaggle of interlaced limbs, two tousled heads, four gangling legs . . . and a bottom. Her bottom. But what was that on it? A tattoo? And what was she wearing on her arms? Some kind of pleated fabric? And what was that noise she was making? A drunken snore? I cleared my throat loudly.

The girl in the bed stirred and nonchalantly leant up on one elbow to take me in. It was then that I realized that it wasn't pleated material I'd seen on her arms, it was wrinkles. And the arse tat was an HRT patch. I stared in horror at the aged visage before me. I felt as though I'd missed the 'muster drill' and now, as the boat was sinking, I had no idea how to find my lifeboat station.

'Can you put your breasts on your chest so that I can lie on them?' Merlin asked his paramour.

'Well,' Kayleigh's mother said to me, 'I promised you I'd break 'em up, didn't I?'

I tried to speak, but every inhalation was a shallow, panicked little effort. My lungs scrambled for air. I felt exactly the way victims recount the experience of having been slipped a roofie – minus the hospitalization and the stomach pumping. What I actually felt like was an autistic person who's been taught to recognize human emotions from flash cards and is left totally bamboozled.

'Thank you for the hot chocolate, Mum. It was so nice of you to take time out of your busy schedule for us.' A halo of steam rose above the two mugs in my hands. Merlin took the cocoa from my rictus grip and passed a cup to the woman next to him, who said, 'Yeah, thanks. Although I think we're gonna need somethin' stronger, pet, don't you? I'm not sure hot cocoa's gonna quite cut it . . .'

PART THREE

21

Hot Love in a Cold Climate

I fled downstairs, taking the steps two at a time, mainly because if I looked at that spectacle too much longer I was worried my retinas would detach. I was already concerned that I might need to get my eyeballs brushed with a steel bristle to erase the terrible image of my twenty-one-year-old son in bed with a fifty-seven-year-old woman. If I had possessed such a thing as a psychological satnav, it would be about to blow up, as I was traversing some mental terrain that was totally uncharted. Everything seemed slow, as though I were moving through deep water. I sat slumped at my kitchen table in a fugue of shock.

'Well, you wanted me to help break 'em up,' were the first words June said when she clumped downstairs into my kitchen moments later.

'But not like this! Ohmygod. What are you thinking? Is this even legal?'

If Kayleigh had been tossed into our lives like a hand grenade, her mother was an atomic bomb in cowboy boots.

'Hey!' June winked at me. 'She who hesitates is celibate, right?'

'You think this is *funny*? This is no time to be glib, although I am fighting the urge to pitch it as a reality-TV show – Cougar Town Meets Disabilities R Us: *These boys have special needs. But hey, so do the menopausal women who love them.*'

'Come on, love. Jeez. Who could blame me? The kid's so good-lookin'. The kind of cute that makes yer eyes pin-wheel.'

'Yes, it's called *youth.*'

'Look, I didn't plan it. I forbade Kayleigh from seein' him. I confiscated her phone. But he's a smart kid. He ran away after, like, one day at some weirdo camp—'

'He's been with you all *week*?'

'—then hitch-hiked back to London and tracked us down—'

'He hitch-hiked?'

'The kid arrived drenched from the rain so Kayleigh put him into one of her T-shirts, which was waaaayyy too tight. Takin' it off, it stuck to his head, so I got a five-minute private view of the sexiest, tightest torso I ever laid eyes on.'

'So you decided to *lay* him. That's disgusting! I mean, what kind of a pervert are you? You're a dirty old woman, that's what you are – a cradle-snatcher!'

'Oh, don't gimme that crap. If I were a bloke, nobody would bat an eye. Besides, it's Merlin's *mind* that really excites me. He's awesome,' she said with reverence. 'The kid kills me. I packed Kayleigh off to my sister's place, 'cause

I promised ya I'd keep 'em apart, then I took Merlin to some slap-up lunch at this posh Frog brasserie joint to cheer him up. He thought "chilled oysters" meant that the oysters were really relaxed, lyin' back and havin' a fag. Can you believe that? I just cracked up . . . Then at dessert time, he wouldn't order tiramisu, because he thought it was called Terror Misu and it might give him nightmares. And when I asked for my tea to be served in a nice china cup, he wanted to know what people in China call their good plates. Later in the day, when we watched some movie on Netflix set in a snowstorm, he wanted to know how the guy who drives the snowplough gets to work. I'd never thought about that. Then, when we watched some Susan Sarandon flick all about Death Row, he wanted to know why they bother to sterilize the needle for lethal injections. I'd never thought of that either! I mean, his mind! Well, it's *mind*-blowin'.'

As she spoke, my astonishment grew by the moment. I couldn't quite take her in: her bar-room-brawler voice, her long, dangly earrings, which looked like an elephant's IUD, and those acrylic Kayleigh-type nails, sharp enough to disembowel a ferret. Then there was her vocabulary – rough and ready, but smart and sassy, too.

'The kid's a crack-up. He's so, what's the word? Exotic. Like the human version of that weird Aussie creature. Wassit called? A duck-billed . . . ?'

'Platypus.'

'Yeah. One of them. That David Attenborough bloke should make some kinda documentary about 'im.'

'Merlin's not some animal in the circus. You're talking about my son! My *twenty-one-year-old* son,' I added pointedly. 'Oh my God. Until now, *Forrest Gump* was the closest I had to a home movie, now I'm suddenly in *The Graduate*, except Anne Bancroft has varicose veins and a smoker's cough.'

'Yeah, well, I wanna rewrite *The Graduate* and make it so that Mrs Robinson gets to keep the guy! Why the blimmin' 'ell not? I read in some mag somewhere that sex is good for older women. It safeguards yer heart, by protectin' against bone loss.'

I clenched my fists in anger. 'You know, I don't think your long-term health is a major concern for you right now.' The pulse behind my right eye throbbed like a heart.

'Don't be so snooty! This is why normal folk hate you lot. You prob'ly sit up in bed at night knittin' your own morals to 'ang on the wall of your bungalow in Boring-on-Sea. Thing is, Merlin adores me. He says I'm an extremely sensual hot-to-trot Love Goddess. I just 'appen to be an extremely sensual hot-to-trot Love Goddess stuck inside the body of a fifty-seven-year-old barmaid.'

'You're old enough to be his grandma, for God's sake!'

'Hey, yer only as old as the man you feel.' She gave me a look that was fizzing with laughter.

I looked at her dimpled knees and floppy biceps, which hung down like a flesh curtain. 'It's wrong, and you know it.'

'Hey, some people worry about the difference between right an' wrong; I'm worried about the difference between wrong and fun!'

She liberally sugared my cup of tea, which was cooling on the table, then stirred it in a leisurely way. The woman was a study in composure. She obviously had a low centre of gravity. I, on the other hand, was spinning and accelerating into the stratosphere. I listened to the whump-ing sound of my own blood in my veins.

'I want you to tell Merlin that it was all a mistake,' I ordered. 'You know it's for the best.'

'Do I?'

'Come on. I'm sure you'd be happier with a man your own age,' I said coldly.

'Jeeezus, no! I never wanted a life of carpet slippers and gassy, farty sheet-sharin', watching TV instead of talkin' . . . Naw, not for me the cankles and the comfy shoes and the incontinence pads. Merlin is the wind beneath my bingo wings!' She let out another self-satisfied chortle, waggling her arm fat.

I shuddered in revulsion. I felt grubby and soiled even having this conversation. 'It has to stop,' I said flatly. 'Now.'

'Why?' she said with equanimity. 'He keeps tellin' me 'ow 'e's longed for a woman of experience. And 'ere I am! I may not be educated, but I'm street-smart. I've got a degree from the School of 'Ard Knocks, with distinction. Plus, he's so uninhibited and inventive,' she said blithely. 'I just want to shag the kid till there's nothin' left but his socks!'

A vision exploded on the screen of my eyelids of their bodies coalescing and blurring, plunging into darkness, until all was black. This was way, way too much informa-tion for any mother.

'Why?' I gasped, more to the universe than to this meno-pausal man-eater. 'Why do these things keep happening to me? Haven't I always been a nice person?'

June snorted. 'Expecting life to treat yer well because yer a nice person is like expectin' ISIS not to behead ya because yer a pacifist. Life ain't fair. That's why you gotta seize yer fun in the sun where you friggin' can,' she said, in her matter-of-fact, earthy way. 'And younger chicks, they clearly don't understand Merlin. Girls like my Kayleigh, they're just a sulk with fake tan on it. Whereas I adore the kid. I'd shack up with him in a heartbeat.'

The incomprehension of it, the affront, reared up like a tidal wave and swept me away. My stomach turned over giddily. 'Don't be ridiculous,' I said, duly horrified. 'You have no idea what it's like living with Merlin . . . You couldn't take enough drugs to even *hallucinate* what it's like living with someone like Merlin.'

'Hey, keep yer hair on, love! I'm not marryin' the boy . . . Although, at my age, there's less pressure on the "till death do us part" clause, right?' she hooted.

I swung my feet off the chair rung and hunched towards her, looking threatening. 'You will see my son again over my dead body!'

'Well, we better put the morgue on standby, hon, 'cause I ain't givin' 'im up.'

On cue, the kitchen door swung open and Merlin bounded in.

'What a mesmerizing and sublime evening I've enjoyed in your spectacular company!' he enthused, bouncing over to the breakfast bar and biting into an apple. 'Life with your daughter was breaking me down. I was struggling. I was having trouble keeping pace, socially, emotionally and pharmaceutically, with Kayleigh and her cronies. But then I met Juicy June, who joins the ranks of the World's Most Smoking-hot Babes of Her Generation. Don't you agree, Mum?'

He gave me his famous candid stare, the pale-blue eyes wide. Once again, I was speechless.

'Every day, I like to think of June sitting opposite me in the bath, reading aloud her favourite poem while wearing a tiara and smoking a cheroot, and getting settled with her fabulous plump arse and her beautiful wide shoulders. You are the ideal bath thought, June. It will help me get through the bath very smoothly when I think about every element of you. You are my bath idol,' he told her.

'Well, thanks, sugar. I've never, in all my life, received such an eloquent and welcome compliment! Thank you very, very much!' Kayleigh's mother giggled like a school-girl before planting a rapturous kiss right on his mouth.

I shuddered once more. 'Please don't kiss her, Merlin!' I said involuntarily.

'Why? A kiss is merely the anatomical juxtaposition of two orbicularis oris muscles in a state of contraction,' he told me, perplexed.

'But don't you want to kiss a girl your own age?' I hugged him to me. He smelt of soap, like when he was a sweet baby – which really wasn't all that long ago, I thought, horrified.

'Kayleigh made me feel as though my heart had indigestion. I now have a second chance at getting some much more rambunctious fluff.' He grinned winningly.

'Rambunctious fluff!' June slapped her substantial thighs with her gnarled hands. 'I've never been called anything nicer.'

I couldn't stand to think of her withered fingers touching my son's soft, warm skin. 'But, darling, June is old enough to be your grandmother.'

'Never forget that it's better being over the hill than under it,' my son told me sombrely. 'June is one of the most fascinating women I've ever had the pleasure of meeting – besides you, Mum. She's teaching me to swear in Russian. She's backpacked through India, crewed a ship around Thailand and worked as a hostess in a Bangkok bar. She can read palms and Tarot cards. She has ridden an elephant, caught dengue fever, gone shark diving and sky-diving, eaten kangaroo scrotum, survived a willy-nilly, dated a Hell's Angel biker, lived rough on the streets, wrestled a crocodile and shot a man in the leg in a bar in Marbella which he was trying to rob. She's also teaching me about foreplay. Sex with a woman with no foreplay is like a gun-slinger bursting through the doors into the saloon, making all the locals turn around and glare at him with unwelcoming slit eyes . . . And this weekend she's taking me to a rock festival.'

'Absolutely not!' My voice sounded so distant it could have been coming from the bottom of a cave.

Merlin looked at me with confused eyes. 'What's the matter, Mum?'

'You are not going anywhere with this woman!' It came out as a barked command.

He lasered me with his blue eyes. 'Why not?'

'Yeah,' June repeated, her dark eyes scalding me. 'Why not?'

'June is one of the few people I can look in the eye and it doesn't hurt,' Merlin explained gravely.

'Sure, I can understand you sleeping with a plain, pasty-faced, foul-mouthed fifty-seven-year-old . . . if, say, you were both stranded in the desert and the only other option was, like, a dead camel slumped by a dried-up watering hole. But otherwise, no way!'

'Plain and pasty-faced?' June balked. 'J'know what? The secret to beauty is to have Nordic parents who give a woman height, hair and the blue eyes of a Viking – otherwise, a girl's just gotta get by on personality an' charisma. Right?'

'*Girl?*' I scoffed. 'Do you *have* a mirror?'

'Merlin looks beyond the superficial. Unlike his friggin' mother.' June glanced from Merlin to me. 'Just remind me, which one of you is supposed to be the educationally sub-normal one again?'

'I'm going to take out a restraining order on you,' I addressed June coldly. 'That's what I'm going to do.'

'Ya know yer trouble, lady? You can't bear to think of a life without Merlin in it. You take a peek through the crack to the emptiness, the big silence, and yer just can't stand it. That's the truth of it. I can't believe you ever even let the kid out.'

'Don't be ridiculous.'

'Out of your *womb*, that is. He's been yer raisin'-friggin'-whatsit all these years. What will yer do without him? But yer have to let him live his life his way. Then maybe *you* can get a life, too, pet.'

I felt my face solidify into a mask of incredulity. 'And who the hell are you to tell me how to live my life?! A boozy, loser barmaid with a delinquent daughter!'

I could see from her sudden fag-ash complexion that I'd hit her where it hurt. 'You're right, love. Life dealt me a bad hand. I've been lied to a lot. And that's exactly why I love your boy. He can't lie. Men play so many games. But not Merlin. When I ask, "Does my bum look big in this?" I know I can count on a true answer. In fact, he reckons it's big enough to be classified as an emergin' nation!' she guffawed. 'He also said that I'm the perfect weight . . . for a twenty-foot-tall woman!' Once more she threw back her head and snorted out a big belly laugh.

'You're not overweight,' Merlin elucidated, 'you're just under-tall.'

'Exactly, pet! Ha ha ha!' June gave another yelp of laughter, followed by a convivial cackle, before concluding, 'Everybody lies these days. Politicians, bankers, advertisers. Ya know, Lucy, yer could make money by settin' the kid up in a Truth Booth. Why don't yer just ask him truthfully what he wants? Go on. Just ask him . . . Merlin?' June swivelled in her chair to face him.

Merlin considered things for a moment, then replied thoughtfully, 'Life is tragically fleeting. One thing I can't remember is my first memory, so will I remember my last? But I definitely want to store up as many happy memories in my joy bank as humanly possible.'

'But you can make *other* memories – happier, better memories – with *girls your own age.*'

'I am not a mummy's boy, Mum. You want me to be a mummy's boy, don't you? You like it that way! Why don't you ever let me choose my own friends?' Overwhelmed by the unfathomable anxieties and emotions eddying around the room, Merlin kicked the kitchen door, making the hinges wince.

I needed to de-escalate the situation fast, to smooth the emotional waters. I took a deep breath, then said, 'Darling, I'm late for work, so why don't we talk about this tonight, when we're both calm and not distracted, okay? With cool heads.' I checked my watch. 'Oh God. I've already missed assembly. Merlin, I'll drop you down at the Job Centre on my way, okay? While you've been at summer camp, or wherever the hell you really were, some new jobs might have come up.' Like, for example, as a monk in a remote, inaccessible, celibate Tibetan monastery, with any luck.

Outside on the street, June doled cash into my hand.

'What's that?'

'The money for the necklace Kayleigh stole. I pawned it. I've got 'er a job as a check-out chick in Sainsbury's, over in Islington, so she can start to pay yer back all the dosh she owes yer. Like I said, she's moved out to live with my sister. We only stayed 'ere last night 'cause she came home to pack her bag. My sis is a parole officer, so there'll be no messin'! So now maybe yer can take the word "bitch" off my resumé? Oh, and I'm not interested in any trust fund neither, if that's what you're thinkin'. The best things in life are free – talkin', walkin', laughin', oxygen and orgasms. So you can either give that money back to Oxfam or put it towards our weddin' reception ... Only jokin'!' She winked cheekily, clocking my stony countenance.

I pocketed the money and unlocked the car.

'So,' Merlin opened the passenger-side door for her with the sweeping gallantry of a French courtier to the Sun King, 'can we drop you anywhere, my passionate puma?'

'. . . Like off the nearest cliff,' I quietly seethed under my breath.

22

Assume the Crash Position

At work that day, the kids might as well have been grilling me about the location of weapons of mass destruction in Iran as the iambic pentameter. I had no comprehension of what anyone was saying to me; I just stood around, my mouth gormlessly ajar. All morning an unpleasant buzzing rang in my ears. My mind just whirred and stopped, whirred and stopped, like a haywire clock.

At lunchtime I just stood staring in the staffroom refrigerator, at a piece of cheese which pre-dated the Elizabethan era and a few sandwiches which would be of interest to archaeologists. But I didn't have the energy to complain that the fridge hadn't been cleaned out at the end of last term. Nor could I even contemplate getting out the milk to make a cup of tea. All I could focus on was the montage playing ceaselessly in my mind of my naked son entwined with Kayleigh's menopausal mother.

After school I drove straight to see my sister. She was just back from North America and having a mani-pedi and her roots dyed at her favourite hairdressers. I perched on the pedicurist's stool by her soaking feet and vented *sotto voce.*

'Is it really so bad?' Phoebe reflected, after I'd brought her up to date on the latest episodes in *Merlin – The Soap Opera.* 'You've said yourself, many times, how unfair it is that older men go out with younger women all the time and nobody gives a damn, but if an older woman goes out with a younger man, all hell breaks loose.'

'But not *my* young man!'

'Well, you are kinda going for gold in the Hypocrisy Olympics, you know, Lu-Lu! Didn't you tear a strip off those policemen for calling you a cougar?'

'Listen, I feel about ageism the way some people feel about homophobia. It's an inexcusable and atrocious reflection on the double standards of our sexist society – unless it's an older woman sleeping with *my* son and then I'm, like, *Call the police!*'

In the bank of mirrors behind my sister's head, my cheeks blazed red, two expressionist splatters of colour.

'Well, speaking as a woman who is out in the Meat Market again, lemme tell you: for every bright, beautiful, sassy forty-year-old woman, there's a bald, bloated male dinosaur swanning around with a twenty-two-year-old swimwear model on his arm. Okay, June may be a little shopworn—'

'A little?! She's fifty-fucking-seven!'

'—but, being a woman of experience, she might be able to teach Merlin a few things. Add a little *savoir-faire . . .*'

'Oh, yes. I'm sure she knows exactly which fork to use to dig out her earwax at the dinner table.'

'So then, what are you going to do? Maybe you can talk to her, reason with her, make her see sense? Find some common ground?'

'"Common" being the operative word. She's a barmaid, for God's sake. And you know how I feel about barmaids, after our feckless father ran off with one and ruined our lives!'

'You can't hold Dad's mistakes against her. You need to work with the woman.'

'How? That woman couldn't be more foreign to me if she were a Papua New Guinean tribeswoman strolling in from the rainforest with an armful of raw yak meat, some piranha ceviche, and some shrunken heads to string on to a necklace.'

'But you've got to admire her chutzpah. June really is a totally brazen bitch, isn't she?' my sister observed with a hint of admiration. 'I mean, imagine it, being able to describe yourself as a twenty-one-year-old's fifty-seven-year-old girl-friend,' she marvelled.

'You've just described a fossil, not a girlfriend.'

'I dunno. Maybe we should try to be more like her and date younger blokes?'

'Merlin's not *dating*, he's joined the National Trust! I mean, the woman's a crumbling edifice.'

'She just wants to feel young again.'

'If she wants to feel younger, why doesn't she try a mummy make-over, or bikram planking, or colonic irriga-tion, or Yogalates instead of having an inappropriate relationship with a special-needs boy with the emotional age of, oh, about twelve. It's paedophilic.'

'But he's not twelve, Lucy. He's a twenty-one-year-old

man. If you had your way, he'd be hermetically sealed off from the world, or constantly protected by a hygienic plastic screen, like a bank cashier.'

'I want him to be independent, I do! But seeing your baby son naked with a woman old enough to be his grandma is a sight most mothers pray they won't live to witness. Imagine if it was *your* son?'

Phoebe took a moment. 'Okay. Okay. Ugh. Yes. I see what you mean. So, what's your plan, then? A duel at sunrise with pistols?'

'Good God, no. She'd kill me in a heartbeat. No. I'm going to offer her money to bugger off. She says the best things in life are free, but, one way or another, you always end up having to pay for them. And everyone has their price.'

'And if bribery doesn't work?'

'Do you know where I can buy a shallow-grave shovel?' I said sourly.

A hairdresser came over to unravel a tinfoil parcel atop Phoebe's cranium to see if the colour had taken. The colourist shook her head before rewrapping the fronds.

'Still, there's one positive thing that's come out of their liaison,' Phoebe rationalized, as soon as the stylist had sashayed away. 'I mean, what a relief to discover that there's one person in the world more annoying and insane than Kayleigh – her mother.'

'She wants to take him to a rock festival this weekend. They're camping.'

My sister shuddered. 'Ugh. At that I do draw the line. Camping is the reason God invented monsoons.'

'I'm soooo, so tired.' I slumped at Phoebe's half-pedicured feet, my head on my knees.

My sister stroked my hair. 'Darling, no wonder! You have to be a number-one athlete in tip-top condition to take on the arduous, marathon role of mothering Merlin . . . or any kid, really.'

'Oh shit, Phoebe. I'm sorry. I'm being so selfish, burdening you with all my problems. Tell me about *you*. How's your life?'

'Nothing like as dramatic as yours. *Yours* is like being stranded up a mountain in Bora Bora with constant volcanic explosions. I'm just busy buying homeopathic penile enlargers for my kids to give their father at his gay wedding tomorrow – the wedding I hope will be cancelled, because Danny will stop drinking at the Bum Boy Bar in the Hot Cock Tavern and come back to me. The wedding I am wife-cotting, as I'd rather gnaw my way through my own womb than have anything to do with Trevor, the odious toerag who broke up my family . . . But, otherwise, everything's just hunky-dory, darl!'

Phoebe's voice had crescendoed in volume. The whole salon had fallen silent and pivoted in her fraught direction.

I put a protective arm around her shoulders. 'You can't have a crisis, Phoebe, okay? My schedule is already full.'

It was true. My nose ached from crying and my eyes stung like nettles.

I drove home, determined to save my son from another romantic car crash. The only trouble was, as usual, I'd forgotten to strap a seatbelt to my brain.

23

The Day that Keeps on Giving

The note was waiting for me on the kitchen table.

Dear Legendary Mum,

I have taken full advantage of being your son and it has been a tremendous plessure to be in your company for these sublime twenty-one years, although at times it has been a rambunctious relationship, especially now that I have become the Artful Dodger of Romantic Warfare.

It's incredible to think that we've been through two extraordinery decades together on this rollercoaster ride. There are so many aspects of your character and demina to admire. You are very pretty and have style, flair and panash and u r a divine goddess of a mother. You look beautiful in every outfit, you have a radiant smile and a mesmerizing figure. I adore u and whenever I see you u always brighten up my day. You are a legend of femanists.

But I would hereby like to resign with immediate effect as your son. Our mother–son relationship has reached a painful parental plateau and it's time for me to explore love in all its exotic climes with my passionate puma.

I hope you have a heavenly and enthralling life. I love you.

From your intriguing and phenomenal son, Merlin the king of swing.

Then, in a bracketed postscript: (*I, Merlin Beaufort, approve this message.*)

It took a moment for the bone-jarring slam of reality to hit me: my son had run away with Kayleigh's mother. But where to? Oh God. Only one person would know June's where-abouts. I scrambled harum-scarum out the door, jammed the key into the ignition and skidded to a stop fifteen minutes later, back outside the hair salon.

'But I'm mid-pedicure and my hair's only half done!' Phoebe moaned as I dragged her out through the rain, foils flapping, and into my double-parked car.

'It's an emergency.'

I thrust Merlin's handwritten letter at her. She scanned it quickly as I careered back on to the main road and turned the car towards Islington.

'"Passionate puma"?' she queried sarcastically.

'Don't!' I tried to push away the mental snapshots of June pouncing on my son like prey then devouring him whole, her limbs writhing in a feeding frenzy of hormonal hunger.

'So I guess it's not a good time to whistle "Maggie

May"?' Phoebe said, sliding Merlin's note into the glove compartment. 'A snow leopard and now a puma? I think Merlin's misunderstood the term "get some pussy".'

I concentrated on the road to clear my mind. Headlights reflected back starkly from the patent-leather surface of the wet bitumen.

'What? No come-back to that "catty" remark?'

'I just can't make jokes right now.'

'*You*, not able to joke around? That *is* serious . . . So where are we going exactly? Do you even know where June lives?'

'No. But I know someone who does.'

'Oh God. Let me guess. The human car crash otherwise known as Kayleigh.'

'I know June's type. I meet them at parent–teacher nights. She's one of those typical big, blousy, boisterous women with broad shoulders and a machine-gun laugh but with a sad and secret soft spot – their child. Which is why I'm going to bribe Kayleigh to take me to Merlin and then guilt-trip her mother into breaking up with my son.'

'So, Kayleigh's the straw that will break the camel-toe's back?'

'Exactly. Although I'm *so* trying not to picture that . . .'

I abandoned the car on a yellow line and bounded up the crowded high street towards the supermarket where June had told me she'd secured Kayleigh a job as a cashier. My sister panted along behind me, the cigarettes she'd started smoking again when her husband abandoned her for a bloke clearly taking their asthmatic toll.

Inside, the joyful electronic chirps of the cash registers

were jarringly at odds with the dull, drooping faces of the shoppers. I pushed through the numbed customers, my eyes raking the rows of tills, until I sighted that familiar shock of pink hair.

A smoky breath of hash mingled with spearmint chewing gum greeted me at the till. 'Shit. What are youse skanks doin' here?' the silver-tongued Kayleigh opined enchantingly.

I reached into my pocket for the wodge of notes June had given me that morning and thrust half the pawned-necklace money at her. 'For you . . . if you take me to your mother.'

'Why should I do owt for you?' Kayleigh's eyes narrowed suspiciously.

'Because she's run away with your ex-boyfriend.'

It took a moment or two for this toxic information to fully register. 'That's rank!' Kayleigh's face flinched at the realization. She made the finger-down-the-throat, tongue-stuck-out gagging gesture I'd been dying to enact myself. 'My mum's a *cougar*?'

'Merlin prefers to call her a puma, apparently.'

'Ugh,' she adjudicated. 'That's, like, proper gross.'

For once, the girl articulated my feelings exactly. 'Right. Which is why I want you to take me to your mum's house. And I'll pay you the rest of the money if you guilt-trip her out of sleeping with my son.'

Kayleigh snatched the cash from my hand. 'Yer doin' me head in now . . . that daft cow's eyes always was bigger than her vag.'

It wasn't quite how I'd put it, but I got her drift.

We waited twenty minutes for Kayleigh's shift to end, then bundled her into my car. As Kayleigh directed me towards

236

Ludgate, I glanced out the window at families going about their lives – the happy, bustling, busy, carefree world of those with normal sons not being shagged by femme fatales old enough to be their grannies.

I found myself forlornly peering through the windows of houses at normal families seated around their kitchen tables, a *tableau vivant* of everyday happiness that I would never know. How I longed to be one of those women whose biggest horror in life is that the supermarket has run out of smoked salmon and kale or that her hubby might wear comedy socks at the weekends and shock their fellow golf-club members.

The street Kayleigh directed us to was a cobbled mews behind a pub, not far from the big pudding dome of St Paul's. The street was too narrow to park in, so we left the car in a precarious position half up on the kerb and clip-clopped over the cobbles towards the tiny cottage. The little doll's house – a converted stable – was so small it would induce claustrophobia in a sardine, but there were flower boxes on the windowsill and a hanging basket of petunias swaying cheerily in the breeze above a brightly painted front door. Story-book cosy and chocolate-box cute, it wasn't quite the lecher's lair and shady den of debauchery I'd envisaged.

Kayleigh explained that June was the manager of the pub and that the cottage came as part of her pay package. She then leant back on the wall and nonchalantly lit up a fag. Her hair, the colour of caramel straw with pink streaks, was straighter than usual, and tattered at the ends. She was chewing gum and a strong smell of watermelon was coming off her. 'J'wan' the key?' she asked, flaring her eyebrows.

I shoved my hand forward, and then, unexpectedly, froze.

Did I? I suddenly lost all confidence and hung back. What was I going to say? How could I win back my son's affections? Right now, my mothering confidence level was so low I'd need a deep-sea-diving suit and a pressurized mini-sub to find it.

Kayleigh blew a pink bubble of gum and popped it with a chipped red fingernail, then extended her palm. 'The key'll be extra.'

'Let's take a look first,' Phoebe suggested, squeezing my hand. With the stealth of ninjas, we tiptoed to the window and, trepidation mounting, peered inside . . .

What I saw in June's kitchen scrambled my brain.

People often describe the most ordinary things as surreal. The word has lost its power. But this was Dalíesque, dripping-faces-on-stilts, lobster-phone surreal. The steady ground became a wild sea, pitching and rolling beneath my feet.

Standing in an improbable cartoonish composition before me were Merlin, June . . . and Jeremy. Hovering on the sidelines was the sticky-beak social worker. A cold wave of disbelief and panic surged through me. What treachery was afoot? It only added to the baroque bedlam that had become my life of late. Various possibilities darted through my addled brain. Was June in conspiratorial cahoots with my scheming ex-husband? The poison of suspicion seeped through my bloodstream like a Russian assassin's polonium.

As I watched through the window, June's arms splayed to hug my boy and he vanished into her saggy, big-bosomed embrace. The sight of it made my skin crawl.

'Open the door!' I hissed at Kayleigh.

She put her hand out to be paid. '*Now!*' I ordered with

homicidal chill. My face in the reflection of the glass had gone as white as Oscars Night.

Shocked into obedience, Kayleigh slid the key into the lock. Once more I glimpsed the little bullied schoolgirl beneath her brittle mask. Spooked, she took off at a clip down the cobbled street. I barrelled into the hall before the door had fully opened. The old, flatulent German shepherd Kayleigh had occasionally brought to my place gave a bronchial bark. As I careened into the kitchen, the conspirators wheeled as one to look at me.

'The truth is, June, Kayleigh doesn't take after her father, she takes after her double-dealing, deceitful mother. I really can't describe my feelings about you right now without recourse to slang terms for faeces,' I spat.

June's clothes were so neon bright she looked like a discarded fruity bit from a tropical cocktail, but her face was far from festive. 'Once more, lady, ya really need to work on yer flippin' people skills.'

'Well, then, explain to me what the hell *he*'s doing here?' I hooked a thumb in my ex-husband's loathsome direction.

'Absolutely lovely to see you, too, darling,' Jeremy purred in reply. There was a self-satisfied smirk playing on his lips which made my blood run cold. With great theatricality, he presented me with an official-looking piece of paper. 'I think you'll find everything in order.'

The glittery-eyed social worker leant forward with greedy inquisitiveness to gauge my reaction.

'What is it?' Phoebe asked in a tight voice.

'My only son, who's a vulnerable adult with a retarded emotional age, is to be handed over to me, with immediate effect,' my nemesis crisply enunciated.

The world seemed to inhale, aghast, and forget for a moment about revolving.

'W–what?' I stammered.

Jeremy's eyes were aglow with chilling triumphalism. 'The Court of Protection, in their wisdom, has granted me emergency guardianship over my son while they undertake an investigation.'

Jeremy's words hit me with cyclonic impact. My world humpty-dumptied, never to be put back together again.

'*Your* son? He's *MY* son!' Like a character in a Disney animation, little black dots danced before my startled eyes.

Phoebe looked to Sonia for clarification. 'Hey, sour-lemon lips. Would you explain exactly what the hell is going on?'

'Court etiquette dictates that you hand Merlin over immediately,' Sonia replied in her brisk, clipboard manner.

' "Etiquette" is just a way to fuck people over without 'em realizin' it,' June adjudicated, narrowing her eyes threateningly. 'There's no flippin' way Merlin is goin' anywhere with the likes of youse scumbags. So youse can bugger off out of my 'ouse, right now.'

Jeremy raised his eyebrows. 'Lucy, do you really want me to call the police to enforce this court order?'

My tongue felt tied. Despite my vast lexicon, monosyllabic words were all I could summon. 'Why?'

Jeremy exhaled, exasperated. 'Must I reiterate your endless shortcomings yet again?' he said, before gleefully rattling off a list of my maternal misdemeanours. 'Kerb-crawling, drug-dealing, encouraging fraternization with a convicted felon – one Kayleigh Abramovich – and, finally, living off the immoral earnings of male prostitution.'

'W–what?' I spluttered.

Jeremy nodded at Sonia, who handed over a file of photos. I glanced at them, dumbfounded. High-resolution images strobed before me: June and Merlin entwined in a twilight embrace outside my house; June and Merlin entering my house, hand in hand; June and Merlin kissing in the kitchen; June and Merlin silhouetted in his upstairs bedroom . . . then, June and Merlin emerging in the morning with me. And, finally, June counting out money into the palm of my hand.

Jeremy gave a mirthless smile. 'I think the evidence is clear. Social Services definitely thought so.'

A sharpening wind gusted down the mews outside, rattling the old windows of the cottage. Jeremy had detonated his bombshell and, shell-shocked, now everyone around him was embedded with emotional shrapnel.

The world seemed to tilt and start sliding towards an abyss.

'Social Services must consider the young man's welfare and best prospects,' Sonia added. The word – *prospects* – held all the fastidious disdain of a Victorian aunt.

June rallied first. The woman might be five foot nothing but she's also big-busted, big-gestured, stroppy, robust, and has the authority to order drinks all round with one tiny hitch of a threaded brow. She rounded on my ex-husband, sucked in her lips and sprayed her words like lead shot. 'Yer mind's in the gutter, j'know that, yer disgustin' pig . . . In fact, yer give pigs a bad name, 'cause they jus' roll in shit. *You* put it in yer mouth.'

Jeremy drew himself up to his full, haughty height and towered over her. 'I'm sorry. But *what* are you, exactly? Some kind of lawn ornament?'

'You've been spying on us?' I asked the social worker, appalled.

'I hired a private detective to prove my case,' Jeremy clarified.

I looked at my ex with horrified astonishment. He was now up there with the world's worst people – oligarchs, kleptocrats, Chinese party officials, Middle Eastern despots, African war lords, deluded North Korean dictators . . . oh, and snooping social workers who look down their noses for a living.

I gawped at Sonia, aghast. 'You don't honestly believe I would pimp out my own son, do you? It's preposterous! Merlin, tell your father the truth.'

Merlin was standing rigidly with his fingers plugged into his ears, humming a Beatles medley. I removed his hands, then asked him the question plainly and simply. 'Darling, will you tell them about your relationship with June?' I urged gently. 'Why are you with her?'

'Well, my passionate puma has exquisite eyelashes. I also love her flubber muscles.' Merlin wobbled the soft flesh of June's biceps. 'And I do so enjoy facial hair on a woman. You see, love knows no boundaries of gender, height, age nor species,' he expounded.

'Species' rather stumped the room, but Jeremy shrugged it all off anyway.

'The testimony of a mentally ill boy will not be given any credence in a court of law.'

'*Mentally ill?!* How dare you speak about him that way. You never understood him.' I took Sonia by the shoulders and only just managed not to shake her till her teeth rattled. 'When Merlin was diagnosed with autism, I realized that

242

not only was Jeremy not on the same page, he wasn't even in the same book, let alone in the same library. He doesn't love my son. All he wants is the dosh from the trust fund.'

'You're the one only interested in money,' Jeremy retaliated. 'You pimped out your own son, for God's sake, to a geriatric barmaid.'

'Geriatric?' June was so angry, her face flushed red with splotches of fury. 'Dear God,' she chanted, 'grant me the serenity to accept the things I can't change, the courage to change the things I can't accept, and . . . *the wisdom to dispose of the bodies of those people I had to kill today because they TOTALLY PISSED ME OFF!*'

'Is that a threat? Sonia, can you record this, please? This will make a very interesting addition to my kiss-and-tell tale, don't you think? Though, of course, a tabloid exposé will be the death knell for your teaching career, Lucinda, that's for sure,' he added, with casual cruelty.

Sonia scrabbled in her bag and pulled out her iPhone, then pressed the Record button.

'Just as well yer both so shallow – I won't 'ave to dig a very big grave to put youse in,' June fumed.

'Another death threat. This time, to a representative of the court! Oh, this day just keeps on giving!' Jeremy beamed.

'Is it me, or is this guy getting harder to love?' Phoebe asked me.

'Jeremy has been open and forthright in all his dealings with you,' Sonia rebuked us.

'Oh, really? When a man like Jeremy tells you he's putting his cards on the table, always take a quick peek up his sleeve. *This* lowlife would even cheat in solitaire,' I hit back furiously.

243

'Lucy has never met a man she couldn't blame,' Jeremy explained to the social worker with a sad sigh.

Sonia nodded, then immediately began peppering me with pointless questions. Was Merlin on any medication? Did he need to pack any books/clothes/music? Was he allergic to any foodstuffs?

I pulled Merlin in close and hung on to him fiercely. 'Come any nearer and I'll sink my teeth into you faster than you can say "grievous bodily harm",' I warned her.

'Right, well, you leave me no choice,' Jeremy said smoothly. 'Call the police, Sonia. This means, Lucinda, by the way, that you'll have breached your suspended sentence. Obstructing justice, disregarding a court order, et cetera. It will mean a jail sentence this time. So Merlin would have to live with me anyway . . .'

The seismic impact of this bleak scenario hit us all simultaneously.

'You'd better swot up on some dialects, Lucy Lu – Chinese, for the Triad members; Jamaican patois for the drug mules; Arabic for the terrorists . . . If only you'd done a ju-jitsu course at the gym instead of Pilates for those pelvic-floor muscles you never use any more.'

I wanted to make a Proustian double entendre or a Dorothy Parkeresque quip but only just managed to hold back the tears. Sweat beads popped out on my upper lip. My eyes started to burn and my chin trembled. I was on the point of flying apart, like a supernova.

'Merlin, darling.' My sister was the first to speak, although her falsely upbeat voice sounded as fake as crop circles, Loch Ness-monster sightings and that *Alien Autopsy* film. 'Why don't you go with your father?'

'No!' he shouted.

'Just for a night or two. It'll be good for you to get to know him, after all this time. It'll be fun,' she enthused half-heartedly.

Merlin clutched my arm with the desperate grip of a castaway to driftwood. 'The father–son contract is null and void.'

'We'll see what the police have to say about that,' Jeremy grumped, unlocking his phone.

'Lucy, don't you think it would be a good idea for Merlin to stay with his dad for a night or two – just while we talk things over with a lawyer?' my sister persisted through gritted teeth.

With the expert ease of a furniture-removals company, Jeremy had boxed me into a corner, leaving me no room for manoeuvre.

'Merlin, darling, are you okay?' I looked deep into his eyes, the better to take his psychological temperature.

'I can cope with the voices inside my head,' he said. 'It's the voices *outside* my head that drive me crazy.' He clung to me like melted marshmallow.

'Sweetheart.' Each breath echoed loud and slow in my skull, as though I were scuba-diving. 'I think going with your dad for a day or two is our only option right now.' I somehow managed to squeeze out a smile. 'And I'll have you back soon, I promise.'

'No,' Merlin said fractiously. He was smelling his fingers compulsively in an effort to self-soothe. 'I don't know him. Does he have a heart of glass or a heart of stone?'

It was hard to breathe. I felt as though I were pushing against packed earth, as if I were buried alive. Fighting Jeremy was like trying to open a coffin lid from six feet under. 'We can Skype the whole time . . .'

'Come on,' Jeremy harrumphed. 'It's time to go.'

Merlin began rocking back and forth, in great distress, humming to himself. He covered his head and contracted into a foetal curl on the sofa.

'June, help me,' I begged.

June leant down and kissed his forehead. 'You don't want yer mum locked up in the old slammer, do yer, darlin'?' Merlin shook his head furiously, as though tormented by mosquitoes. 'Then go with yer dad, pet. Just for a night, okay?'

Merlin slowly stood up. His clothes hung on him like flags in dead calm. He looked at us, slack-faced and dead-eyed.

'Okay, Puma. I'll obey your command, but only to keep the unicorn out of captivity,' he said. 'I don't think unicorns would do well in a zoo, Mum, do you?' My heart churned painfully. 'But Dad's not going to eat me, is he? He won't dislocate his jaw and swallow me whole?'

'No, darling, of course not,' I said, although I couldn't be sure.

'All right then, but I'm going under duress. Do not forsake me!' were Merlin's final words to me – and then he was gone.

When the door closed, I gave in to grief. It gushed out of me – a haemorrhage of sorrow, an arterial wound. Calamity had fixed me with its merciless eye. How had this happened? How had Jeremy managed to win, yet again? All the man needed was a pointy black beard to complete his look of Prince of Darkness from some medieval-church gargoyle carving.

June handed me a slug of whisky. Even though Merlin had told me she wasn't much of a drinker, extreme circumstances meant that the woman was already lapping at her second tumbler.

'Don't cry,' my sister soothed as I let out another

harrowing sob. 'We'll get legal advice. We'll fight this in the courts. We'll get him back, I promise you.'

'Bugger the courts,' June said. 'Justice is a lottery, and women never win. We need to take the law into our own 'ands.'

'How? Jeremy's ego is so indestructible that denting it can only be achieved by several months of strategic bombing. The man's just so tough,' Phoebe said meekly.

'In my experience, if a man's too tough, its best to parboil him for a few hours before bashin' 'im with a meat tenderizer . . . So, tell me more about this trust fund.'

Phoebe filled June in on the sordid details, concluding with, 'Basically, the man graduated with Dishonour from the International School of Corrupt, Amoral Bastards. But how to prove it?'

'I reckon we break into his 'ouse and 'ave a sniff around.'

'Break in?' Phoebe discarded the possibility with a swift shudder of revulsion.

'Yeah. To search for clues.'

'Clues to what?'

'I doan know . . . financial irregularities, fraud . . . Must be loads of shit that creep's tryin' to 'ide. The jerk told the judge 'e wants the best for Merlin, right, but 'e's prob'ly already spent the trust-fund dosh on a yacht or a Porsche or somethin'.'

I caught my reflection in the mirror. All my eye make-up had washed away. I looked drained – much like my bank account and my belief in the criminal justice system. I clutched my stomach, trying to hold back the terrible hurt inside.

'Okay,' I suddenly heard myself say, 'but I'll need to find some hardened criminal to help me, not having been privy to learning such skills at teacher-training college. I mean, how do burglars do it? We need to get a jemmy . . . What *is* a jemmy, exactly?'

'Jesus, Lucinda! Are you serious? You don't need a jemmy-wielding felon, you need a shrink – and *now*,' my sister said, alarmed.

'Let's just go case his place,' June suggested. 'J'know where the weapons-grade jizztrumpeter lives?'

'Yes,' I said.

'No!' Phoebe said emphatically. 'We are not "casing" anything. Who are we all of a sudden, Cagney and Lacey?'

'Well, June and I are going to the Dark Side. And you should come, too,' I said, steeling my resolve.

'Thanks so much for the offer,' Phoebe replied sarcastically, 'but if you don't mind, I'm just trying to hold my head up high and not cry as I walk determinedly through the dying embers of my failed and suddenly single forties.'

'Well, exactly! I mean, what have you got to lose, Phoebe? Your husband's marrying his gay lover tomorrow and your kids are over at his place for the wedding rehearsal, so it's not as though you have anywhere better to be right now, is it?' I persisted.

Her pretty face fell. 'Well, I *am* due for a mammogram. They squash your tit into a sandwich maker, but it's no worse than your average divorce,' she replied bitterly.

'Please come with us, Phoebe,' I pleaded. 'Not to break in, okay? Just to keep an eye on Merlin.'

'Let the lawyers handle it, Lucy. Yes, Jeremy's vile, but he's not going to hurt Merlin. Your over-protectiveness has become obsessional.'

'But you heard what Merlin said: "Do not forsake me!"

What does his fucking father know about him? Nothing. Even if he is aware that Merlin has OCD, will he know he calls it CDO because it has to be in alphabetical order? Will he know that he likes his toast cut into triangles, but not on Wednesdays? Will he know he only eats marmalade on Mondays? Does he know about barefoot Tuesdays? Will he know not to chew around him? And that he doesn't like different foods touching on his plate? And that he can't stand food of a certain colour? Will he hug him when he has a meltdown? No! No, he will not!! Only *I* know all those things! Because I love him. I love him so, so much, it hurts.' My voice was so loud the glasses and cups on the shelf were rattling.

'Okay, okay,' Phoebe said, soothingly. 'I'll come.'

June put a comforting hand on my shaking arm. 'We'll take my car – you're in no state to drive,' she said. 'Plus chocolates. And cake. A lot of cake. And whisky.'

'Oh God,' my sister sighed. 'But only if we go via the hairdressers.'

'Yeah, what gives with yer friggin' hair?' June asked, putting a chocolate sponge in a Tupperware container, slapping down the lid and burping it tight.

'I'm a work in progress.' Phoebe patted her foils in trepidation.

'Aren't we all, love?' June laughed, tossing her car keys up in the air and catching them with insouciant ease. 'You okay, pet?' she then asked me.

I glanced around June's spotless kitchenette. 'Put it this way, I'm just glad that you have an electric oven.'

24

The Crème de la Crim

That night, my maturity and sound judgement became strikingly evident when I took to crying hysterically and stalking my arch-enemy by staking out his house in the company of the woman who was debauching my vulnerable twenty-one-year-old son. To make matters worse, I was accompanied by my saner sibling, a sibling who had recently transmogrified into a raging homophobe after not noticing that her groom was gay. (Surely the fact that Danny wore one of the bridesmaid's dresses to their wedding rehearsal should have been a *clue*, right? Meet my sister – the Queen of Denial.)

June hung a suicide left into Holland Park and nosed her battered rust-bucket into the kerb opposite Jeremy's manicured house. The wide wooden shutters were thrown open, revealing the palatial drawing rooms of his Georgian mansion. The house, ablaze with light, bathed his heirlooms in a golden glow.

'Fuck me,' June whistled, '*someone* got diddled in the divorce settlement, didn't she?'

'Don't worry. One of these days I'll be out of therapy,' I said, training June's horse-racing binoculars on to my ex-husband's luxurious interiors, searching for a sight of Merlin.

'Therapy? A therapist's nothin' more than a pickpocket who lets yer use yer own fingers. Fuck that. Revenge is the best therapy in the world. So, 'ow ja wanna get back at the bastard? Plant some drugs? Set 'im up in an 'oneytrap sting with an underage chick? Burn down 'is 'ouse?'

My eyes snagged on to a magnified Jeremy standing at his bedroom window. He was locking lips with a glamorous young woman who was so well-endowed it looked as though she'd taken a bicycle pump to her chest. His usual type. Probably an intern at his law firm. Even though I'd seen it all before, I still felt the familiar stab of betrayal. He'd left me for a similar breed, a TV star whose bra cup size was higher than her IQ.

'Why don't we just kill him?' I proposed. 'Think about it. I'd be out of the maximum-security psych ward in, say, ten years. And then there'll be a TV miniseries waiting, plus a podcast serial and a lecture circuit.'

My sister gasped from the back seat, histrionically waving away my words. 'I don't like the turn this conversation's taking. In fact, I don't like being here at all. Two hours ago, you hated this woman, and now you're in cahoots. It's not right—'

'*That's* what's not right!' I gestured up to the bedroom

window, where Jeremy was unbuttoning the blouse of the female less than half his age.

'Hey, girls, if we're gonna 'ave a catfight, let's get some mud or jelly an' make some flippin' money out of it,' June suggested.

'I still think we should just tell the police and let them handle it,' Phoebe persisted.

June found this side-splittingly hilarious. 'J'know what? The police force of Great Britain is not exactly overflowin' with Mensa candidates, kiddo, lemme tell yer.'

'June's right. Besides, Pheebs, who do you think the police are going to believe? A respected barrister-at-law? Or his embittered ex-wife, a foul-mouthed barmaid who's lost her toy boy, and a homophobic trolley dolly deranged by the fact that her hubby's plighting his troth to his flight attendant boyfriend in front of her estranged kids on the morrow?'

'Oi! Who the fuck are you callin' foul-fuckin'-mouthed?' June said with mock-bitterness.

'And please don't remind me that my husband is knotting his nuptials with his cart tart.' I watched in the rear-view mirror as my sister fumbled in her bag for her cigarettes. 'My over-cooked hair has gone a weird shade of orange, so I'm depressed enough already.'

Phoebe's locks, which normally hung in two perfect blonde parentheses around her delicate face, were now a weird carroty colour and scraped back into a severe pony-tail. It boinged around at the back of her head, like a puppy dog nervously wagging its tail.

'You know, you really *should* go to the wedding tomorrow, Phoebe. It might help bring closure and you'll finally quit smoking.'

'Jesus. Since when did you become a social worker? I can't believe you haven't started wearing a beige tent dress and Birkenstocks . . . Let's just go home right now and call Social Services and tell them our side of the story.'

'It's pointless, Phoebe. Jeremy always wins.'

I passed my sister the binoculars and tilted her head up towards Jeremy's second-floor bedroom in time to witness my ex's expert digital dexterity in the bra-unhooking department.

Phoebe was quiet for a moment, before conceding, 'We don't have to actually *kill* Jeremy. Maybe we could just maim him a little – enough so that he has to go to hospital, where, hopefully, he'll contract a flesh-eating virus.'

'Now you're thinking.' I leant back over the car seat and patted her hand.

'I'm thinkin' too,' said June, 'about the epidemiological ramifications of scorpion envenomment.'

'What?' My sister and I reacted in unison. 'Epidemiological'. My brain just felt too tired for that word right now.

'Yeah. Merlin told me about it,' June mused. 'We could put a scorpion in his bed. Kills instantly. Or there's oleander tea. That poison leaves no trace, apparently . . . Your kid's a walkin', talkin' encyclopaedia, I'm tellin' ya.'

'Where *is* my darling boy?' I asked anxiously, wresting the binoculars back from Phoebe's half-varnished talons. I'd tried calling his mobile a hundred times, but there was no answer. My eyes raked every floor, back and forth, until I finally detected a shadowy figure sitting forlornly in the dark by an attic window. I sharpened the focus until Merlin's sad face coalesced into frame. He was slouched in a chair, headphones on, staring blankly into the rainy street.

My heart lurched, and blood beat thickly in my temples. I must have given a little moan of despair, as June immediately cracked the cellophane on a box of chocolates she'd packed for the stake-out.

'So tell me. Why-ja ever fall for a prick like him?' she asked, handing around bonbons.

'Good question!' Phoebe exclaimed. 'I've never understood how the two of you got together. But I wouldn't be surprised if it didn't involve a Satanic ritual on his part at some point.'

I sighed deeply. 'My pick-up line to Jeremy was "Is that an unabridged dictionary in your pocket or are you just pleased to see me?" He was suave, educated, erudite—'

'And cold as hell,' my sister added, helping herself to a violet cream.

'Well, fuck me,' June said succinctly. 'An upper-class, Oxford-educated privileged white male who turns out to be a gangrenous-dicked troglodyte. What a freakin' surprise!'

'It wasn't a marriage, really,' I clarified. 'It was more like a long one-night stand.'

'Here.' June retrieved a flask of whisky from her magical Mary Poppins-esque handbag and passed it my way, saying, 'Medicinal.' Taking a grateful swig, I decided that perhaps I *would* momentarily remove the word 'bitch' from her resumé after all.

I trained the binoculars back on Merlin's attic prison. I hit his number on my speed dial once more, but the mobile Jeremy had given him was clearly switched off or, worse still, had been confiscated. I wanted to be with him so much. It was a hard, physical longing, like a craving for air when trapped underwater. He moved out of view and, a few minutes later, a light came on downstairs. I readjusted the focus on June's binoculars, and there was my angelic boy by the window, forlornly peering at the evening sky. My heart scrambled. Was he okay? Had he eaten? Was he crying? How could I reach him?

'I'm going in for a closer look,' I announced, already half out of the car. 'Maybe I can get his attention.'

June put a reassuring hand on my arm. 'We're gonna get that prick,' she promised me. 'If the worst comes to the worst, I know a bloke with a few car-boot-ripened corpses. The wily geezer could easily whack in another . . .'

Of course she did.

'Jesus, Mary and Joseph.' My orange-haired, previously agnostic sister sunk down low in her seat and started praying as she fumbled for another fag.

I slipped into Jeremy's front garden, disturbing a flock of egrets en route. They strutted back towards Holland Park, their long, aristocratic necks and grey, feathery frock-coats giving them the air of Etonian students striding purposefully about on prefect duty. They seemed to look down their beaks at me with disdain. Yep. Even my feathered friends knew I was a failure as a mother. Just as I was manoeuvring myself into a position on a low-lying tree branch, from which I would be able to wave at Merlin, Jeremy suddenly reappeared at his bedroom window and opened it wide, talking all the time into his mobile. I scrambled back down the tree trunk and hit the ground as if tasered. I lay, winded, in the rooty embrace of the oak, wincing with pain but unable to call out. The undergrowth was full of the whisper and scurry of small creatures which I hoped weren't rats. A 4x4 trundled by, tyres crunching through gravelled depressions, belching petrol breath into my face. I stifled a cough and spasmed with the effort not to splutter.

Soon after, some mites, famished and unafraid, began to feast on my face and hands. I couldn't swat them away, or my cover would be blown. As I listened to Jeremy's smug, self-satisfied voice, I pondered how a middle-aged, crossword-addicted English teacher and mother of one had come to be lying half crippled in an insect-riddled ditch sucking on jeep exhaust? It was the type of question I'd asked a lot of late. I just hadn't been myself since before the summer. It was as if my calm, ordered brain disc had been wiped and replaced with the IQ software of, say, a single-cell amoeba or a reality-TV contestant.

Jeremy was having a marathon conversation with a client, so I tried to settle into my impromptu hiding spot. A flash of lightning twisted in the dark evening sky, followed by the low-throated rumble of thunder. A fox streaked past, shivering through the hedge into the park like a ghost. And then came the first plop of rain – which quickly turned into a downpour. There was nothing I could do but huddle, shivering, into the tree roots and try to judge how long it would last by listening to the cadences of rainwater running down Jeremy's drainpipe.

I just lay in the dirt, making inventive promises to a God I didn't believe in to let Merlin be okay. Just as hypothermia was setting in and I was seriously considering amputation of my frostbitten nether regions, Jeremy ended the call and moved away from the window. I attempted a dash to the shelter of the car, but the security light came on and I dived back into the shadows.

Fifteen minutes later, I was just gauging my chances of

crawling around the garden perimeter to avoid the light sensor when the front door creaked open. I hunkered down once more. Peeking through plant fronds, I saw Jeremy standing under the portico. His look was one of studied insouciance. He'd changed out of his suit and was wearing Pucci suede loafers with no socks and distressed denims with a starched white shirt, cuffs crisply rolled up his tanned forearms. There was always something calculated about his most nonchalant gesture, statement or attire. Unlike my perpetual state of chaos of late, everything in his life was planned with the pinpoint precision of a wartime commander.

His young girlfriend appeared at his side. He pulled her into his body for a kiss – a long, luscious farewell kiss, his hands on her hip bones, leaning his body weight into her slight frame. I remembered being kissed like that by him, the heady delight of it.

'Sorry I can't come to the party with you,' I heard him say in his velvet voice, 'but I'm stuck with the oddball brat. I'm sorry he asked if your breasts are real. He's such an embarrassment. If only I could shove him back into the condom vending machine for the refund, eh?!' he joked.

I felt the heat of rage flush across my face but stayed silent and stock still.

'I'm taking the boy to see my lawyer in the morning to sign some paperwork. He wants to go to his uncle's wedding in the afternoon – his gay uncle's wedding, can you believe? What a dysfunctional family! I said no, but on second thoughts it would give us some time to explore every inch of those very real and beautiful breasts of yours. So why not meet me here tomorrow, about six? I can be your aperitif before you head off for your Freshers' Welcome what-not . . .'

Freshers? A uni student in her first year. She was eighteen, then. I cringed.

'I'm thirsty already, Jerry,' the poor girl purred.

Jerry? I winced at the informality. It made him sound so harmless.

London was going through an unseasonable cold snap. It was so chilly that moments earlier I'd been wishing I could buy some hot roasted chestnuts on the high street to put down my knickers. Passers-by were sporting the bank-robber look, faces shrouded in black scarves. Big Ben was probably huddling up to the Houses of Parliament for warmth. Lap dancers in Soho were no doubt wearing flannel G-strings. In the alleys around Liverpool Street Station, men's tongues would be freezing on to street-walking hookers . . . But not me. I glowed hot with anger. Red-hot, flaming fumes of fury seemed to be leaping out of my body – the flames of pure, molten hatred.

I might have leapt from my lair and gone for his jugular there and then if a large, growly dog hadn't suddenly sprung out of the shadows behind my ex. Desperate not to be detected, I shrank down and focused my gaze on the ground – a cigarette butt, a beer-bottle top, a crumpled crisp packet . . . Finally, they stopped kissing, and Jeremy's latest conquest passed me on her way to the tube. The front door closed, silencing the quarrelsome canine, and then, with a thud, the windows were shuttered closed and Merlin was stolen from me all over again.

Phoebe squelched to my side seconds later with an umbrella, ducking out of the security light's intrusive beam. 'You could have been hit by lightning! Are you okay?'

'I *was* hit by lightning – I'm scorched emotionally. Can't you see me smouldering?'

'Come on, sis.'

'He's got a dog,' I said, once I was safely back in the warmth of June's car.

'Of course he has a dog,' my sister said, in an effort to cheer me up. ' Somebody has to do the brain work.'

'What the hell are we going to do now? Even if we break in, the dog will devour us at the door.'

'I bloody love dogs,' June enthused. 'I saw that big, beautiful Doberman through the doorway. 'E's flippin' gorrrgeous.'

'He's the hound of the Baskervilles is what he is! He'll take off a whole leg and half your labia with one leap.'

'Awww, 'e's only a wee puppy,' June insisted in a baby voice.

'Only a puppy? Where are you from? Transylvania?'

'That explains a lot. Back away from the vampire,' my sister warned, covering her neck with both hands.

June pulled her tasselled poncho jumper over her head and passed it to me. 'Why do poor old Transylvanians get such a bad bloody press?'

'Well, there was that Transylvanian queen who liked to bathe in the blood of virgins,' Phoebe contributed. 'She was a tad merciless.'

'Merciless! That's exactly what we need to be with Jeremy,' I said. A little spider had ridden into the car on my jeans leg. I unwound the window and let it crawl off my finger on to the ground.

'Jeezus,' June scoffed. 'You two are about as merciless as a soufflé.'

But my teeth were chattering so violently I could hardly hear her.

'Fer God's sake, take off yer wet top and put that on.' June pointed to the thick poncho draped across the seat between us. 'It's pretty bloody 'ard to be merciless if you're like, coughing up 'alf a lung from friggin' pneumonia. And drink this.'

I did as June suggested and sighed with relief at the warmth of the wool on my icy skin and the burn as the whisky hit my bloodstream.

'Great. That's settled, then. As soon as Lover Boy goes out, we go in. Leave the pooch to me.' June cracked her knuckles. 'Okay?'

And so we watched and waited. Eventually, we all went quiet. Phoebe and June dozed, but I watched the house all night for another glimpse of my son. I kept vigil until my eyelids glittered with sleeplessness and the car pitched around me like a rolling ship. Finally, I must have slumped into sleep, curled up against the door, because I jolted awake to a dishwashy dawn with a neck cramp and a hangover the size of the Netherlands . . . only I hadn't been drinking much the night before. Just those two warming tots. No. It was the dead lead weight of anxiety that was making my head throb. An Andes-sized range of angst loomed up before me. My son was being held captive by a callous maniac and I was relying on a predatory puma to save him. Who was writing this script? I asked myself for the millionth time.

The indolent light of morning dawdled, taking its time. My body was stiff from where I'd dozed off against the car door. While I waited for the others to stir, I examined the seatbelt crease on my face in the vanity mirror behind the passenger-seat sun visor. Oh, the glamour!

A leg cramp took hold so I got out of the car to stretch. Jeremy's crescent wrapped itself around a picture-perfect private park fenced off from the public. By eight a.m. it was echoing with the nasal assault of nannies bringing dogs or sprogs to heel. 'Sebastian, down!' 'Fido, up!' 'Peregrine, come here.' 'Speckles, stay!' The raucous vocal onslaught finally woke my two partners in crime, who grumbled into consciousness.

June staggered off to fetch coffees and buns from the high street while I continued to keep watch. After a hit of caffeine, the cloudiness that had taken over my brain the night before dissipated and I was starting to think clearly. I now knew precisely what had to be done – I had to break into my ex-husband's house, avoid a death-spasm chomp of his canine's slathering fangs, then ransack his office to find any evidence I could present to the courts to get back my child. Either that, or clobber him to death with his own polo mallet. Polo mallet? No, a rocket launcher was more what I had in mind.

At nine o'clock Jeremy's house stirred. The kitchen shutters were thrown open, and fifteen minutes later Jeremy was at the door. From the cover of June's car, I saw him preparing to leave for the appointment with the lousy lawyer I'd heard him telling his girlfriend about – an appointment which would surely involve Merlin being coerced into signing over power of attorney to his ruthless father. I watched Jeremy raise the barrel of his collapsible umbrella and fire it at the incoming rain before he Fred Astaired down the stone steps.

A moment later, Merlin, all hollow eyes, trudged gloomily behind his father. My heart skipped a beat to see my darling boy so despondent and crestfallen. I dug my fingernails into the palms of my hand to stop myself from calling out to him.

'Is it possible to cry under water, Dad?' I heard Merlin ask in a small voice. 'Have you ever wondered that?'

Jeremy ignored him and pointed at the passenger side of his BMW. 'Get in,' he ordered coldly.

If my eyes could shoot out lethal rays like comic-book superheroes can, I would have annihilated my ex-husband there and then.

After they'd driven away I applied another imaginary layer of stiff-upper-lip gloss, then joined my accomplices on the pavement. We huddled together against the rain and gazed up at Jeremy's fortress. The house, all locked up, seemed to be holding its breath. Attack dog, security lights, window grilles, dead locks – the building was Fort Knox-fortified. Basically, Jeremy had every defence, bar a shark-filled moat and quicksand pit.

'So, um, without the aid of a battering ram or perhaps some Semtex and a US Navy Seals team, how exactly were you planning on breaking in?' Phoebe looked June up and down. 'I'd say the most athletic thing *you've* ever done is tear open a condom packet with your teeth.'

But before Phoebe could make more disparaging comments, June produced a large metal crowbar from her huge handbag with a theatrical flourish.

'Don't tell me! A jemmy!' I enthused.

'Yep.' June's eyes lit up with the evidence of past illegal exploits. 'At least we know the prick doesn't 'ave an alarm.'

Her voice was citrus sharp. 'The Doberman provides that . . . Which is why I picked up this slab of meat from the butcher on the high street this morning and mashed my diazepam into it. I buy 'em off a punter who comes down the pub. 'Gets me off to sleep after a late shift.'

'What?' Phoebe's face was stricken. 'Oh, Christ. So now, if the Old Bill don't get us for breaking and entering, the RSPCA will arrest us for dog-disabling. Oh, this plan of yours is just getting better and better.'

But she was left arguing with June's shadow, the words dying in her mouth as our ringleader barrelled up the steps to the front door and shoved the slab of sedative-laced sirloin through the letterbox slit. When the cacophonous barking subsided, she led the way down the side passage to the old coal chute.

'I used to clean 'ouses around here,' she said, by way of explanation, 'so I know all their secrets.'

Wielding the jemmy with expert ease, she levered open the trap door of the chute before disappearing feet first down the slide inside. Ten minutes later, the side door creaked open and we were in.

I felt along my veins a tingling joy almost frightening in its vengeance. So began my career as a criminal mastermind – well, maybe as a rather spayed and mangy cat burglar. I just hoped I was a cat burglar with, if not nine, at least two lives.

25

Buggery Bollocks and Fuckity-fuck-fuck

The air of the house was languid with roses and White Company candles coupled with a comforting aroma of floor wax and potpourri and – well, money. I walked through the kitchen into the drawing room, with its ornately carved seventeenth-century sideboards, bulbous armoires and dining chairs so lavishly upholstered and heavy it seemed the delicate Georgian townhouse might collapse under their weight.

When the heater gave a tubercular wheeze and rattled a wet sigh, I jumped with alarm and looked around wildly. We should never have come. What had I been thinking? This was a stupid idea. Taking advice from June was like taking hairstyling classes from Donald Trump.

Breaking and entering, trespassing . . . Dear God. I could see the judge in my mind's eye, his white hair floating atop his aged head like a cumulus cloud – just before his countenance turned all stormy and he sent me to prison. I suddenly felt as though I'd lit the fuse on a Molotov cocktail. On reflex, I took a step backwards.

Phoebe was also wavering. 'Okay, well, it's been nice, but I had better go now, because I forgot to say that I have plans for tonight. Plans that actually involve living a little longer.'

June, decoding our facial expressions, shouted, 'Lighten up, girls! There's no goin' back, not once you've gone to the Dark Side.'

Beyond the drawing room was the hall, where the dog lay panting. I drew back in stark terror, but June just bustled towards it. Phoebe and I followed in single file, hugging the wall. June fearlessly prodded the hound with the toe of her rhinestone-studded cowboy boot. When the big beast didn't stir, she dragged him by his collar into the living room and closed the door. Then she took the stairs, two at a time, turning at the top to gesture for us to follow.

By the time we'd tentatively crept up on to the landing, June had located Jeremy's office and was beckoning us in. 'Right. This bloke's ego's big enough to cast its own shadow – correct?'

'Shadow?' Phoebe scoffed. 'Jeremy's ego's so big it has its own climate.'

'And the twat's a slimy, two-faced liar, right?'

'Two-faced? He's the most traitorous living thing on earth. Unless there's an aged Nazi hiding out in the Argentinian jungle,' I amended.

'So the creep's bound to keep some trophies of his evil achievements, right? Phoebe, take the desk drawers. Lucy, attack the filin' cabinets. I'll sniff out all his secret nooks and friggin' crannies. I 'eard 'im tell his little chick 'e won't be back till six, so *go*!' she ordered.

Like cadets being drilled by a parade sergeant, Phoebe and I immediately obeyed orders.

After an hour of dedicated snooping, June came and stood at the office door for an update. 'Found anythin'?'

I shook my head. 'I can't find anything incriminating. Not so much as a parking ticket.'

An hour later, when we still hadn't located anything even remotely implicating, Phoebe's pinched expression spoke volumes.

Outdoors, in the squelching world, rain dribbled down from a lifeless sky.

As the dull grey day began to die prematurely in the wet window and we still had no evidence, I felt deadened by desolation. The impact of Jeremy's treachery sank into my bones. Merlin was right. His father was a snake – a big, sleek jungle snake who swallowed people whole, without a qualm. He devoured them slowly, with subtle cunning, an inch at a time, so you'd barely notice you were being eaten alive. First me, then Sonia the social worker, then the judiciary. And now, clearly, my poor Merlin was to be his next victim.

As time seeped away, my melancholy became tinged with self-pity. The grinding hollowness of failure took me over. Jeremy was going to get away with it. Again. The reality impacted on me like a punch to the stomach. My tongue felt too swollen and dry to speak. Words came, but the sounds were harshly alien. 'He's won,' I whispered. 'Let's face it.'

June shook herself like a wet animal. 'Bugger that! We've got more than four flippin' hours till 'e's back. Maybe the slime-bag's 'idden stuff in the bedroom?' she boomed, and led the way there.

It was a grand room, with an imposing king-size four-poster bed and wall-to-ceiling mirrors. We began rummaging through drawers and searching the backs of cupboards and had just become fully engrossed in our under-the-bed sleuthing when we heard the unmistakable sound of the front door opening.

The room froze. All that moved were optic muscles as we three women played frantic eye tennis. This was the moment on a flight when the captain announces that we have a 'minor engine problem'.

My heart kickstarted into life again and began a percussive pounding which made my whole frame tremble. 'But he said he wouldn't be back till six!' I gasped. My watch read two p.m.

'Maybe it's the cleaner?' Phoebe whispered hopefully. 'Or what if it's some psycho burglar maniac?'

'May I remind you, Phoebe, that *we're* the psycho burglars in this particular scenario!' I hissed.

My sister and I skulked out on to the landing and peered hesitantly into the hall below. In bespoke brogues, Jeremy had arrived, and was calling out to his dog. There was someone behind him on the outside step, subduing an uncooperative umbrella.

Instinctively, I took a step backwards, knocking over a Damien Hirst-type taxidermy sculpture of a small, deceased shark. Needless to say, I knew just how it felt. With the precision timing of a seasoned barmaid, June caught the artwork before it thudded to the floor.

Phoebe then ran back through the master bedroom door as though hunted by a pack of wild dogs. She jigged from foot to foot like a Samoan hot-coal walker. 'Buggery bollocks and fuckity-fuck-fuck,' she whimpered. 'What are we going to do?'

I figured regurgitating my breakfast would probably not be the most appropriate reaction.

'Not much of a bloody guard dog, eh? Must be out the back shagging the neighbour's Schnoodle,' we heard Jeremy say.

His companion's tinkling laugh alerted us to the fact that they were ascending the stairs. I spasmed with fear.

'Hide!' June urged, as their voices grew nearer. She tried to shove me into the cupboard, with the grim determination of an airline passenger attempting to thrust some inappropriate object into the overhead baggage compartment. Phoebe tried to clamber in after me. As we elbowed each other for space, June dropped to the floor and scuttled under the bed. Suddenly cast in a French bedroom farce (only minus any *bon mots* or witty innuendos), I dived out of the wardrobe and on to the floor and scrambled in under the valance.

Footsteps. Murmurs. The bedroom door opening. The sound of a zip. The creak of bedsprings. Then, a few moments later, a low moaning. This was quickly followed by some rather vigorous entwining on the bed above. The strange, disembodied sound drifting down to me was clearly one of pleasure. I closed my ears against the squelchy noises. I tried not to breathe. I kept every inhalation so shallow I feared I might hyperventilate. My heart was thumping in my chest like one of Kayleigh's favourite synthesized dance tracks: *dooomf doomf doomf.* It was hard to believe they couldn't hear it up there above me, even through the pocket-sprung designer double mattress. Jeremy and his big-breasted young girlfriend were bouncing about on the bed so energetically I began to think I was at a funfair, on a ride called, perhaps, the Whirl-'n'-Puke. The orgasmic gasps of Jeremy's lover were now so theatrical I felt sure I could charge tickets to his bedroom as a major themed attraction. Acid-green envy ran lava-hot in my veins. It had been so long since I'd made any noises like that.

' . . . Jerry, darling . . .'

Then I heard his voice. 'I worship you. Oh, my love . . .'

I lay there in a stupefied trance. Jeremy was normally so parsimonious with his affections, yet here he was, uttering endearments in honeyed tones, muffled only by the odd gnaw on a nipple.

I wasn't sure if I was more depressed by the fact that this asshole ex of mine was getting so many more orgasms than I was these days or by the fact that he was vocally caressing his lover with such adoration. I curled in on myself, mesmerized with horror. It was just as well I was lying down and not standing up in the cupboard like Phoebe, as I wasn't sure my jelly legs could have supported me.

After half an hour under the bed – an environment well known for not having much fluff-free oxygen that might enable you to breathe properly – my nose began to tickle. I lifted up the valance a little to get some air. A pile of male and female clothes were mingled on the carpet floor right by my head.

And then I saw the shoe. From the way my hair follicles prickled, I knew that what was going on above my head, and which had caused my blow-dry to become snagged on the bedsprings, was something quite out of the ordinary – quite out of the ordinary indeed.

You see, after leaving me, my ex had dated, then dumped, in chilly succession, a TV domestic goddess, a high-profile divorce lawyer, a lap dancer, a banker caught up in a bonus scandal and a beauty queen. But a Birkenstock-wearer was not his usual prey.

Lifting the valance higher, I peered into the huge mirror on the bedroom wall opposite. My brain rejected what my eyes so clearly saw. From this vantage point, it was also impossible not to notice that the social worker was not a waxer. I jabbed June in the side with my elbow.

'What?' she whispered.

'It's Sonia. The sanctimonious social worker.'

It was dark under the bed, but the white crescent of June's smile was clearly visible. Her lips went through a rubbery repertoire of contortions as she tried to hold back her amusement. She was twitching like a junkie with the effort of not laughing. I, too, felt a fizz of exhilaration zing through my veins.

And so it was at the stroke of two forty-five on a cold October afternoon that I finally got the upper hand over my bastard of an ex-husband.

The absurdity of it all struck me so hard that I doubled up in a paroxysm of mirth. I was chortling so hard I launched into a coughing fit worthy of a tuberculosis ward. The guffaw which erupted from June's mouth sounded like a moose passing a kidney stone. She bellowed. She roared. She clutched her stomach.

The bed stopped creaking. Two male feet planted

themselves on the floor next to me. Followed by an inverted head. My ex's inverted head.

Jeremy was too dumbfounded to react – he just ogled me, upside down, the blood rushing to his brain. My ex-husband simply stared at me for a full minute in a wide-eyed parody of disbelief. I couldn't have had more effect if I'd fired a missile into the home stretch of the Grand National.

I burst out from under the bed as though pepper-sprayed. And there she was. The social worker, wearing little more than a vinegary expression – well, besides sky-blue eyeshadow and a woven Tibetan wrist bracelet.

Jeremy, the velvet-voiced charmer, was totally lost for words. The only sound from his lips was a flatulent sibilance. His penis shrivelled before my eyes. It now resembled a stringy-necked baby buzzard Bear Grylls might unearth from its nest on a frozen clifftop. His expression was that of a man who has been contemplatively collecting driftwood on a beach and has just caught a tsunami in the small of his back.

Revenge was a wet, thick thing alive in my mouth. All I wanted to do was explode into more hysterical laughter. I wanted to snort, howl and generally laugh until my lips fell off. But I somehow contorted my face into a mask of sobriety.

'I know you never regarded marriage as an exclusive carnal arrangement, but two women in twenty-four hours may be a first even for you, *Jerry*.'

'What?' The social worker's bewildered expression would be caught in aspic in my memory forever more.

'Oh, sweetie, have you not worked out that Jeremy Beaufort is a sexual kleptomaniac?' I asked her, my voice dripping with condescending scorn. 'Good God, woman. You have the perceptive powers of a coma patient. Can't you see that he's just manipulating you to get to my son?'

Glaring hotly, Jeremy knifed to his feet and scrambled into his clothes. 'You broke into my house!'

I narrowed my eyes in contempt. 'Yes. Perhaps one day I'll be flooded with remorse.'

'I'm calling the police.' He pawed at his phone. 'Breaking and entering. I think you'll find that's a definite violation of your suspended sentence.' His voice rang out harshly in the still room. 'You are going down.'

'Um, I think the police will find that's actually your social worker's forte,' I double-entendred.

'You're trespassing on private property.' A familiar frostiness had crept into Jeremy's voice. 'I'm sure the police will be interested in your low-life companion, too. Who exactly *is* this thing you seem to have walked in on the bottom of your shoe and smeared all over the carpet of your life of late?' he demanded, as he laced up his brogues.

June loomed over Sonia's naked body on the bed with a companionable air. 'Well, well, well,' she chuckled with gloating glee. 'I kicked over an old rock and look what crawled out. Truly am-*ayyyyzzz*-in'. Posh boy and his social worker flunkey. Well, my de-ah fellow,' she parodied Jeremy's posh accent. 'This is *terribly* rum, innit, Lucy? But wait. What? No chocolate mint on yer pillow? No complimentary truffles up yer tart's twat? What kind of host are yer?'

'Yes, let's call the police,' I agreed languidly. 'That's a brilliant idea – then we'll have an official record of your illegal liaison ... I knew you were a slimeball, Jeremy, but having sexual intercourse with your son's social worker is the slipperiest, most vile behaviour you've ever demonstrated.'

'Intercourse?' June scoffed. 'Where the fuck are we? Church friggin' Fellowship? What Lucy means is she can't believe you're bonking the woman who has the power to get you custody of your kid.' She pointed at Sonia, who was scrabbling her clothes up off the floor. 'Pooh. What's that pong?'

'Corruption sewage?' I suggested helpfully.

'Hey, Sonia. "Social worker" is yer job description, right? And yet yer also clearly an accomplished knob-polisher, too. Who knew? What a multitasker! Ya must add it to yer friggin' CV.'

'Yes, what *does* it say on your job description, Sonia?' I interrogated. 'Social worker-cum-strumpet?'

'Strumpet?' June laughed at me. 'Where-ja get these words, Lucy, a friggin' antique shop? Still, Sonia, I imagine the way you behave in a case says a lot about you, for example, if yer shaggin' yer client, that reveals yer a lyin' slag.'

As Sonia fumbled for her glasses and frantically threaded her legs into Marks and Sparks cottontails, I had to admit that she didn't look like a femme fatale. No. She looked as though she were about to compete in a curling event in Norfolk, or a needlepoint workshop for the Brownies. As she layered on her grey bra and beige smock and shoved on her Birkenstocks, she seemed more likely to be here to restock an aquarium or feed the worm farm after digging about in the basil bed than to illegally shag a client.

'Jeremy and I have a deep and beautiful connection,' Sonia announced self-righteously.

'Really? And did it not cross your mind that you're not

his normal type – which is an anorexic model with
store-bought boobs?'

'Or a filthy-rich divorce lawyer who puts 'er cocaine dealer
on speed dial?' June chorused.

'Or a naive teenage fresher with a Daddy complex?' I
prodded.

Jeremy glared at me, furious that I'd been spying on him.
But, this time, I held his ice-blue gaze until he looked away.

'After a suitable amount of time we'll move in together
and we will care for Merlin appropriately, with boundaries
and discipline,' Sonia said, attempting to regain her professional mode of drilled belligerence.

'Oh, really? So tell me, when you took up Jeremy's case,
did he insist you leave the majority of your brain cells as a
deposit?'

'We're in love.' Sonia's piping voice shimmered with sug-
ary sincerity.

'Oh, you poor shmuck. Nude swimming in a shark tank
would be ten times safer than being in a relationship with
this man. You think you're going to get a marriage pro-
posal but all you're going to get is chlamydia. Oh, and the
sack.'

'This is a complete invasion of privacy.' Sonia's voice was
querulous.

'You'll definitely lose your job,' I added, 'after an internal
investigation—'

June hooted. 'I think she just 'ad one of those! Haha!'

'You'll be suspended without pay—'

'And not from the ceiling by yer nipple tassels neither.
Haha!'

'—for maintaining a sexual relationship with a client

while presenting his case. It's misconduct of the highest order.'

'—or lowest, actually.'

'You're a Trojan social worker. I'll press charges. You'll go to prison, where you'll be a pariah.'

'Yeah, 'cause all prisoners 'ave 'ad their kids taken off 'em by interferin' social workers like you. You'll probably get knifed.'

Reality finally flashed into Sonia's eyes. Terror pulsated in her veiny temples. 'P–please . . .' It was as though a toffee had glued itself on to her molars, impeding speech. 'P–p–please don't report me.'

'We won't need to, the press will tattoo "client shagger" on your forehead, which means you'll never get a job any-where ever again either.'

Sonia gnawed fretfully on the inside of her cheek, her familiar frostiness now evaporated. 'The press? Jerry?'

Jeremy gave a sheepish grin, like a schoolboy caught out in some juvenile mischief. 'Lucinda' – his tone was one of pained geniality – 'this is beneath you.'

'No, *that's* beneath you.' I pointed at the snivelling Sonia. 'She hasn't got a leg to stand on – literally, having illegally thrown it over her client.'

'Come onnnnn,' Jeremy purred. 'I'm sure we can all shrug this off. After all, sex doesn't mean anything. What are we? Victorian prudes?'

'Doesn't mean anything?' Sonia's eyes darted nervously to his.

'I say we just turn a blind eye. For old times' sake.'

'Really? 'Cause I say, congrats on winning the World Bas-tard Championships, Jeremy. I now realize you've clearly got a special reserve tank of bastardly behaviour stowed away inside you for emergencies.'

My ex-husband was a portrait of earnestness. 'You're a reasonable woman, Lucy. Now I'm sure that, as two smart, practical, pragmatic people,' he said unctuously, 'we can come to a mutually beneficial arrangement.'

'We sure can!' June enthused. 'As soon as ya arrange to squeeze out a gold-plated agreement signin' over the trust-fund money to Lucy. Then, and only then, will we bugger off out of yer life.'

Jeremy cast a scornful eye over June and then, to my surprise, laughed right in her face.

'Laughing at jokes only you can hear? Ya poor fuck,' she said.

'It's your word against ours. And who's going to believe an embittered mother on a suspended sentence for kerb-crawling who's lost custody of her child, or her lowlife accomplice, who's attempting to blackmail two upstanding citizens falsely accused of carnal fraternizing?'

His eyes, when he laughed, remained as dark and glassy as a stuffed animal's.

June looked in my direction and raised a worried brow. My expression mirrored hers. Just when raw panic was taking hold of my internal organs, I heard Phoebe's voice.

'May I cordially present . . . the evidence.' In all the drama, I'd forgotten that she was still hiding in the walk-in wardrobe. She emerged now, her iPhone aloft, the whole sordid ordeal captured in moist detail on her video camera.

Now it was June's turn to laugh in Jeremy's face. She made a fist and jerked her elbow back hard. 'Yes! I'd say we got yer by the goolies,' she added with a triumphant chuckle. 'Prepare to start talkin' in a 'igh-pitched voice, dip-shit.'

Yes, blackmailing my ex-husband gave me a knot of guilt in my gut, but it passed in a moment, like acid reflux.

It was clear from Jeremy's crestfallen face that Phoebe had just triggered the fuse on the suicide vest that was going to blow up his life.

'So, shall we discuss our options?' my sister asked reasonably.

'Not that you 'ave any, yer noodle-dicked knucklehead!' June snorted.

'I'm sure the Department of Social Services will be interested in your split personality, Sonia. In public, demure, serious and righteous, but in private, orgasming for Britain.' Phoebe turned up the volume on her phone footage so we could fully appreciate Sonia's vocal crescendo.

Sonia immediately dissolved into a puddle of self-pitying lachrymosity. She cried like a kid, big whopping *wa-wa-waaaas*, complete with wheezing and shuddering.

Jeremy and I stood facing each other, silent as tombstones. Dark crescents bloomed in the armpits of his shirt. His fingernails, professionally buffed to a porcelain sheen, were shaking. His stare was a hard, cold laser.

Breaking the strained silence, in his usual smooth, sophisticated, Eton-educated, poised and polished way, Jeremy finally hissed, 'You cunts.' Then he lunged for Phoebe's phone. His rage mirrored that of the Incredible Hulk. He did everything but turn green and burst forth from the seams of his trousers.

But all those years as a barmaid meant that June was prepared. As they grappled, she extracted what looked like a hairspray canister from her cavernous handbag. Thus armed, she strutted towards Jeremy, stiff-legged, nose up, like a dog scenting a fight. Aiming the nozzle in Jeremy's deranged direction, she simply pulled the trigger. He screamed as the spray hit his face. Like a boxer, he rocked from one Italian-leather-shod foot to another. He stamped, listed starboard then dropped to the floor, writhing, knocking over a side table on his way down.

'Pepper spray,' June explained. 'For feminine protection.'

The house, so engrossed in its own charmed life, suddenly seemed to lose its composure. A framed picture of Jeremy and his pompous parents slid to the floor at his feet and smashed, symbolically. Proving that fate does occasionally possess a sense of humorous hubris, the painting's undignified departure revealed a safe screwed deep into the wall.

'Well, well, well, ain't that interestin'.' June's tone was one of droll jocosity. 'I wonder what could be in there?'

'Let's find out, shall we?' Phoebe said. 'But first of all, Sonia, it's time to cough up that paperwork. Just pretend it's a furball, you sex kitten.'

Behind her spectacles, at the centre of the thick lenses, the social worker's eyes shone with guilt and terror. Even though, under normal circumstances, she could win an award in the Jargon and Obfuscation Championships, the woman seemed unable to speak.

'The paperwork,' Phoebe reiterated, tapping her iPhone to re-run the sordid viewing. 'Now!'

Terrified into acquiescence, the formidable Sonia now became as docile as a child. She opened her bag, extracted the relevant files and passed them over to me. I quickly cast a horrified eye over Sonia's notes on Merlin. 'Suicidal . . . violent' – her typed report had warped my gentle son into someone insane and dangerous.

'"In need of full-time care in a residential home"?' I read aloud, seething. 'You falsified his records and doctored your account to appease Jeremy? Oh my God. I take it back. You two really do deserve each other.'

'Drop all complaints and quash the case and you'll never hear from us again,' Phoebe told her. 'Otherwise . . .' She hit the Play button once more.

Sonia nodded, blurting, 'Yes, yes, I'll go on sick leave . . . actually, I've got to go right now. I completely forgot. I've got a medical appointment.'

'Really?' Phoebe jibed. 'Something lethal, I hope.'

A thud or two of her Birkenstocks on the polished wooden stairs and Sonia was no more.

Jeremy was still writhing in agony, rubbing his eyes relentlessly. In his more restrained moments, it sounded as though he was in labour.

'Yeah, that must hurt . . . But not as much as seein' yer son's trust fund goin' down the crapper, eh?' June yowled in derision.

Eyes streaming, Jeremy looked up at me from the floor with such rumpled perplexity I nearly burst out laughing all over again.

'Okay. I'm ready to do a deal. Just get rid of that maniacal slag, so we can talk.' As Jeremy nodded in June's direction, his voice rose half an octave, losing much of its well-bred intonation in the process.

My brain was clear – miraculously clear. I moved slowly

towards him, as if drawn by the inexorable pull of a magnet, bent down and slapped him hard across the face.

'You know, June's ex-boyfriend once called her a slag and she stuck his balls into the garlic press then made them into a hanging basket strung together with his femoral artery,' I warned him, before standing on his left hand. I indicated for Phoebe to stand on his right hand and for June to sit astride his chest.

'Tell us the code to that safe, or June here will stake your nuts out over an ants' nest.'

Jeremy, eyes still streaming, remained tight-lipped. Not even a wrecking ball could dent his immense self-assurance. But June was a one-woman demolition squad.

'Or I could just sit on ya till yer little more than a splodge on the carpet,' she offered, placing her cowboy boot on to his neck and pressing down on his thorax.

'Either way, I predict an imminent attack of death,' I added.

'O–o–okay,' Jeremy spluttered. His garbled monotone signalled that he'd understood my message.

June lessened the pressure on his jugular so he could spit out the four-digit code for the safe.

I left him spread-eagled beneath the barmaid, the nozzle of the pepper spray aimed at his face, while I punched the code in. The safe door abracadabra-ed open, revealing a neatly stacked pile of cocaine pouches, plastic bags and digital jeweller's scales.

'You hypocrite,' I castigated.

I pushed the drugs aside and riffled through the legal-looking documents below. I quickly found the trust-fund files, and the letters from the bank revealing the depth of

Jeremy's debt, including correspondence indicating that his house was mortgaged to the hilt. Phoebe, who had been busy ransacking Jeremy's briefcase, brandished the legal document he'd made Merlin sign that morning handing over all power of attorney to Jeremy Beaufort Esquire.

I crossed out Jeremy's name and inserted my own. June, pepper spray cocked, forced Jeremy to initial the change and sign over full custody rights of Merlin to me, for ever more.

'You're a callous, cruel, gold-plated prick . . . but, apart from that, yer a prince,' June said, trussing him up, then tethering him to the bedposts with four of his own designer silk neckties.

'Your poor, clueless, gullible girlfriend can untruss you later – though I think it may dull her appetite, come aperitif time,' I mocked insolently.

The rain had stopped and the green smells wafting up from the garden were sharp, wet and delicious. I was just savouring my sweet victory when I clocked Jeremy's face. He looked angry, yes, but not quite angry enough. Experience had taught me just how expert my ex was at slithering out of trouble. I paused to think. I glanced down at the dashing arabesque of his signature on the form. Why hadn't he put up more of a fight? My mind raced. What was to stop him from claiming that he'd signed the papers under duress? Was his bribing of a social worker with sexual favours enough to convince a court that he had attempted to pervert the course of justice? I needed something that would get him struck off the roll of legal practitioners or, even better, imprisoned.

Out in the hall, I punched a number into my phone. 'Yes,

may I speak to the custody sergeant, please? Tell him it's . . . tell him it's Loony Lucy . . .'

By the time I joined the others downstairs, the doggy diazepam had worn off and some fierce barking was detonating from behind the closed dining-room door. June squawked out a laugh as we bounced out of the front door. 'The name's Bond . . . June Bond,' she said, blowing across the smoking barrel of an imaginary pistol.

Once we were safely in the car, I leant over the seat to hug Phoebe, congratulating her on having had the nous to record their whole sordid sexual encounter.

'Pretty shockin', eh?' June said.

'What, that he was shagging his social worker? I know! I would never, ever have guessed that!'

'No, that an upper-class bloke was 'avin' sex without a ridin' crop, whipped cream and lederhosen,' she chuckled.

'Yes, that, and the fact that, when he came, he didn't call out his own name,' Phoebe clarified.

We howled with laughter, spluttering and shrieking, holding our sides in hilarity and relief. June's little car rocked on its suspension, the windows steaming up. It was a good ten minutes before we had recovered enough to head off to find my darling son at Danny's gay wedding.

As we drove along, still laughing, I thought back over the day. Everything that was happening felt exaggerated, as though we were in a movie. I kept looking for stunt men and make-up girls. Maybe Merlin was right and we were in a play? Maybe life really was just a strange experiment being carried out on a lesser planet?

But, either way, it was a momentous day. A day that would

always loom large in my memory. Like John Lennon's assassination, or the death of Diana, or the disovery of the Higgs boson, I would always remember for ever more where I was on the day that I finally won the war against Jeremy Beaufort Esquire, Bloody Bastard the Third.

26

We Interrupt This Marriage to Bring You a News Bulletin

Defeating Jeremy – well, in the end it was like Darth Vader being felled by a paper cut. With biblical drama, the fog began to lift. My life had been so black and white of late, but now, with Jeremy destroyed, colour began seeping back into the world. I slipped into the moment like a hot bath.

For our celebratory drink, I directed June to a pub near the church on Marylebone Road where Phoebe's ex was marrying his male trolley dolly. As Jeremy had confiscated Merlin's phone, I texted his cousins to let him know that we were next door in the pub and to make sure Merlin understood that he was no longer in his deranged dad's custody. Dylan texted back to say they'd pop over after the ceremony to say hello. The hostelry combined the exotic ambience of a Jamaican brothel with the charming cosiness of an inner-city drug den, yet I felt so elated and joyous it could have been the upper deck of a super-yacht or the palatial interior of the Taj Mahal.

When a Tina Turner song came on the jukebox I catapulted to my feet and leapt about the room with the same gusto as Jessica Ennis-Hill running for the pole vault.

When the song ended and I joined my two collaborators at our table, I hugged my sister hard.

'Phoebe, you saved the day! Your hubby may have come out of the closet, but thank God you had the brains to go back in . . . and then film through a crack in the door. Full-time career woman, mother of two, sarcasm queen and mistress of espionage . . . Is there anything you *can't* do?'

'Well, my expressive dance needs work,' she said, throwing back a tumblerful of wine. 'I'm getting pissed, by the way.'

'Do you think that's a good idea, darling? Your kids know we're here. They could walk in at any moment.'

'Hey. My ex is marrying my best male friend from work and my hair's gone orange. So, if not now, *when*?'

'The girl's gotta point,' June agreed, topping up Phoebe's glass from the bottle on the table.

'And June – well, we couldn't have done it without you.'

'Hey, the pleasure's all mine. That ex of yours is such an oily individual it's a miracle no sea-birds or seals was injured in the flippin clean-up.'

'Well said! I'll drink to that.' Phoebe toasted June's comment with another huge slug of alcohol.

'I just wish you'd let me maim him a little more. I 'ad me 'eart set on makin' the dipshit sit on his paper shredder while it was goin' full speed. 'E deserves no less, after the way the toe-rag's treated you, Lucy,' June said with great dignity.

There was a certain poise about the woman, despite the

flashy rhinestone cowboy boots with their slightly eroded heels. You got the feeling she could easily be a retired actress somewhat down on her luck, or maybe an eccentric professor of prehistoric mastodon mating habits or some such. I astonished myself with an impulse to hug her. I reached across the table and squeezed her hand. It's impossible to say which of us was more startled.

'It was all worth it, for Merlin's sake,' she continued. 'That amazin' boy. That kooky kid's so topsy-turvy. Trouble is, that won't go down well with people who don't understand 'im. Like most of the girls of his generation . . .'

A comment like that should be stepped around as carefully as a dozing ISIS sniper. And so I did. 'Another drink, June?'

'I mean, the kid's unique. What other boy his age sees beyond the superficiality of beauty?' she persevered.

'Still, it'll be nice when he gets the chance to meet girls in his own age bracket,' I said pointedly.

We prowled around the edge of this conversation like Cold War spies.

'I mean, is there anything less attractive than a woman in her fifties trying to act like a dewy-eyed teenage fawn? Desperately trying to stay young,' I persisted. 'I tried that Retin-A cream once. It's just a great way to have large chunks of your skin peel off and waft to the floor during aerobics class.'

'Which is why it's so great that Merlin don't care about looks,' June emphasized.

I chose my next words carefully. 'Which is also why I'm glad you'll stay *friends*—'

'Friends? Jeez! Well, we're a bit more than friends, I hope, pet!'

A list of reasons why June should not be with Merlin ran through my mind like the headlines along the bottom of the TV screen mid-news programme. She was too old. He was too impressionable. She was taking advantage of his naivety. It was seedy. Seedy? Hell, it was wrong. 'He's young enough to be your grandson!' I complained for the millionth time.

'Hey, if the world was a logical place, men would ride side-saddle.'

'That's your answer?' I asked, gobsmacked.

'No. My *answer* is that I love the kid. And you can't do nothin' to pull us apart.'

It wouldn't sink in. June's words were slipping straight off the surface of my mind. I breathed out, not even having realized I was holding my breath. 'You're honestly contemplating continuing your affair with Merlin? After all he's been through? You can't be serious.'

'I'm serious all right. I've never met a more gorgeous guy. The kid's a gentle genius. Totally without guile, yer know? Jeez, the boy's more disarmin' than a UN peace-keepin' mission.'

My normally robust brain cells staggered about, bumping into imaginary furniture. It took an immense effort to concentrate on what June had just said.

'Anyways, what does the age difference matter? I want a flippin' age armistice. The point is, I get the kid. And 'e gets me.'

'What *matters* is that you're manipulating him. The simplest toy, one which even a senile old woman can operate, is the toy boy.'

'It wouldn't matter if I was a bloke and Merlin was a girl, would it? Look at your ex, bonkin' a schoolgirl and nobody turns a friggin' hair, but when it's an older woman with a younger fella, the shit hits the morality fan. Yer reckon yer a feminist, but yer just a flippin' hypocrite.'

Our brief truce was over. Tableware-throwing was about to resume.

'I won't allow it,' I said ineffectually. My voice was that of a drowning woman. Fixing Merlin's life was what I did, but how could I fix this? Which psychological assessment meeting did I need to attend? Which form should I fill in? Which course did I need to enrol him on? What pills did I need to prescribe? In which over-heated council office did I need to queue, holding a Styrofoam cup of instant coffee in my shaky hands to beg for a pittance of help?

'D'yer love Merlin?' June asked me fiercely.

'What? Of course! I love him more than anyone on the planet.'

'Well, if yer love somebody, set 'em free. That's what the song says. Let 'im go, Lucy. Let the kid make his own mistakes.'

'You don't get it, do you? I'm not just his mother, I'm his carer. It's my job to worry about him.'

'Yeah, well, by my calculation, you've only got, oh, forty or fifty years of worry ahead of you, so don't peak too friggin' early, pet.'

'I don't want to be over-protective, but I'm the one who knows him best and knows what's best for him.'

'Really? But what's best for *you*? Yer so obsessed with yer love for the kid that yer've left no room in yer heart for anyone else. Yer need to get on with yer *own* life. Go out and get laid, woman. I mean, you've got no boyfriend, and no friends that I can see, besides yer sister, and *she* ain't got no choice in the friggin' matter. Right now, it seems to me that yer usin' Merlin as an excuse to opt out. Stop livin' through yer boy and go out and get your own freakin' life!'

Phoebe, fresh from her tipsy dancing around the jukebox, staggered back to our table. 'So what did I miss?'

'This!' I said, and threw my wine in June's face.

June made a lunge for me then, and hooked her nails into my hair. 'Throwin' wine . . . that's the kind of thing what could get a woman's nose broken—'

'June!' Phoebe shrieked.

'I'm just puttin' it out there in the universe,' she rebuked.

'Stop it! Both of you!' Phoebe ordered in her most commanding 'fold up your tray tables for landing' voice.

'Girl fight! Catfight!' some knuckleheads at the bar chanted drunkenly. I heard a glass smash, but I couldn't see anything, as June and I were locked head-to-head, like a couple of menopausal moose.

A girl-on-girl fight in a bar offers many disadvantages – namely, rowdy onlookers with mobile phones, the ensuing humiliating footage posted online, and possible police arrest. But a smashed glass in the face is a boon for both plastic surgeons and undertakers worldwide.

So raw was our mutual anger that our clash really might have ended in a bloodbath if Merlin hadn't fortuitously appeared with his cousins at the door of the pub. He called out our names and something immediately altered in the air between us – and June and I pulled apart.

'What a robust evening!' Merlin said by way of greeting. 'So, how are your lives developing? Are you having any relationship difficulties? Adults aren't really adult, are they? They're just in adult disguise.'

'Merlin!'

I hugged him with a relief that was so intense it was almost painful. 'Darling, are you okay? I missed you so, so much.'

Merlin gave me a look of distant, almost sweet, abstraction. 'I've been trying to smudge the edges of me. But I'm starting to think the edges of me are the best bits.'

My heart gave one big bang that hurt my chest. 'They are, darling, they are.'

Meanwhile, Phoebe's kids – Dylan and Julia – were attempting to show their inebriated mother photos on their iPad of the registry office wedding ceremony and the following church blessing. Phoebe refused to look. Her kids finally gave up. Despondent, they left the iPad on the table and slouched over to the jukebox to choose a tune. June picked up the tablet and scrolled through the wed-ding snaps.

'Jeez. 'Ow could yer not know that yer hubby's gay? The man makes Liberace look like a coal miner.'

'Well, come to think of it, he did love opera and mani-cures.' Phoebe sighed.

'And he always got very excited about shirts he bought on sale,' I added. 'Remember?' I asked my sister.

'Yes. Plus, there was the fact that he liked me to take him roughly from behind with a strap-on.'

Wine spurted out of June's nose this time. Clearly, the habit was contagious. But then Phoebe's kids were back and 'It's Raining Men' was booming out of the jukebox. As Julia sang the lyrics to her truculent mother, Dylan badgered her to call a parental truce and go over the road to join the wed-ding party, to let bygones be bygones.

'Or bi-gays be bi-gays,' June interrupted.

Merlin listened intently for a moment, then put his hands to his face to shield his eyes, tilted his head upwards and addressed the ceiling.

'Aunt Phoebe, I heard Mum telling Grandma on Skype that if you don't go to the wedding you risk alienating your offspring. And that, as a Woman of the World, you should just suck it up.'

Phoebe narrowed her eyes at me. 'Did she now?'

'She did say we should never say that to your face, though,' Merlin added.

'Then why are you saying it?' I sputtered, aghast, my own face turning puce with embarrassment.

Merlin kept his eyes fixated on the ceiling fan. 'I'm not saying it to her face, am I?'

'Thanks for the loyalty, sis,' Phoebe commented sourly.

'Well, the truth is, Pheebs, I don't like this change in you. Neither does Mum. Since Danny left, you've become a tough crowd of one. But I have good news.'

'You found my real sister?'

'Oh, ha ha. Now Danny's married his boyfriend, you can *move on.*'

As I said, my sister has a tendency to pull at her hair when she's thinking, and has been known to suck on a strand when plotting a plan. Well, she was sucking the life out of an orange frond now. She was chewing on that strand so ferociously it was a sure sign of a major campaign.

'Oh God. You're scheming something. What?' I insisted, alarmed.

'You know, I think I *will* go to the wedding party. If only to rain on their gay parade.'

'Oh, Phoebe, don't do anything mean. You'll have a brief

moment of delicious vengeance, then months of waking in the middle of the night, replaying the mortifying moment flooded with self-loathing, pulling the blankets over your head and just wanting to disappear into an alcohol-deadened coma.'

'I'd better stock my cellar, then . . . Kids?' she called out. 'Okay. I'll come. Lead on.'

'Don't be the bad fairy at the wedding, Phoebe,' I pleaded.

'All the fairies at that wedding are bad, Lucy.'

Merlin, unaware of the emotional avalanche he'd just dynamited, slipped into the seat between June and me and then looked from one of us to the other.

'You're one of my oldest friends, Mum. You have such charisma and panache. I love my extraordinary, beautiful mother, who has the most lovely clavicles. When did we meet? Have my looks changed since then? I think I have a mesmerizing personality, don't you?'

'Well, yes, yes, I do.'

Merlin kissed my hand with grave tenderness. 'I'm sorry I've been such a difficult child. And I want to thank you for allowing me to be your son. And for the nurturing and cherishing. You are a living legend and from now on I will honour you by calling you Doctor – no, Professor – Lucy. But I'd just like to make an announcement that I will no longer be requiring your full-time mothering services, as I too have now *moved on* . . .'

June turned to Merlin and smiled with delight. I, however, felt a dolorous tug at my heartstrings. I steadied myself against the table in preparation for a body blow. 'You've moved on?'

'Yes . . . with Michael.'

'*Michael?*' June and I chorused.

'Yes, I'm a little bit gay, apparently.'

I set my glass down very gingerly, as though it were made of Baccarat crystal. 'You're gay?' I asked quietly.

'Well, yes. So I've recently ascertained. As you know, Uncle Danny has just married his male partner in the church over the road. And during the ceremony I met this dazzling homosexual man. He has a vast array of talents. He's a musician, a poet, a chef and an International Man of Mystery. He's an octopus, juggling with all his testicles.'

'His testicles?' June repeated, stunned. Bafflement and incomprehension contorted her face into a mask of dismay.

'Merlin, wait. Who is this bloke, exactly, with all these tentacles?'

'It's a secret, I'm not supposed to tell you, but the homosexual man I'm keen to impress is just over there.' He surreptitiously pointed towards the bar.

Merlin's 'secret' whisper could have been heard by Inuits digging ice holes in Alaska. June and I swivelled as one to see a good-looking young man in his twenties straddling a bar stool. He wore the rudimentary gay uniform of designer trainers, no socks, skinny cropped jeans, a long, fitted denim shirt, a fitted short navy blazer with a pocket square, and rounded tortoiseshell specs. Unlike his regulated sartorial ensemble, the man's smile seemed charmingly authentic.

'Gay sons make excellent companions for their mothers, what with the shoe-shopping, opera and Kylie concerts. So you should be ecstatic at this turn of events, Mother,' Merlin added cheerily. 'Although Michael's parents don't see it that way. Not judging by the death threats.'

'*Death threats?*' Again, June and I spoke in unison.

'Mainly from the local imam.'

'Michael is Muslim?' I asked.

'Oh yes,' Merlin said matter-of-factly. 'It's not Michael, it's Mikaeel.'

I put my head in my hands. 'And we're off!' I muttered under my breath.

June was bug-eyed with disbelief. 'Yer can't just "go gay", pet. No way . . .'

I placed a restraining hand on her arm. 'Let him make his own mistakes,' I paraphrased sarcastically. 'Let him make his own way . . . If you love somebody, set them free. Isn't that what the song says?'

'Bloody hell.' I could hear a world-weary laugh surfacing in her voice. Then she guffawed – a hard, almost guttural sound which turned quickly into a sob.

'I'm know I'm big for my brain, Mum, but I think I'm growing into it,' Merlin explained. 'Don't you agree, June?'

June controlled herself then, and gave a rueful half-shrug. 'Good for you, kiddo. It's been great knowin' yer, hon—' She tried to say more but her voice cracked again. She cleared her throat irritably to disguise the emotion. 'I think I've gotta bit of a cold comin' on.'

'Yes, there's something going around,' I said, to aid her ruse.

June took a deep, shaky breath, pulled herself together with all the strength she could muster, then addressed me cheerily. 'Hey, at least you don't 'ave to worry about pregnancy.'

'The interesting thing about life,' Merlin suddenly philosophized, 'is that you can never get that day back. Or that hour. You can never be in the same year. This moment will never come again in the history of the world, which is why you have to embrace love, that rubicon word, with all its transformative powers,' he said in his honey-buttered tone. 'And why you should act with passion. And *carpe diem* like there's no tomorrow ... True love sews sequins on the world, doesn't it, Mum?'

He was watching me intently, like a prize pupil. I instantly pictured him as a little boy, splashing around in the sea as he vaulted backwards away from me, somersaulting out of my arms into the deep blue. I took a ragged breath and, with every ounce of willpower in my being, replied, 'Okay. Have fun, kiddo.' I used my breezy Lauren Bacall/Bogart voice, only this time it didn't sound as inauthentic as tinned asparagus. It sounded warm, genuine, real. I shrugged myself deeply into my son's embrace, my head on his chest, near his heart, and inhaled his familiar, reassuring scent. 'I love you, Merlin.'

'Ditto, Mum. The thing is, I've always felt that I needed to be fixed. But maybe I'm not broken? And, as far as "normal" is concerned, "normal" is just a cycle on a washing machine. That's what Mikaeel says. And labels – well, they're just for jars.'

I gulped. No one has ever invented the word I needed to describe how I felt right then.

'I'm returning to the revelries now but, before I go, can I get you a cup of tea or anything?' he asked, which, in Merlin terms, was the equivalent of offering me his lottery winnings, or an internal organ, or his first-born child. I was deeply, deeply touched.

'I'm fine,' I told him. And I was.

'And so, the Love Mission goes on!' he exclaimed. And then off he went – my vivid, original, odd, effervescent son, the garlic in my life's salad. Sure, garlic was not to everyone's taste, but anyone who didn't like garlic was not welcome at my table, because how bland and tasteless life would be without it.

27

Special Needs

An empty pub in England is as rare as a radical Islamic State joke book, but with the departure of Merlin, Mikaeel, Phoebe and her two kids, and with most of the drinking clientele spilling out on to the street to groove along to Danny and Trevor's wedding-reception medley of gay anthems, which were blasting forth from the church court-yard, June and I suddenly found ourselves alone.

We looked at each other, not sure what we were, if not adversaries. We listened in silence for a while to 'I'm Every Woman', 'Dancing Queen', 'Tainted Love', 'YMCA', 'Macho Man' and, aptly, 'I'm Coming Out'.

'How 'bout I buy you another drink?' June finally said.

'Good God, no. I think I've had enough.' I slumped across our table.

'Jeez, is *this* any way to treat yer former daughter-in-law?'

'I suppose you know that's not remotely funny,' I replied, though I could feel a smile welling up.

'J'know what? There are times when it's extremely bad manners to stay sober. Hen nights, stag nights, weddin's – especially the weddin's of ex-hubbies to their new gay partners. Um . . . after a cancer diagnosis . . . when yer kids finally fly the nest. And when they invariably bloody move back in . . . when yer only son tells yer he's gay . . . and when yer toy boy trades yer in for a younger model. Not to be drunk at these times makes a woman look heartless, deranged or like a flippin' android.'

She signalled to the barman for another bottle, then plonked down companionably next to me. 'J'know, this could well be the turnin' point in yer life, Lucy.' She was nursing her glass in both hands, a wintry gesture out of place with the sweaty, overheated atmosphere of the bar. 'What j'yer call it? Yer epiph-i-what's-it.'

'My epiph-i-what's-it? I assume that to be a medical term for alcoholic poisoning?' I said, as the bottle of white wine was placed before me. ' "Epiphany", is that the word you're looking for?'

'I've learnt a few life lessons in my time, j'know that?' June then proceeded to count them off on her varnished fingers. '1) Life ain't fair. 2) Don't ever shag your best pal's hubby. 3) Try everythin' in life except crystal meth and Morris dancin' – unless it's both at the same time. And 4) Don't live through yer kids.'

I couldn't make out her mood at first, but then I saw the white crescent of a smile peeking above the froth on her pint.

'Kids always leave, see? So a girl's gotta get her own life. Otherwise, you've got nothin' left when they go.'

'That's easy for *you* to say, June. I'll always be umbilically attached to Merlin. It's not so easy to have your own life when your child has special needs.'

'Hon, you have needs, too, many of 'em special, I'm sure.' She winked. 'So . . . exactly 'ow long is it since you've 'ad a fella, pet?'

'What? Oh God. Years.' I thought back to my last boyfriend – an Aussie rock muso, Archie, who'd asked me to accompany him on a world tour. Oh, how badly I'd wanted to head off into the hedonistic sunset . . . only I couldn't leave Merlin.

'Years? Jeez. You must 'ave a libido the size of flippin' Venezuela by now.'

'Not really. I'm afraid I've rather gone off men.'

'Yeah, but not *all* men are scumbags. Look at Merlin – the sweetest angel on the planet,' she said wistfully 'Na. Yer gotta date again. There's plenty of time to be old. You're still hot.'

'Sure . . . it just comes in flushes now.'

'Yer can forget all them patches and 'erbs and doses of mares' urine. Toy boys are the best ever cure for the meno-pause, lemme tell ya! . . . I love your son. But hey, I'll get over 'im. Couple more glasses and I'll be there.'

I thought I saw a tear in her eye, but it was most probably a trick of the light.

'It won't take me long to meet another fella. I mean, check me out – I've got cheek, chutzpah, sex appeal in spades, me own boobs and teeth, me own mews cottage and car. Plus, I can do a little light breakin' and enterin'. What's not to love?' She discreetly tugged the wedgie crease out of her skirt bot-tom. 'Let's go out on the town and become born-again sluts!'

I couldn't remember the last time I'd flirted. It was a skill from my girlhood that I'd grown out of, like, say, cartwheeling or slow dancing. 'No, no. I couldn't. No way,' I flustered.

'Why the hell not? What are you most scared shitless of?'

'Um, waking up in bed with Bill Cosby after drinking Rohypnol?'

'That rat's in security lockdown, so a one-night stand with a hot-to-trot Love God can't possibly freak you out, can it?'

'You're nuts, do you know that?' I said indulgently. Now that Merlin was no longer in her clutches, I could allow myself to appreciate her no-bullshit brio and punchy charm.

'Yep!' June drained her glass, jerked me up to standing, then yanked me out the pub door. In the St Marylebone parish church square opposite, Phoebe's ex-husband's wedding guests were dancing on the cobblestones. 'I Will Survive' was blaring from the speakers and the matron of honour, a drag queen called Cinnamon Brown, who was looking understated in a lemon lamé ballgown and a pink tiara, had just leapt into the fountain. A conga line of drag queens was circling her, headed up, much to my amazement, by my homophobic sibling.

'Well, that sister of yours clearly gave her ex a piece of her mind, didn't she?' June hooted. 'She's not so much rainin' on their parade as bloody well leadin' it.'

I found myself giggling, too, the tipsy laughter acting as a kind of instant analgesic. Once we'd regained control of our senses, June and I leant on to the street railing, curiously comfortable in each other's company. With London exclaiming all around us, we serenely watched the proceedings. Phoebe spotted us by the fence and, spilling Prosecco from a plastic cup, frantically gestured for us to join in. The gay best man stopped licking a huge chocolate male torso to pour pink bubble bath into the fountain.

June jabbed me in the ribs with her elbow. 'What-ja say? Shall we?'

The alcohol was now coursing through my veins. I felt like a wilting plant being watered and brought back to life. And then I heard myself say, like a carefree kid, 'Yeah, okay.' It was my relaxed, laid-back, happy-go-lucky voice – a voice which sounded slightly false from disuse.

A few moments later, June, my new and totally unexpected friend, was grinding her hips up against a man half her age, who, I suddenly realized, was the vicar. Behind her, Phoebe was pre-boarding a handsome male flight attendant with the words, 'He's straight! Doors to manual!' She then patted her pudenda, her posterior and her mouth, screaming, 'Your entrances are here, here and here!' I noted with delight that she was also taking a long, smokeless tote on an e-cigarette.

Atop the stone steps leading into the church, Merlin was running through his eccentric dance repertoire. Beside him was Mikaeel, diligently mastering the moves to the Typewriter, Angel Wings and the Jumping Bean. Nor was he being what my son called 'overly Caucasian' in the dance department. Mikaeel was wiggling and waggling bits of his anatomy he probably didn't even know he *had* before. I watched them for a moment – Mikaeel laughing; Merlin all limbs and eyes and ardour. My son's face was alight with hope and excitement. The air was positively buoyant with his presence.

I was standing there in the middle of the cobbled church courtyard, surrounded by the swirl of joy and laughter and the crimson cascade from the fountain, with bubbles of silliness pop, pop, popping all around me, just watching my beautiful boy, when I felt a firm grasp on my upper arm. I caught a glimpse of a blue uniform in my peripheral vision. Startled, I turned to see Jack, the custody sergeant.

'Oh God. What have I done now?' were the first words out of my mouth.

'I just came to say that, thanks to your tip-off, we found the cocaine in your ex-husband's safe, and the amount is clearly not just for possession. That's above a trafficable quantity there. The guy's in the game. Which is why he's been arrested and charged and is unlikely to get bail.'

'Thank you. Oh, what a relief!'

'But I'm afraid you're under arrest, too.'

'Oh God.' My heart sank. 'What for? Breaking and entering? Trespassing? Grievous bodily harm? My sister and June had nothing to do with it. It was all my idea . . .'

The custody sergeant raised an amused brow. 'You're actually under arrest by the Fun Police, as it's come to my attention that you just aren't having a good enough time.'

And then he swept me up into his strong, muscled arms for a waltz around the frothing fuchsia fountain. Coming out of the spin, he leant me backwards, then nipped a line of kisses down my throat, setting off a chain reaction zinging and pinging through my erogenous zones and making the hairs on the back of my neck stand up. It had been years since anything this thrilling had happened to my nape. I realized it had been decades since anything had made me go moist in the extremities like this. Hell, I don't think anything this exciting had *ever* happened to my extremities.

I was just savouring the dizzy delight of being swept off

my sneakered feet when my sozzled sister appeared at my side.

'Lu-Lu, do you know that your son is now off dating an unspecified gay bloke who may or may not remember to use condoms and may or may not be addicted to glitter balls and Abba dance tracks?' she drawled at me. 'Does he even *know* this Mikaeel guy? Did you give him the lecture about safe sex, by which I mean not getting tinsel on his tackle and—'

I put my hand up as though stopping traffic. 'Do you know what, Pheebs? No more lectures. It's Merlin's life. Things may go wrong, or they may go right. But' – I took a deep breath before I could garner the strength to utter the rest of the unexpected sentence, the most unexpected sentence that had ever left my lips – 'but I'm just going to jump off that bridge when I come to it.'

I then did the only thing that any exhausted, world-weary, overwrought, exhilarated, liberated, frazzled, sozzled, flying-blind, making-it-up-as-I-go-along, loving, doting, beautifully clavicled, part-meerkat, half-unicorn, owlish, bat-shit-crazy special-needs mum with special needs of her own could do – I seized the custody sergeant, grabbed his peachy posterior with both hands and bloody well kissed his hot, hungry mouth – a born-again slut at last.

Acknowledgements

My mother gave me the greatest gift imaginable – three wise, warm and witty sisters. Thanks to Jenny, Liz and Cara for enduring my first draft with minimal bribery (pedicures and pina coladas). Your nuanced notes were invaluable.

Thanks to Mum for doing the daily crossword with me, to keep the old brain cells pumping, and to my food fairy, Mimi, for all those gourmet parcels, and to my daughter, Georgie, for keeping me on my toes politically. (Hell, you keep me so en pointe, I could join the political corps de ballet.) To all my cherished family and friends, especially Sandi, Ruby, Penny, Helena, Ronni, Nell, June, Arron, Mark, Craig, Geoff, Patrick, Billy, The Gerts and most of all Brian, thanks for the warm laughs at cold times.

I'm also incredibly grateful to legal-eagle pal Kirsty Brimelow, QC, who guided me through court-room and prison-cell procedures with such patience and precision. Thanks also to Detective Niall O'Carroll for not arresting this book for inaccuracies and sending it down for life.

To my publishing team, you birthed this, my sixteenth book, with the least possible pain, making you my creative epidural. Particular thanks to my perspicacious editor, Francesca Best, who taught me that good editing is best fuelled by dark chocolate. To my publisher and dear friend Larry Finlay – thanks for constantly championing my work. Same goes for legendary agent and great mate, Ed Victor – the Ed-ocet missile of the book world. Thanks to Maggie Phillips and the team, too. And to the incomparable Karen Reid and Sally Wray – thanks for making it such fun on the road, despite the odd stalker. (Surely a tautology, Ed?)

But my most heartfelt thanks of all must go to my autistic friends and their families, for sharing their stories of all the angst, hilarity, trials and tribulations that go with looking for love in a neurotypical world. And, of course, my deepest gratitude goes to my son, Jules, who has taught me that there is no such thing as normal and abnormal . . . Just ordinary and extraordinary. I love you.

And here's to someone actually inventing Lucy's Autinder or Tinder-ism, a dating app to help those on the spectrum to find true love.

Kathy Lette first achieved *succès de scandale* as a teenager with the novel *Puberty Blues*, which was made into a major film and a TV mini-series. After several years as a newspaper columnist and TV sitcom writer in America and Australia, she's written twelve international bestsellers in her characteristic witty voice, including *Mad Cows* (which was made into a film starring Joanna Lumley and Anna Friel), *How to Kill Your Husband (and Other Handy Household Hints)* (staged by the Victorian Opera), *The Boy Who Fell to Earth* and *Courting Trouble*. Her novels have been published in fourteen languages around the world.

Kathy appears regularly as a commentator on the BBC and Sky News. She is also an ambassador for Women and Children First, Plan International, the White Ribbon Alliance, Ambitious about Autism and the NAS.

Kathy lives in London and can often be found at The Savoy (where she was writer in residence) drinking a cocktail named after her. She is an autodidact (a word she taught herself), but has honorary doctorates from Southampton Solent University and Wollongong University, plus a Senior Fellowship from London's Regent's University.

Kathy cites her career highlights as teaching Stephen Fry a word and Salman Rushdie the limbo, and scripting Julian Assange's cameo in *The Simpsons'* five-hundredth episode.

Visit her website at www.kathylette.com and find her on Twitter @KathyLette and Facebook/KathyLetteAuthor